A
WOMAN
MADE
OF
SNOW

Also by Elisabeth Gifford

The Lost Lights of St Kilda
The Good Doctor of Warsaw
Return to Fourwinds
Secrets of the Sea House

ELISABETH GIFFORD

A WOMAN MADE OF SNOW

CORVUS

Published in hardback in Great Britain in 2021 by Corvus, an imprint of Atlantic Books Ltd.

Copyright © Elisabeth Gifford, 2021

10 9 8 7 6 5 4 3 2 1

A CIP catalogue record for this book is available from the British Library.

Hardback ISBN: 978 1 83895 321 8
Trade paperback ISBN: 978 1 78649 909 7
E-book ISBN: 978 1 78649 910 3

Printed in Great Britain by TJ Books Ltd, Padstow, Cornwall

Corvus
An imprint of Atlantic Books Ltd
Ormond House
26–27 Boswell Street
London
WC1N 3JZ

www.corvus-books.co.uk

To Joan and Francis

CHAPTER 1

FIFE, 1949

Wrapped in darkness beneath the trees I watch rain falling on the earth where I have slept for so long. Light from the cottage windows stretches across the lawns, but it does not reach me. Find me, I whisper. Give me my name. Some nights I will take myself up to the bedroom where they sleep and whisper to the woman. She turns in her dreams, stretches an arm out towards the child nearby and I think perhaps she has heard me, but in the morning she will blame her dreams on something else. I breathe into the wind as she comes out to hang up squares of white cloth. Find me. Tell them who I am. She looks around, pulls her cardigan tighter across her chest and goes back inside.

But now, at last, something is changing. The rain, so heavy and persistent for days on end, starts to pool on the lawn behind the cottage. Roots that have grown unseen for years, reaching out beneath the soft soil to pull away bricks in the old drain, finally finish their work. Mud creeps inside the channels until the water has nowhere else to go. The lawn becomes a sheet of moonlight. The space where I sleep fills with water stained red by the rich oxides of the earth. Water lies shining across the lawns, seeps beneath the kitchen door until the stone flags are gone under a sea of moonlight.

In the morning, they will splash through the kitchen, come out and ask each other what has caused the flood. And I will be waiting for the spades to be brought out, for the scrape of metal through soil, blades digging down to unearth the roots tangled in bricks.

Find me, I whisper. The flood waters shiver in return. I look beyond the trees to the roofs of Kelly Castle and I wait.

It is time.

CHAPTER 2

NORTHAMPTON, 1944

Caro leaned forward over the wheel, praying Gertie wasn't going to splutter to a halt again. All she could see of the road ahead were two faint cones of light filled with swirling mist and a succession of pale trees looming up on the edge of the forest before they faded back into the dark. She'd been having nightmares recently of breaking down in the middle of nowhere. The garage at Peterborough had checked the wheels, tightened the bolts so there'd be no repetition of the time the back wheel rolled away, but Gertie badly needed new tyres, which, they'd said, could take weeks to come. Caro blinked. Something ahead on the road. The shape of a man, pale as a phantom in the faint headlights. Squinting, she made out an American GI uniform. No ghost then. She was about to stop and offer a lift, as she often did for soldiers walking back to base, but as she drew alongside she saw that he was one of the black Americans. She immediately drove on, disappointed with herself in the same instant. It was just seeing him appear from nowhere had given her a start. That was all. She drew to a halt, waited till he caught up with her, leaned across and wound down the window.

'Hello there. Would you like a lift back to your base?'

'If you're sure, ma'am.'

'Of course. Hop in.'

He opened the door and squeezed in next to her, filling the space with his height. His skin was dark, patches of shine in the moonlight, his smile wide and white.

She drove on again into the darkness. She noticed him wincing at the tiny space illuminated in front of them.

'I must tell you, I was surprised you stopped, ma'am.'

'Goodness. I quite often give one of you chaps a lift back.'

'But never a black one before.'

'That's true, but does it make a difference?'

'It shouldn't. Still think you've got some guts though, ma'am. Don't know many women back home who'd stop like that. An attractive woman, on her own.'

So she gave him the talk. 'I always find that if you expect the best of people, make it clear to them that that's what you expect of them, then that's how they behave. One has to trust people to be their best selves, you see, then they won't let you down.'

'And it always works?'

'I did have one chap, very homesick, poor boy, who put a hand on my knee, but I gave him the talk, and he took that hand right back.'

'I'm sure he did, ma'am.'

'Oh, and it's Caro. Caro Winters.'

'Desmond, ma'am.'

'I always think it must be so hard for you GI boys being stranded in the middle of nowhere. So far from home and family.'

He took out a photo from his wallet, held it to her left. Caro could just make out a woman with three small children in front of her.

'What a beautiful family you have. You must miss them dreadfully. I'd show you a photo of my fiancé if my hands were free. We're getting married on his next leave – that's if they don't cancel it again. Of course, it's not going to be anything grand. Impossible to get enough sugar to make a wedding cake now, even with everyone chipping in their coupons. Quite hopeless. But I must say, and I tell everyone this, I've found my rations go a lot further since I registered as vegetarian. One gets a really decent piece of cheese, you see, and pulses. And on principle it's better too, don't you think?'

'I could never refuse a steak. But I'm still thinking how it's very late to be out here on your own, ma'am. Caro.'

'I'm used to it. I lecture at the training camp near Peterborough once a week, but my digs are a beastly five miles away. I drive all over the place lecturing in village halls and such. It's important work really, bringing culture and education to working people, keeping morale up. Preparing people's minds for after the war, you see, when there's going to be a need for us to come together and really think about what we need to do to make society better. Don't you think?'

'I do, ma'am.' He nodded to himself. 'Quite an old car you've got here though.'

'Yes, poor old Gertie, should be enjoying retirement but she keeps going. Fortunately my father gave me a crash course in spark plugs and combustible engines. I'm a pretty dab hand at changing the oil.'

'I'm full of admiration for you, ma'am. And grateful for the lift.'

'You're more than welcome. We must all do what we can to help.'

There was a loud bang. The car listed down violently in the back corner, a dragging noise of rubber flapping on tarmac.

Caro braked. 'Damn if a bloody tyre hasn't gone again.'

By the light of a small torch they studied the deflated tyre. Caro was tall and well built, with what her mother referred to as childbearing hips, but her companion was even taller. It dawned on her, standing next to him, how very alone they were. From deep in the dark forests around them, an unnamed animal screamed.

'Right. Spare tyre,' she said heartily, glad of his help manhandling it off the back of the car. But opening the tool box, she found herself hesitating for a moment as he held out his large hand for the wrench. She directed the watery torch beam while he jacked up the car, chilly air creeping up her legs and under her skirt until the beam shook in her frozen hands. Every so often, she breathed warm air into her woollen gloves.

'You're very efficient. Is this the sort of thing you do for a living?'

'I'm a teacher, ma'am. Elementary grade. As is my wife. But our car back home is also temperamental.'

For the first time, she noted the two stripes on his shoulder.

He stood and wiped his hands on a handkerchief. 'Ready to go.'

'All I can say is thank goodness you came along when you did or I'd have been stuck here all night.'

He opened the door for her. She got back into the driver's seat.

She dropped him off at the gates of his base. With the detour it took twice as long as usual to get back to her digs, the fog so thick she could barely manage fifteen miles an hour. Once, she startled awake and found herself driving over the rough edge of a field. She kept singing after that, any old nonsense to keep awake.

Dear Mrs Potts had left a light on in the hallway of the little railway worker's cottage where she and Audrey – lecturing in Greek drama and philosophy – were lodging. She'd waited up, in hairnet and dressing gown, and made Caro a cup of tea and a hot-water bottle. Told her off roundly when she heard why she was so late. Caro didn't mind. She was secretly rather proud of her ability to make good friends across the classes, with people like Mrs Potts. Once the war was over, class was not going to mean anything after all the country had been through together. War was horrid, but it stirred you up, made you realize what mattered, what you were capable of. Caro was relishing her post, the work of it, the satisfaction of knowing she was good at something that made a real difference – even if she wasn't quite as frighteningly brainy as Audrey.

Caro tiptoed into the room she shared with Audrey, got changed in the dark and slid into the freezing bed. She picked up Alasdair's photo from the bedside table and planted a kiss about a third of the way down, picturing the apple-shaped cheekbones, his shy smile and mischievous eyes, the lick of auburn hair that was held back by his regimental Glengarry cap, a Cameron Highlander's badge pinned to one side.

She and Alasdair had only known each other for six months when he had been called up. He'd asked her to marry him the same week. Students in Cambridge, they already knew the shape of their future lives together. They would both work as lecturers at London universities, he in English, she history. Somewhere in the future, she saw rooms crammed with cigarette smoke and people just like them, debating the new world into being. Living in London, of course, meant that they would be a long way away from his mother in Scotland, and she felt a little guilty about that, but the sleeper train was marvellous for the way it whisked you from London to Edinburgh overnight. They'd go up at least twice a year. It had been such fun when she'd travelled up with Alasdair to visit Martha in what was effectively a small castle, three ancient towers joined together with a later Jacobean section, a giddy, impossibly high silhouette of turrets and corbels next to a bosky walled garden. Alasdair had finally owned up to his background the afternoon they came out of a lecture on Orwell, given by the Labour Society to which they both belonged. 'Not that it means we're wealthy. Far from it. The castle eats up any money Mother has, I'm afraid.'

Of course, after the war, people wouldn't accept that some had castles and others had nothing. Just as all this gumph about class and race and about what women could and couldn't do simply wouldn't stand any more. Her father had always taught her that a woman could work as well as any man while he was showing her how to slice ham and haslet for customers at his Food Emporium, the Fortnum & Mason of Catford. The fierce, unmarried women teachers at Catford Girls' Grammar – each with a sad story of a lost soldier from the Great War, if you could get them in the mood to tell it, the teacher staring absently out of the window as the class of girls listened rapt – they all drummed into the girls that there was more to a woman than having babies. There were exams. And doing very well in exams. Because one day, the gels would have careers.

She pulled the eiderdown up round her shoulders. The room was freezing but Caro smiled into the darkness, trying to imagine the future. She saw herself and Alasdair together, striding out hand in hand, sharing everything. It was quite hard to be specific on the details, but she saw many deep conversations, an unbroken closeness. Their life would be much like their time at Cambridge, but deeper, richer, and with their own furniture.

CHAPTER 3

FIFE, 1949

This morning, she was definitely going to be on top of things. She was awake before the baby, though her heavy breasts felt itchy with the need to feed her soon. She checked inside the crib, the child flat on her back, arms fist high to her head, the pink cheeks and lips of a cherub. She felt a gush of intense tenderness for the tiny being, followed by a sharp answering crackle in her breasts and a flood of wet down the front of her nightie. She grabbed yesterday's blouse from the back of the chair and pushed it down the neck of her nightshirt to mop up the flow. Pulling it out and leaving it on the pile of washing, she tiptoed downstairs, ducked down to look at the rising sun slanting across the old drying lawns. It would reach through the deeply recessed window for at least part of the morning before leaving the kitchen in gloom again. Today she was going to get the washing done early, get it out to dry in the morning breeze. The bucket of nappies in the back porch was crying out for attention but for now it would have to wait. This moment was hers.

She fetched down the red enamel coffee pot they'd bought in Italy on their honeymoon. Not an elegant china and gilt affair that you might find in the drawing room of Alasdair's mother or the provost, but the honest utilitarian kind that farmers and peasants all over Italy would be using at this very moment. She put the kettle to boil on the range, leaving the whistle open to make sure there would be no shrill scream prompting Felicity to begin hers. She balanced the tin filter on the pot's neck and poured hot water through the grounds, the earthy smell redolent of sunshine and the tiny pension on a hillside that had overlooked the Amalfi coast. Memories of all the gifts of the sun: ripe lemons and red peppers, olives and fragrant coffee, sun warming the resin in the cypress trees to the rise and fall of cicadas. All things that were in short supply in Fife.

The plans they'd had for them to both teach at one of the London universities had not come to pass. She had fallen pregnant with surprising ease, nine months after the wedding. She'd felt a little embarrassed that she couldn't manage things better, ambushed by her own fertility. Alasdair's only offer of a post came from St Andrews. It was an excellent university. As a result, they were now living five hundred miles away from London and three hundred yards from Martha.

She tipped oats into a pan, poured water over them and set the pan on the cooker. The water in the jug was almost gone, but she wasn't going to fill it now. The squeaking of the pump beneath the bedroom window would startle Felicity awake, so she allowed herself this moment to settle on the chair, one elbow on the scrubbed top of the pine table, bare feet up on another chair. Immediately, as if Felicity could see her off duty, a wail started up from upstairs. Caro sipped the coffee defiantly, hoping. No sound of Alasdair stirring as the siren continued. She dropped her head, put down the coffee and went back up to the bedroom.

Felicity's nappy had slipped out of the leg of the rubber pants, just enough to soak the cot sheet. She picked her up, the child inconsolable with some belief that she might never be fed again despite the score of times she'd latched on throughout the night. She gave off a yeasty smell of old milk mixed with ammonia. Yelling or not, Felicity needed changing before any feed was possible. Another nappy for the bucket. Caro really needed to empty it out, pump water for a new lot of soiled ones. All the water for the cottage had to be pumped by hand and the electric generator was temperamental and often cut out, but it had seemed a small price to pay. After their honeymoon camping in the fields of an Italian family who lived off the land, tomatoes and bread and olive oil, this tiny cottage seven miles outside town on the border of the Kelly estate had seemed to Caro a statement of all they wanted in life. The fact that there would be no rent to pay had settled it. Alasdair's small assistant lecturer's salary would be their sole income for a while.

'Darlings, I can't think the old Laundry Cottage will be comfortable enough. At least come live with me in the main house,' Martha had said. But Caro loved their little cottage, the romance of it, the simple Arts and Crafts beauty of things made for work.

Caro settled herself in the high-backed rocking chair by the range and pulled the tartan blanket around her shoulders. She fitted Felicity onto her left breast. Felicity pulled away, stared up at her for a moment and smiled, then bobbed back and settled to her feed, tapping on Caro's chest bone as if applauding. These new, beatific smiles were fleeting reward enough for the wild and sleepless night that had gone before – almost. Every day a little change in what the child knew or could do. She tucked the blanket around both of them and began to rock, considering what was left in the cupboard that might make an impressive supper. Half a loaf, a bag of lentils, a cauliflower. She began to write a list of things that Alasdair must pick up in town during his lunch break. Caro had extended a standing invitation to Martha to dine with them every week. With Alasdair's mother so close, popping by unannounced at all hours – hello, dears, just me – Caro had begun to feel like the sole guardian of their privacy. Alasdair – and it was one of the things that made her love him so much – seemed incapable of saying no to his mother. The resulting placatory weekly invite to her had seemed to Caro extremely generous, given the intense planning entailed by a proper meal with a tablecloth and napkins. Caro was secretly trying to educate Martha not only into restraining her visits but also into enjoying pasta with tomato sauce, a simple salad drenched in olive oil, and other recipes from Elizabeth David that she'd clipped from a magazine. Recipes that Martha had so far failed to enjoy judging by her hearty and profuse compliments, as if cheering on the laggard in a race.

So it had seemed unfair of Martha, after such a generous offer, to continue to drop in at all hours, unannounced.

Yesterday, Caro had finally had enough. She had tried suggesting, now that the cottage had a phone line, that Martha could ring before she popped by. Check if it might be convenient.

A look of surprise and hurt appeared on Martha's face. 'Oh well, of course, dear. If you think I am intruding. I didn't mean to be a nuisance.' In future, she promised, she would always ring first.

In the end it was all sorted very simply – after a few uncomfortable moments. It was always best to be clear. So Caro was going to make something tonight that would convey that Alasdair's mother was welcome and cherished.

Alasdair appeared in his pyjamas, walking on the balls of his feet, turning his toes up against the cold flagstones, hair adorably rumpled.

'Is that coffee?'

'In the pot.'

He took his favourite mug, poured the rest of the coffee into it. Gave another sniff. 'Is something burning?'

'Damn. It's the porridge. On the back of the range. Can you give it a stir?'

'It's fine. Perfectly edible really.' He watched her as he stirred, a sleepy smile on his face. 'You look like a cross between a Renaissance Madonna and an Indian squaw in that blanket.'

'It was chilly this morning. Means it should be a beautiful day later.'

He put a bowl of porridge in front of her, a spoon by the side, kissed her on top of her hair. She breathed in the soft cotton smell of his blue pyjamas, the sleepy perfume of his skin.

Someone rapped loudly on the front door.

'That's early,' said Caro. 'Maybe the postie? It's been at least a week since I had a letter from Daddy or Phoebe.' She heard a familiar voice in the hallway and her heart sank.

'This is cosy,' said Martha as she appeared in the kitchen, shrugging off her coat. A tall woman with a long face, hair fastened up with many pins, and a definite, energetic manner, Martha had a way of filling any space. 'Ooh, is something burning?' She located the saucepan on the stove. 'One has to watch porridge like a hawk. And I'm so looking forward to coming for a bite of supper later.'

She settled at the table. 'Now I know I'm not following the new rules, ringing before I come and see my grandchild, but this isn't a visit as such. I just thought I'd pop by to see if Alasdair would like a lift into St Andrews since I'm going in anyway. So much nicer than having to wait for that bus. Alasdair dear, your feet must be cold. Have you no slippers?' She glanced over at Caro as she said this.

'New rules?' asked Alasdair but Caro was too busy fishing for the blanket that had fallen away, uncovering her breast, to try and explain. And what sort of wife would be rude enough not to make a cup of coffee and sit chatting, while Caro watched Martha's eyes rove around the messy kitchen she might have had time to clear up if Martha had given her warning, and if she'd not dropped in yesterday to bring over a couple of Alasdair's old baby blankets, with their slightly rank smell and yellowing wool, and then stayed to chat.

It was never restful when Martha was there. Always something that would worry her and that she must helpfully point out, or dropping hints she was surprised Caro was still breastfeeding Felicity at nine months. Worst of all was when Martha decided to do something useful, energetically emptying the larder to clean the shelves and putting everything back in some improved order, finding shirts that needed ironing, because a man must have a clean shirt for work.

Felicity started crying.

'Do let me take that child,' said Martha standing up and holding out her arms. 'It will give you a moment to get washed and dressed, dear. Mothers need time to themselves and you are looking awfully worn out.'

Alasdair had already commandeered the little bathroom. She went into the bedroom, lay down on the unmade bed and it was glorious, a few minutes of child-free truanting. She woke to Alasdair shaking her shoulder gently, dressed in his blue shirt and new trousers.

Caro saw the surprise in Martha's eyes to see her still in her nightgown as she took the sleeping Felicity back. She heard their cheery voices disappearing, the thud of the door closing. They left behind a feeling of failure. As the car pulled away, Caro saw that they had also left behind the shopping list. At least Alasdair had left the ration book too.

She wrestled the nappies into the twin tub, did the necessary things with a rubber hose to drain the water into the sink, put them through the mangle by the back door and pegged them out on the line. Hoisted them up with the prop to let the breeze catch them. Ten white terry-towelling flags signalling her victory, even if in a past life she would have considered such things flags of surrender. She took the list and the pushchair and the baby and walked to the end of the drive and along the lane to wait for the bus into St Andrews. The market stall, the grocer, the butcher's. She'd had just enough coupons left. She piled the shopping under the pushchair and walked Felicity back along the Scores, between the Victorian mansions and the far view of West Sands, the sea going out like a wrinkled brow. She walked on past Alasdair's imposing grey stone English department, a vast mansion overlooking the sea, and thought of him working away inside. She manoeuvred the pushchair down to her favourite place, little Castle Sands, and fed Felicity in the shadow of the red sandstone bluffs, eating a quick lunch of broken-off bread and cheese. She picked up a pebble-smooth piece of sea glass, green as an emerald, and slipped it into her coat pocket. Felicity's perfectly formed, downy head cradled in her hand, the tiny weight of a precious little cantaloupe; she tried to remember this, to settle it in her memory even as the moment was passing.

If she hurried there'd be time to pop into the library before the next bus back – she felt defeated and stale if she didn't have a book on the go – and there'd still be plenty of time when she got home to put a lamb ragout with thyme into the oven to cook slowly. After being worn down by hints from Martha that she should feed Alasdair 'properly', Caro had begun cooking meat again. An apple charlotte made with fresh butter and served with cream. It would take all her ration points but it would be simple and memorable. Martha would feel cherished and welcome.

Cutting up between the old fishermen's cottages, she was surprised to spot a familiar figure across the market square coming out of the Balmoral Hotel. It was Alasdair. He was talking animatedly with a petite woman, her dark hair cut in an elfin style, an elegant red suit in the new fashion. They were smiling in the way that people do who've just had a rather good lunch in a posh hotel. The woman moved to kiss his cheek. Alasdair hugged her. Caro watched as, with hands in his pockets, he headed back to the department, his head tipped in that way he had when he was humming to himself.

Why hadn't she called out to him, hurried over with a wave? It wasn't just the thought of being introduced to the elegant woman in the red suit, Caro in her seen-better-days coat, her windblown hair, the grocery-laden pushchair. There was something more that she didn't entirely care to examine. She'd felt a need to observe. She knew she was being quite silly, acting as if there was something illicit in what was almost certainly a working lunch with some colleague that Alasdair had failed to mention before. She could still run after him – darling, who was that I saw you with – but she knew Alasdair would need to get back to work, doing whatever it was he did in his study. And besides, she wasn't the sort of nervy and needy woman who spied on her husband.

She turned and pushed Felicity doggedly towards the bus stop. But the unsettling feeling that she'd witnessed something disloyal refused to go away. At the very least, the Balmoral was famous for its fussy three-course meals with wine and waiters – when Alasdair knew perfectly well she was cooking a special meal that evening. And a meal in the Balmoral was going to dent their weekly budget horribly. Perhaps she'd just cook an omelette later since he'd be positively stuffed. Or perhaps – and this was what she felt like doing as she hauled the shopping off the pushchair and folded it to get on the bus, Felicity on one hip – perhaps she'd go ahead and cook the lamb, with lots of potatoes, and a very large apple charlotte for pudding. Let Alasdair tell her he didn't feel awfully hungry.

As soon as she got back, the phone rang.

'Darling, bit of a hurry,' Alasdair began. 'Good news. Don't worry about cooking this evening. Mother's inviting us over to Kelly. She's got a wonderful idea she wants to run past you.'

'I've just been into town to do the shopping for tonight. You left the list.'

'Oh, I am such a nitwit. Sorry, darling. You've already done the shopping. That is bad luck.'

'Not luck exactly. By the way, I saw you across the marketplace, as you came out of the Balmoral.'

'Really? Darling, why ever didn't you come over and say hello?'

'You looked as if you were in a hurry to get back to the department.' She paused. 'You were talking with a rather smart-looking person, a woman.'

'You mean Diana. An old family friend. Have you never met Diana? She's just moved back here and she dragged me in for a catch-up and a bite to eat. If only I'd known you'd be in town. We could have all eaten together. Anyway, we'll talk tonight. About Mother's idea.'

'Alasdair, I can tell you now that I am simply not going to agree to move into the castle. I need – we need – space away from Martha, room to be a family.'

'It's nothing like that.'

'What then?'

'Look, darling, and don't be cross, but it's just that Mother's noticed that you seem a bit down.'

'She thinks I'm a bit down?' Caro suddenly felt tears welling up. Was she down? Anger that Martha had noticed. Relief that someone had noticed.

'She was thinking you might like some sort of project?'

'A project?' Caro allowed herself a bitter laugh. 'She doesn't think I'm busy enough already?'

'Some time to yourself. A chance to do some research again. It would be an actual post, darling, archivist to the estate, rooting through family records and letters and putting them in order for Mother. And you'll like this – perhaps you might even solve the family mystery.'

'How do you mean?'

'It's never been something my family talk about much, but no one has the slightest idea who my great-grandmother was, other than that she was a Mrs Gillan. I even tried to find out more about her once or twice, but every last trace of her has been excised from the family records. Just the sort of sleuthing through archives you're so good at.

Oh, and don't worry because Barbara could help mind Felicity when she comes in, or Mother. But we'll talk later.'

'Alasdair, I don't think–' He was gone. But even as she put the black receiver with its smell of Bakelite back in its cradle, Caro's spirits were beginning to lift. The idea of having her own work to do again, a door through which she might walk into her old life for just a little while each week. Was it possible? The idea of tracing this vanished relative was certainly intriguing. She started folding a pile of nappies from the laundry basket.

Of course it was marvellous to have a baby and people simply didn't realize that caring for a child took easily as much thought and intelligence as any thesis, and was equally absorbing and rewarding – in its own different way. But the rustle of papers at a calm desk, following through a thought. Someone else holding Felicity for a while.

Perhaps she was too harsh on Martha. Surely it wasn't beyond Caro's wit to try and get on with her better. After all, they had so much in common. They both adored Alasdair and they both adored Felicity. Or was this simply another ploy of Martha's to some obscure end? It was always hard to work out what Martha was really thinking.

Caro looked down at the skirt and short-sleeved blouse and cardigan she was wearing, had been wearing for a couple of days now. There were stains on her shoulder, the skirt in need of ironing. Yet she made sure Alasdair had his clean shirt each day. Felicity was always beautifully dressed in tiny, adorable, clean clothes. When had she become the last priority in the household?

While Felicity was asleep Caro took a hurried bath, rolled on her girdle from pre-Felicity days and snapped on her remaining pair of good stockings. Not wearing a girdle was, after all, considered a sign of bad breeding in certain circles. But she had to roll it straight off again in order to breathe. She put on her favourite red skirt, and the embroidered peasant blouse that Alasdair had bought for her in Sorrento, pinned up her thick hair. She rooted around in her bedside drawer and found a lipstick. Stood and gazed at the woman in the mirror.

Who was that woman? Hard to know these days. Having a child had broken up the pieces of herself and handed them back in an order she didn't recognize, with the expectation that she would immediately know how to incorporate nappy buckets and feeding schedules and ways to cook turnips into her daily life. The Caro she knew had excelled at university, loved her post as a lecturer during the war. But post-natal Caro was a strange, Picasso-like woman made of opposing elements. Often overwhelmed with self-doubt. The rolling days of motherhood gave no prizes or pay packets to chart progress, just small chores that would need repeating as soon as they were done, and a dispiriting, overwhelming feeling of never being in control of events. She missed capable and confident Caro, dashing around the country, lecturing to upturned faces in village halls, able to clean a carburettor or expound on Shakespeare's plays equally well. She had admired that Caro.

A stirring from the pram in the hallway. A small grunt. She picked up Felicity and was given that beaming toothless smile. Wide-open eyes filled with such glee fastened on hers and the world tipped into joy again, one of those moments that reordered everything that had come before. She cradled the child in arms that were plumper than before, and realized that she felt strong, capable. Blessed. Standing at the open door of their life to come.

CHAPTER 4

Early morning, a line of light around the edges of the tall shutters. Charlotte can feel a mounting energy in the air that won't let her stay in bed. Six faint chimes from the clock in the drawing room below. No one about except for the servants moving like ghosts through the hidden passageways of Kelly, dusting, laying fires.

She slips from bed, crosses the floorboards and folds back the white shutters to see the larches bright with early sun, gold light on green. Beyond the castle roofs smoke is rising from the chimney of the Laundry Cottage, where the water will be set to boil for the day's wash. No point going to see if Mary will be free, not until Mary has finished the morning tasks for her aunt. Last summer, and the summers before, Charlotte could fetch Mary from the cottage at any time of the day and they would run through the woods, Oliver and Louisa joining in their games. But now everything's changed. Mary's been given an apron, a worried frown on her face when Charlotte asks her to come out so they can wander through the fields together. 'Not till I've finished the ironing, Miss Charlotte.' And Mary will be shut away with the hissing flat irons, folded sheets airing on rails above her like a village of white Bedouin tents floating in the air.

Charlotte opens the wardrobe door slowly, pausing at each creak so as not to wake her sister in the room above. In the inlaid mirror she catches sight of a sliding image of last night's work, the dressing table with scissors next to an ivory comb, fistfuls of hair spilling onto the floor. She looks away quickly, thinks of Louisa's pillow with its crown of curling rags. It will be a long time before Charlotte sleeps in curling rags again.

She feels around on the floor of the wardrobe, ignoring the hateful new dress hanging above, and pulls out a pile of Oliver's old clothes. Hurrying now, for the morning's already getting away from her, she drags on the trousers, tightens the belt on the last notch. She's not as broad as Oliver was two years back. Pulls on the Aran sweater, its oily wool hinting of sea voyages and adventures. No time for socks, she laces up the boots, runs a hand over her hair. She hasn't got used to the new weightlessness.

The girls' rooms are in the oldest part of the castle in the North-West Tower, built in the Dark Ages and from which the castle has spread out in layers of increasing elegance and ambition. She winds down the stone staircase that opens out onto the chapel in the Tower Room below, crosses it to reach the drawing room. Charlotte can just about remember visiting Kelly as a small child of four or five, when Aunt Sylvia and Uncle Gregor had first purchased the castle. It was still a ruin then. She remembered great holes in the roof two floors above the drawing room, snow drifting down and piling up on the wet floorboards, dark ravens swooping and hopping through the rooms, cawing their displeasure at being disturbed. How cold it had been and how tightly Papa had held her in his arms because it was too dangerous to run through the rooms. She could remember Aunt Sylvia's excitement, her arms waving as she outlined all the things she was going to do to bring the castle back to life, a tall figure in violet capes and skirts, nodding flowers in Aunt Sylvia's hat. Why can't she remember her father's face better? Or her mother's? Because she had had no idea that one day she would need to remember them.

She thought they would always be there, a constant part of her, Father kind and solid, Mother warm and petite in a green woollen dress.

Crossing the back of the drawing room with its silk chaises and white-painted panelling – hard to imagine it as a ruin now – she comes out on the main staircase. She glances over the banister to the sunburst of black-and-white marble tiles of the hallway below, catches the shadow of a maid disappearing through a door. No one else about.

She creeps down, along the back corridor, and bursts out of the back door, four storeys of windows still sleeping blind above her. Breaking into a run, she's soon near the Laundry Cottage and glimpses Mary's aunt at the back, sleeves rolled up, casting grain to the chickens.

Of all the places that Charlotte loves in Kelly Castle, the Laundry Cottage is her favourite. How many times has she sat at the pine scrubbed table next to Mary, thick slices of a new loaf spread with yellow butter by Mary's kindly aunt, Jean, while the coal glows red in the range and the white linen airs on the rails above? Mary has become as much a sister as Louisa, in all their summers growing up together at Kelly. At Christmas and in summer, as soon as the boarding school term was over, Charlotte and Louisa would go not to their aunt, their official guardian, and her house in a gloomy street in Glasgow, but to the home of the Gillans, Uncle Gregor, Aunt Sylvia and their son Oliver. Not that they were a real aunt and uncle, but they had been such good friends of Father's that the girls had always called them such. Uncle Gregor said that the air in the countryside was so much better for their lungs than the sooty air of town. And such healthy lungs they had too, according to Aunt Sylvia, who wondered if Charlotte must always shriek like a banshee in such an unladylike way.

Charlotte frowned as she passed the cottage but carried on. It wasn't that Charlotte wasn't welcome at the cottage any more, but lately, Mary's aunt had made it plain to her that it wasn't kind to run in and out of the cottage at all hours, tempting Mary to come out and play. This summer, Mary had to work.

Mary, she knew, was tolerated by Aunt Sylvia, as part of Aunt Jean's household. A better life for her here, Jean said, than going straight into the jute mills that were the destiny of most Dundee girls. At Kelly there was fresh air and good food and a chance to go to school in the village. But now that Mary was old enough to work, her aunt was hoping, expecting, that Oliver's mother might find a place for her niece soon among the housemaids. Otherwise Mary would have to return to Dundee and join her other aunts in the jute mill, its air thick with fibres that clogged the lungs, its thundering machines that left the girls half-deaf.

The same jute factories that had paid for Kelly Castle.

'And please, Miss Charlotte,' Aunt Jean had begged her, 'no more remonstrating with Mr Gillan about the mill conditions. They'll think it's me who has put you up to it, or Mary, when we are hoping, as you know, to hear soon.'

Mary's loss of freedom was not the only thing making this summer so strange and disappointing. Charlotte had always pitied Louisa's attempts to be dignified and seemly as the older sister while she and Oliver vied to climb the highest tree, or to shoot the straightest home-made arrows. Louisa pale and anxious on the sidelines. But lately, Oliver had shown not the slightest interest in making pirate dens. It was Louisa he noticed. He'd even praised the blue of Louisa's dress, how it matched her eyes. Oliver, who had never once noticed or cared about clothes before. A horribly upsetting betrayal. Charlotte did not have a high opinion of boys in general, but Oliver had always been a constant friend; now, however, it was as if he'd forgotten who she was, who he, Oliver, was. He'd even laughed when she'd dared him to race her to the top of the old Scots pine on the lawn. Said girls didn't climb trees.

Angry tears pricked her eyes. While they'd been away at school that year it seemed that someone had decreed that childhood was over, a closing-down of what a girl may or may not do – and a forewarning of the hardening of roles to come that she saw in the lives of the adults around her.

Well, Charlotte was not going to accept it. She would stay true to herself and true to the things she loved. And in time, she was sure of it, Oliver and Mary, and even Louisa, would come round to her view that nothing was as fine as the freedom they had shared here at Kelly, long, light days whooping around the grounds, Oliver leading the charge, even Louisa sometimes forgetting herself, running with skirts bunched up, voices echoing against the hills.

Striding fast across the lawns towards those hills, the old boots darkening as they splashed through thick dew, she dived into the rhododendron bushes, found the break in the low iron fencing that marked the boundary to the estate and entered the cool world of larches and birch trees. She took off her itchy hat, ran her hand again over the strange shortness, the tender changes of temperature on her scalp. Her head so light she could almost float.

No, she wouldn't think of the gloomy bedroom, or the long black strands of hair on the dressing table. Her stomach turned over with a flutter of dread all the same.

She followed the boots where they wanted to go, taking wide steps up soft banks of pine needles, climbing higher through shaded avenues of slender pine trunks, the treetops above crowding together to whisper their secrets.

Then out beyond the woods where the whole coastland lay open and bathed in brilliant morning colours, magenta soil, bright green corn, or the dark green of cabbage fields that were almost navy. Beyond it, the sea; and a little further along the coast, beyond where she could see, lay the Tay Estuary and the port of Dundee where ships travelled out across the world, to India, to America, to Russia and the Arctic. And one day – she took a deep breath – one day, she too would set sail in just such a ship.

Going back down the hill she began to feel the lack of breakfast – and the lack of socks. The left boot had chafed a sore patch on her ankle making her walk with her foot on one side. And with the rooftops of Kelly growing larger, she felt a wavering of courage. Those handfuls of hair in the gloomy bedroom were very final.

She took the longer route back, skirting unseen through the saplings round the back of the drying lawns. Sails of radiant white sheets now hung in the shafts of slanting light that would pole over the garden as the day progressed.

Briefly, she caught sight of Mary moving behind the kitchen window. Headed back to the castle with a feeling of exile.

Creeping back in through the servants' door, she could hear Annie singing in the back kitchen, Tom Griddle's flat footsteps along the stone slabs of the passage. She ran back up to her room, slipped inside. Jumped when she saw Louisa sitting on the bed, skeins of black hair in her hands. Louisa's fair hair was very much still on her head, brushed into ringlets and held with ribbons. She was wearing the blue morning dress that suited her so well.

'How could you? Have you forgotten that we are guests in the house, Charlotte?'

'As if I'm allowed to, for even a minute.'

'Where precisely do you think we will go each summer if not to Kelly? Oh, why must you be so difficult?' Tears landed on Louisa's lap, leaving dark spots on the blue cotton.

'You don't have to cry, Lou. It's a few handfuls of hair, not the end of the world.'

Louisa huffed with exasperation. 'We're not children any more, Charlotte, playing castaways in the woods.'

'Better if we were.' Charlotte kicked the end of the bed, her lips set.

'And such lovely thick black hair. I was going to help you put it up for the first time. And after Aunt Sylvia had that beautiful new dress made for you.'

'This? This beautiful?'

Charlotte dashed to the wardrobe and pulled out the dress, held it in front of her; an ugly, fussy thing that Aunt Sylvia had ordered in Perth, since Charlotte should have something suitable for her age now, as almost a young lady. A muddy lilac stripe overlaid with encrustations of lace at the front, buttoned wrists and a long buttoned bodice that would need a maid with a button hook to get out of, a scratchy ruff of lace around the neck. A large silk bow on the back making it difficult to sit down comfortably.

'I think it is charming. And ladylike,' said Louisa.

'It's a fancy pudding with so many flavours it's inedible, and all to show how kind Oliver's mother is to orphans. I'll never wear it.'

But even as she shoved it back into the wardrobe, Charlotte knew Aunt Sylvia had a way of making sure that she would.

Charlotte pulled on her oldest and most comfortable day dress. The hem was a little short of late, but all the better for running. She felt the itch of tears in her eyes again, for the cool wind on her face when she and the other children used to race across the lawns together, laughing and calling out.

As to the hair, there was nothing to be done – save using a pot of glue. Louisa chose a large velvet tam-o'-shanter, soft enough to pull down and cover Charlotte's hair completely.

'A lady may wear a hat indoors while dining,' she said, doubtfully.

'At breakfast?' said Charlotte.

One behind the other, with solemn steps, they descended the tower staircase.

'If Father had lived. . .' whispered Charlotte.

'I know, dearest. But please try and remember that we are fortunate to be here,' whispered Louisa. 'It is only for Uncle Gregor's friendship with Father that we are invited here each year.'

And perhaps for his feeling of guilt, though that was never said. It was Uncle Gregor who had underwritten their father's Arctic expedition, sent out in the hope of discovering new sources of whale oil. The Dundee jute mills could not run without it. After the expedition was lost, he had also accepted the privilege of underwriting Louisa and Charlotte's education, relieving the elderly aunt when their boarding school term ended, the girls arriving in a series of green-and-gold summers and crisp winters, watching the gradual restoration of the old building from ragged, ivy-hung sandstone walls to a beautiful Scottish mansion house filled with medieval furniture and rare paintings.

The tower steps ended at the little chapel room. In it hung the portrait of Aunt Sylvia's brother, William, for ever a handsome young man of nineteen in a blue Admiralty jacket. William had also disappeared in the Arctic, but some twenty years earlier than their father. He had been lost with the Franklin expedition that had been sent out in the hope of finding the fabled northern trading route and which was lost without a trace. And if anyone might think that Aunt Sylvia's loss would make her more sympathetic to the girls' loss, then Charlotte could have told them what was implied by every headache or injured tone from their hostess, or fit of nerves that left her in bed for days: Mrs Sylvia Gillan's pain was too vast and all absorbing for any such thing.

Above all, the girls knew to never, ever mention the terrible lies that had circulated around the Franklin expedition some years ago. It had taken Charlotte a long time to understand what the lies were supposedly about, and the significance of a pot of half-cooked human bones the Eskimos claimed to have found, along with a silver plate engraved with the name of Franklin's lost ship. Aunt Sylvia agreed with Lady Franklin – and even Dickens agreed in his journal articles – that sons of Empire and Admiralty could never have committed such heinous crimes, even if they were starving to death in the Arctic wastes. No, it was the Arctic savages, the Eskimos, who had murdered William and his fellow officers as the men tried to struggle home across the snowy deserts. And it was the Eskimos who had spread the vile lies in an attempt to cover the evidence of their own murderous crimes.

Now Aunt Sylvia hated the entire Eskimo race with all her heart and Charlotte's relations with Aunt Sylvia had not been improved by the time Charlotte had made a campfire in the woods and cooked something called cannibal stew. Which Aunt Sylvia had found out about when all the children were very sick from the mushrooms that Oliver had added.

The chapel led out onto the long drawing room. At the far end Charlotte caught sight of Oliver springing up from where he'd been kneeling, hurrying through into the breakfast room. She wondered why his ears were burning red.

CHAPTER 5

KELLY, 1949

Martha had set out an early supper in the walled garden, the sun brilliant on the squares of lawn intersected by gravel paths and borders of flowers. Against the deep blue summer sky, the castle with its tall square tower houses, its corbels and hanging turrets bulging out at the top, looked impossibly romantic, a uniquely Scottish place that had grown around a large fortified tower house, amended and added to over the centuries. Martha carried out cold salmon, potatoes in mint butter and a jug of iced cordial made from the garden's raspberries.

Barbara had stayed on to help, a short and motherly woman with grey hair and a deep Fife accent. She paused to look into Felicity's carrycot, clucking at the darling sleeping inside.

'The problem is,' Martha explained, 'and it's bad news, but I have to tell you that I can't see how we can keep Kelly going without asking the National Trust to take on at least part of the castle. As you know, it's always been a struggle since the death duties after your father passed away made such a terrible hole in our finances.'

'Mummy, you should have told me how bad things were getting,' said Alasdair. 'There must be something we can do to keep the place, surely. We've managed before.'

'I know, darling, but an old girl like Kelly needs a constant influx of cash, just to keep up with the repairs. And I don't want to hold on to her until things get so bad that it's just the owls and the rooks living here again.'

'The owls and the rooks?' said Caro. 'The inscription above the door. "This mansion snatched from rooks and owls. . ."'

'"For honest ease and restful hours." Yes,' said Martha, 'that's it. When Duguld's great-grandparents, Sylvia and Gregor, first saw Kelly it had been abandoned for fifty years. The castle really did have only owls and rooks living here. Then the Gillans came by one winter. They found great holes in the roof and snow on the floors, birds' nests poking out of the fireplace in the hall, but fell completely in love with the castle. Poured much of their considerable jute fortune into bringing Kelly back to life. So one feels a responsibility, you see. I wouldn't like to be the one to let things get out of hand again and one has to face facts.'

'But this National Trust thing, it seems rather drastic. There really is no other way?' asked Alasdair with a frown.

'Not that I can see. And believe me, darling, I've tried to find one.'

He looked glum. 'I can see it could make sense in lots of ways, the democratic thing to do and all that, after all, but the thought of people tramping through the house and gardens, our home. It takes a bit of getting used to.'

'I know, Pudding, dear.' Martha rubbed his shoulder affectionately. 'But the worst of it is, it's not even certain that the National Trust will want Kelly. And if not, then I can't see any option but to sell to the American hotel chain that's more than keen to buy Kelly to cater to rich golfers. As you know, they've been pestering me relentlessly. I've no idea how they got wind of our situation.'

'But that would be terrible,' Caro blurted out. For all that she sometimes chose to disapprove of Kelly, she couldn't imagine losing it, the place where she had envisaged Felicity playing in the gardens as she grew up, or sleeping sometimes in the blue-canopied cot that had once belonged to Alasdair and to generations of Kelly babies.

'I absolutely agree, Caro dear, but I must say they're horribly persistent. They even inveigled their way in for a tour of the place a few months ago. Had the cheek to make me an offer, there and then. A very large sum, in fact. But to hear them talking about all the things they'd rip out to make way for the myriad new bathrooms they'd need for their golfers, it was heartbreaking. Made one feel like the great unwashed. They were full of compliments about dear old Kelly, of course, but I could see they had a very poor view of our make-do-and-mend ways. And as for my art studio in the old stables,' Martha said, a catch in her voice, 'that, it seems, would be just the thing to make garaging for cars.'

Caro noticed tears welling in Martha's eyes and blinked away answering tears in her own. Every room in Kelly bore the mark of Martha's loving restorations and additions, all done on a shoestring. The golden silk-and-lace canopy in the main bedroom that looked so elegant, made from dyed parachute silk and an old wedding veil. The patchwork quilts and antique furniture that graced the rooms, Martha had found in junkyards and the jumble markets, nursed them back to life in her workshop where she also painted. Everything done on the tiniest budget, but with such flair and resourcefulness that it all looked wonderfully in keeping with the castle. Her energy was breath-taking; the wooden panelling she had restored, the salvaged Persian rugs. Martha's heart and soul were in Kelly, and to see that all torn apart by a hotel chain with no feeling for the unique Arts and Crafts atmosphere that made the ancient castle into a home, it would be too painful to endure.

'We'll just have to persuade the National Trust to help,' said Caro. 'How can they not want Kelly?'

'That's where you could come in, dear Caro. You see, it would help our case greatly if we could hand them an archive of Kelly's history and the people who lived here. Alasdair's father – and I'm always so sorry you never met Duguld – was working on just such a history before he was taken from us so suddenly. He documented Kelly's early beginnings and its inhabitants most thoroughly, but the items relating to his own family – and there are boxes and boxes of them – are still in his office waiting to be sorted through, going all the way back to 1820. I'm afraid I've never been able to face sorting them out, but now it's become rather pressing.'

'It sounds like the sort of research I did at Cambridge,' said Caro. 'And I'd so love to, but with the baby, of course, I'm afraid I couldn't do it justice.'

'That's the brilliant thing,' said Alasdair. 'Mother was saying she thinks the estate would be able to justify paying a small honorarium, enough for Barbara to come in for a few more hours and help with Felicity, just as she used to with me and Pippa. And then, of course, I'll be here to help out at the weekends if you wanted to crack on with it. And Mother's always here.'

They heard a loud barking. A black Labrador came bounding across the grass. He put his head on Alasdair's knee, then bounded off again. Alasdair's sister Pippa appeared along the gravelled path, the same pale red hair as Alasdair, and the same energetic gait. She wore a white summer dress with yellow roses, a cardigan over her shoulders, a silk scarf tied at her neck.

'I didn't know you were here, you ruffian,' she said, kissing Alasdair. 'Hello, Caro. Mother.' She kissed the air in their direction and pulled the dog back from sniffing the carrycot. 'I'll put Max in the stable.'

When Pippa came back Martha updated her on her new project to save the castle. Pippa already knew about the offer from the hotel. 'I didn't think you'd have time to go rooting through all the old boxes, Pippa dear,' Martha added.

'Oh gosh, no. I'm afraid I'm far too busy. Caro will do a much better job, I'm sure.'

'And Alasdair mentioned there's some mystery around a missing bride,' added Caro.

'Gosh, that,' said Pippa. 'Isn't it odd? We don't know who our great-grandmother was other than that she was a Mrs Gillan. We know she had a child, our grandmother, Eugenia, a legitimate child who inherited the castle, so we assume the woman in question must have been properly married to our great-grandfather, but that's all we know – no first name, not a trace of her. Not even an actual marriage certificate. Record's been scraped clean. I don't know what she did to deserve such obliteration but it must have been rather dreadful.'

'How can someone do something so terrible that she deserves to be erased from her own child's memory?' said Caro.

'I always wondered if she simply wasn't up to the mark,' said Martha. 'Perhaps Oliver married for love, someone like a maid. Something that would have been unthinkable for Victorians like the Gillans. Since their fortune came from the jute industry in Dundee, they would have been considered rather *nouveau riche* tradespeople by many of the Fife aristocracy back then, and probably quite sensitive about such matters. Even your grandmother had the same outlook. I think Eugenia was rather shocked when Duguld brought me home, a galumphing art student in a velvet-and-silk creation I'd made on the art-school sewing machine, a silk headband across my brow that I was rather pleased with at the time. Not at all the county-set girl Duguld was supposed to bring home. Poor Eugenia. Duguld was only meant to attend art school to get such ideas out of his system before becoming a lawyer. I always found his mother rather critical. And so standoffish. Almost a recluse. A tiny little woman in black who hardly ever spoke unless it was to tell you about some error you had made. When I first came to Kelly as a bride, I was so unhappy I vowed I'd never make the same mistakes that Duguld's mother made. I'd try to be much more open and welcoming if I had a daughter-in-law.' She smiled at Caro.

Caro returned the smile, but felt an odd disconnect. Was Martha really saying that she felt herself to be open and welcoming? So was it Caro herself then who was being difficult in finding Martha so intrusive and quite frankly critical? Or was Caro simply misreading things and overreacting? Going mad, perhaps? She gave her head a mental shake. She needed to get a grip.

After supper, Martha led the way up to the Long Room, a Jacobean gallery panelled in lime-washed oak, the white plaster ceilings studded with rosettes and embellishments like an upside-down wedding cake. Four tall windows looked out over a long view of cornfields. In the far distance the deep blue sweep of the sea faded into an immense sky. A stack of old photograph albums had been set out on a side table, the tooled leather faded and worn at the corners.

'Do look through them,' said Martha. 'And I'll fetch the family tree from the library.'

Caro leafed through the stiff pages, family portraits in cardboard frames, women in wide-skirted silk dresses with narrow waists and lacquered curls, men with bushy sideburns and long frock coats.

'How wonderful to have so many family photographs from the very beginning of photography documenting the family,' said Caro. 'It's very unusual.'

'St Andrews was a centre for the new art,' said Alasdair. 'The university has quite a collection hidden away in the archives, apparently.'

Martha came back with a roll of paper. She spread it out to show generations of Gillans inked in like the roots of a tree. One thing drew the eye: in place of Oliver's wife's name was a black square of ink so layered and scratched into the paper that the pen had made a tiny hole at one point. Even holding the paper up to the light, as

Caro did, it was impossible to read what lay beneath. The word 'wife' had been scrappily inked in below it with the date 1883. A line led down from the couple to a child, Eugenia Gillan.

'Duguld's mother was hopelessly confusing when I asked her about it. I felt sure she must have known more than she claimed to but I wasn't encouraged to probe. Very touchy on the matter. I always felt, though, that in a house like this where there's room to store every last item, there must be something, some clue as to who the woman was.'

'You mean there's an awful lot of old junk in Kelly's cupboards that someone really ought to throw out,' said Pippa. 'By the way, is it time for a small whisky? Shall I?'

She opened a door in a scene of hills and trees painted on a wall panel and brought out a bottle and four cut-glass tumblers.

Sitting himself between Martha and Caro on the Knole sofa, the three of them ensconced within its high sides, Alasdair picked up one of the albums and began turning the pages. He paused at one. 'So is this Oliver? He of the missing wife? He's younger than in the oil painting in the hall, but you can still see it's him.'

Martha and Caro leaned in and studied the tall, slim man. He had high, round cheekbones and the sort of sculpted and open face that must have made people like him.

'That's right,' said Martha. 'Your great-grandfather. And now that you're the same age as he is in the photo, you do look remarkably alike.'

The fire had been banked down for the night, the mesh guard pulled across to stop any stray embers rolling onto the rug. Martha and Pippa had gone down to the kitchen with the tray of glasses and coffee cups and Alasdair had taken Felicity's carrycot up to their room. Caro was glad they'd agreed to stay over in the end, to save taking Felicity back to the cottage in the chill air and waking her. She knew she should be following Alasdair up and taking the chance to sleep while Felicity did but she lingered on, caught by faint but intriguing whispers of Alasdair and Felicity's features in the faces in the old photographs. Odd when you thought about it; all these people were related to her child in a way that she would never be. And she could feel too the old buzz of curiosity that she'd so loved as a student, hunting through documents and letters in the university archives, piecing together lives and stories.

As she closed the album, she already knew she was going to agree to Martha's suggestion – couldn't wait to get started, in fact. And it was an honour in a way, for Martha to entrust this project to her as if she appreciated her achievements. Caro had, after all, been one of the first women to be awarded a degree at her college in Cambridge.

She was going to go downstairs right now and tell Martha that she'd love to take on the project.

Clutching an album she wanted to ask a question about, Caro made her way down the main staircase, treading carefully in the half-light, one electric lamp on down in the entrance hall. Reaching the ground floor, she could hear voices through the open kitchen door, Martha and Pippa talking. Good, they were still there.

'I thought Diana married that chap and moved to New Zealand with him.' This was Martha's voice.

Caro paused at the foot of the stairs, listening.

'She did, but seems it didn't work out,' Pippa replied.

'Does Alasdair know she's back?'

'Apparently.'

'I always thought she and Alasdair might make a go of it some day.'

'We all did, Mummy. Diana certainly did. And of course with her family being loaded. . .'

'She's a dear though, isn't she, Caro?' Martha replied with emphasis.

'Oh Mummy. But don't you find her very grammar school and suburban? And let's be honest, Alasdair got engaged in such a rush, the war and all that. And so young. It was more or less a holiday romance with a ring. It will have been Caro who pushed for it.'

'Alasdair has made his choice, and we will support him in that one hundred per cent.'

'Always the trouper, Mother.'

Frozen three steps up, Caro felt an odd prickling along her arms and neck, a pulsing of blood under the skin that felt like a flush of shame. She turned and tiptoed back upstairs, a queasy mixture of emotions melting the assessment of who she had been a moment before.

Caro had always been rather proud of how she managed to get on with most people – with a little effort. If you expected the best of people, then they would respond in kind. But when it came to Martha and the rest of Alasdair's family, time and again all past experiences failed her. The last time she'd felt this stumped had been in Form Four, when Marjorie Price had told the girls that Caro was no longer part of their wretched gang and they'd ignored her for a whole week.

She quietly climbed back up the stairs, anger and frustration also rising inside her chest, and with it, a growing feeling of stubborn kinship with the woman so thoroughly erased from the family tree. By the time Caro reached the door of their bedroom in the Jacobean tower house, she'd made a vow to herself that she was going to pull the poor woman from the shadows.

And yet – and this was the thing that made Caro hesitate – what if the truth turned out to be some terrible scandal that Martha might wish had stayed secret, that even Caro might regret unearthing and having to tell Felicity about one day?

CHAPTER 6

At the far end of the drawing room, Oliver folded down his lanky frame to try and coax the new kitten out from under the console table. He could hear the voices of his parents through the open breakfast-room door.

Mama was saying that she would not go with Papa and the children to see the new ship that Papa had invested in, her blood being thin after a bout of summer influenza. There was a pause, the clink of metal, Mama watching Agnes spoon kidneys from the silver chaffer on the sideboard onto her plate – that's sufficient, thank you, Agnes. But when Papa told her that the boat's co-investor, Lord Lochinver, would also be there to view the ship, and that Lady Lochinver and her daughter would be joining them for a late luncheon at the Castle Hotel, then Mama said perhaps she would come after all. Which showed, Oliver supposed, that Mama was very keen on a splendid meal.

'However, I wonder if it might be best for Louisa and Charlotte to stay behind this morning,' Mama said. Here Oliver raised his head to listen. 'Oliver spends so much time in the company of those girls. And it's not that I mind them staying so often and for such a long time, but there are things to consider, things about which I am not entirely happy.'

Oliver waited to hear more about these things that displeased Mama, but heard only a scraping of butter on toast. Had it been the time they had broken the window in the library, playing cricket, or the time they had taken the pony and Charlotte had sprained her arm falling off? Papa muttered something about duty and doing the right thing.

'Of course we will do our duty,' Mama replied tartly. 'But no matter the obligations you feel towards Strachan's girls, they are, when all is said and done, not family.'

A reply from his father, which Oliver could not catch.

A sharp chink of a teacup set down on a saucer. 'Why it is always assumed that because Oliver is an only child I am content to welcome this regular incursion of two extra children? And, as a good Christian, I do welcome them, every summer, but as you well know it is not easy. Charlotte is two steps away from becoming a complete savage, try as I might to guide her. One would expect more manners at thirteen, and so underfed-looking and sallow in spite of all she consumes. Louisa may be more biddable in character, and passingly pretty with that fair hair, but she's fast approaching an age when attachments are made, as is Oliver, and sweet as Louisa is, she's hardly suitable.'

Oliver's ears had begun to turn pink as it dawned on him what his mother was implying.

'Fortunately, boys develop much more slowly than girls in these matters – Oliver is still a child really – but that doesn't mean he's safe from the little tricks of someone with schemes.'

'Come now, Sylvia. Would it be so bad if Oliver were to choose Louisa one day?'

Another fast scraping of a knife on hard toast. 'Not while I have breath in my body. There. That's how strongly I feel. This throwing together of young people is not fair on Oliver. He needs to meet more suitable prospects. The Lochinvers' daughter, I hear, is most accomplished. Will have her own fortune. And besides, do I need to point out that the Dundee docks, dirty as they are and with the wind coming in straight from the sea, are no place for young girls?'

'Sylvia, I can assure you that the Earl Grey docks will have been thoroughly sluiced down today. It'll do the girls good to breathe a sea wind. Think how disappointed Oliver will be if we set out without them.'

'My point entirely.'

Oliver could hear the voices of the two girls inside the chapel that led off the back of the drawing room. Any moment now they would come out through the door. Not wishing to meet them for reasons he hardly wished to examine, his ears burning red, Oliver scrambled up and hurried into breakfast ahead of them.

'Are you cold, Charlotte?' Aunt Sylvia asked, frowning at the velvet beret that Charlotte had chosen to wear through breakfast.

'A little,' she replied, touching the bonnet to make sure it was still in place.

'There,' said Aunt Sylvia. 'You see, the girls are feeling the morning's chill. Wouldn't you prefer to remain here this morning rather than catch a cold?'

'My dear, if you are concerned about the wind, then none of us shall mind if you wish to stay behind,' said Uncle Gregor mildly, folding his newspaper.

Aunt Sylvia changed into her new emerald-green walking suit with its waterfall of pleated skirts, a bustle held by a rose at the back, a tiny velvet pie of a hat. The French seamstress from Dundee had assured her that she had the height to carry off the very latest Paris fashions, even if she looked rather wider in the mirror than the illustrations once the dress was done, the narrow waist elusive.

As she entered the carriage to join her husband, Sylvia found that Charlotte had decided to bring Mary from the wash house with her, of all things. The two of them were crushed into a corner of the carriage in a demonstration of how little space they both took up, the reasonableness of Charlotte's demand. Mary wore her best green cotton, a brown jacket, but she made a poor contrast beside the girls in their good woollen capes with large mother-of-pearl buttons. The two girls looked out at her with those accusing eyes of orphans, but Aunt Sylvia saw it all. Charlotte had not expected her to come and thought she would be able to persuade Mr Gillan to allow this latest fantasy of hers. Rather than spoil her husband's mood, Aunt Sylvia decided to say nothing, for now, but her lips were set in a line that Charlotte recognized. A missed meal, some treat she would think up so that Charlotte could be denied it. It didn't matter; it was a price Charlotte would be ready to pay.

No, thought Aunt Sylvia, as the carriage picked up pace towards the station, even when Charlotte was not sulking, one could not call the girl pretty. Striking, perhaps, with her smooth, black hair, dark brown eyes like little polished coals, but it was all ruined by that direct and challenging glare, lips pressed together as if planning some revolution in the future. Even Louisa, softer and more attractive in features, had a disappointing sallow tinge to her skin, a pressed-in little nose and features as if life had borne down on her too hard, the dark circles under her eyes of those who worry more than they sleep. Try as she might, Louisa had not mastered the skill of making others feel comfortable, which is, after all, the sign of good breeding and character.

After the green quiet of the woods and fields around Kelly Castle, the dockside was an assault on the senses. The air rang and shuddered with the noise of iron wheel rims on cobbles, with hammer blows and the shrieking of gulls. Pungent smells piqued the nose, tar and the reek of whale fat from the boilers' yard, new-sawn wood and the sour tang of seaweed. In front of them lay the wide brightness of the Tay's water, on the far side low hills of darker silver. Above, a white, open sky. Whalers and fishing boats were massed along the wharves, masts moving with the water's swell. Landward, the forest of Dundee's factory chimneys climbed the hill, plumes of smoke racing away to the sea.

The entrance to the Earl Grey wharf was graced with an archway of fanciful Gothic brickwork. This abrupt piece of theatrical scenery had been dropped in the middle of the dockyard hustle, paid for by the rich of Dundee, so that Her Royal Highness Queen Victoria could pass beneath it each time she disembarked from her yacht on the way to her residence in Balmoral. Now, Mr Gillan led his wife through and the girls and Oliver followed behind.

The Lochinvers were already on the quayside, Lord Lochinver talking with the captain. The gentlemen shook hands, Mrs Gillan in her bright green fluttering attentively around Lady Lochinver's more sombre grey dress and pelisse.

'So what d'you think?' asked Lochinver as they paced along the quayside. 'Double hulled, reinforced at bow and stern with metal plates. She could stand a full winter caught in the ice and not be crushed. Not that we intend any such thing. She'll be back home with the boat full of oil and baleen before the winter.'

'It's certainly high time we chartered our own whaling boat,' said Mr Gillan. 'It will mean the end of being at the mercy of the oil merchants at Panmure Street at last, with their raising of oil prices year on year.'

'Aye, but we'll still be all chasing a lessening number of beasts,' said Captain Watson, a dour, stocky man in a dark suit with a seaman's banded cap.

'Which is why we need boats like this. She'll be strong enough to push north through the ice to new grounds with this new steam-powered engine. And sturdy enough to overwinter, don't you think,

Watson, should we need to consider freezing in the boat at Cumberland Sound in future?'

'Aye, the barque would withstand the ice if she's frozen in somewhere sheltered enough, but that's not your worst problem. The long dark does things to a man's soul. You'd need to pick a crew sound in mind and body to withstand an Arctic winter out there with no one but each other and the natives for company.'

Mr Gillan turned to make sure his wife was not listening. 'Speaking of natives, tell me about this Eskimo fellow you've brought back from Pond Inlet then, Watson.'

The children had already taken the opportunity to cross the wooden gangway that led to the boat, a few precarious and springy steps above the dark seawater, hands grasping the prickly rope, and they were on the wooden deck with high sides, a fort under siege crammed with barrels, coiled rope, iron tools and weaponry. A sharp wind sliced across. Three masts loomed above them, the tallest higher than any pine at Kelly, hung with webs of thick rope swaying with the sea's sluggish momentum. Charlotte ran her hand along a hessian ladder rising up into the sky, put her foot on the lower rung and pulled up to feel herself cast upon the boat's sway.

A man in a thick, loose jacket and trousers, a fur hat with flaps tied up at the crown, came over. So close they could see his yellow teeth and smell his tobacco breath, a musky tang of smoke and old oil from his jacket.

'How d'you do?' said Oliver, holding out his hand. 'I'm Mr Gillan's son.'

'I don't care if ye're Her Majesty Queen Victoria's bairn. Touch aught and I'll skelp the lot of ye.' He retired to sit on a barrel, took out a roll of tobacco, cut off a wad and sat chewing, his red eyes trained on them.

The children walked to the far end of the boat and around the black funnel of the new steam engine, explorers no longer but interlopers. They braved two turns around the decks and then returned along the gangplank and wandered away to the head of the pier and the harbourmaster's observation tower. They could hear an unfamiliar noise, and the closer they got, the louder it became. A wailing, guttural, human voice, but with no words they could understand. They turned the corner of the tower and stopped. In front of them was a creature with a silky brown torso and legs clad in shaggy white bear skin, with long black hair, and the face of a man but with eyes too long and wolfish, the cheeks with strong planes like flinty rock. He was beating out a rhythm on a paddle of stretched skin, his voice rising and falling in a wordless sinewy chant.

'Is it a bear?' asked Mary.

'It's an Eskimo,' said Oliver. 'It's a real, live Eskimo.'

'Well, what a strange, unnecessary noise he's making,' said Louisa. 'Why ever do you think he does it?'

'It probably makes perfect sense to him,' whispered Charlotte fiercely. 'It's only strange because you don't know the words. Listen. I think it must be about snow, and birds flying home. And all the things he's missing.'

'I ken it's aboot rising up a good wind to tak' us all the way to Greenland,' said a voice behind them. They turned to see behind them a ship's boy, a round cloth cap pulled down over his ears, a woollen scarf hiding most of his jaw. 'The Eskimo men know how to cast a spell to rise up a wind.'

'Oh well, that's nonsense,' said Louisa grandly from her height above the boy.

'Really?' said Oliver, stepping forward. 'How does he do it?'

There was no answer. The singing stopped. The Eskimo remained looking into the light above the water. Then he turned and walked back along the cobbled pier to the boat. A sudden flurry of seagulls appearing above his head before wheeling away to the fishing boats. The boy shrugged and followed him.

'He's the cabin boy for the *North Star*,' said Oliver. 'One day it will be me stepping onto a barque, leaving with the wind to see the frozen north. That's what I'm going to do. Set off with the explorers.'

'I don't see how when your father is expecting you to learn how to run the mill, Oliver,' said Louisa.

'And your mama would jump on the boat with you too to make sure you were wearing your muffler and gloves the whole journey,' teased Charlotte.

'I'll leave at dawn and tell no one,' said Oliver. 'I will.'

'No one?' said Louisa quietly. 'Not even your friends?'

'I'll tell you,' said Oliver. 'But you must promise not to breathe a word. And I'll come back again.'

Charlotte stuck out her hand. 'Well, I'm coming too. Pact. We should be the Kelly Explorers' Society. A secret one.' She made the others all hold out their hands and shake together.

They walked back towards Oliver's parents. Trailing behind everyone else, Oliver and Louisa had joined hands for the briefest moment. And yesterday, Oliver had whispered to Louisa that he loved her. But holding her beret on against the wind, Charlotte saw nothing of this.

It was, in the end, a satisfactory day, Charlotte felt, as Mary and she sat side by side in the dining room of the Castle Hotel eating roast beef and potatoes and then currant pudding with custard, Mary tolerated because the Lochinvers were famed for their philanthropic acts and it cast a fair light on Mrs Gillan to treat her servant girl so well.

In the little war that she waged with Oliver's mother, Charlotte had a feeling that today she had won. It was awfully warm in the hotel dining rooms, however. Charlotte, without thinking, reached up and pulled off her beret.

A silence fell round the table.

'Has Charlotte been ill?' said Lady Lochinver, concern in her voice. Ready, it seemed, to make her excuses and leave as soon as possible if the girl had had a fever.

'Not at all,' said Mrs Gillan with a reassuring smile. 'In full health as you can see, and benefiting so much from the sea air today. Dear, do put your beret back on lest you take a chill.'

A silence fell around the table, Mrs Gillan now realizing her mistake in insisting that Charlotte was in good health. There was only one other reason for a girl to have her hair cut away – and that was to remove vermin. Lice.

The Lochinvers did not linger, barely touching the Queen of Puddings and small trifles, Lady Lochinver giving their excuses that they must hurry to a sudden urgent appointment.

The children finished their meal in silence, Aunt Sylvia dreadfully calm. She spoke only to call over a waiter, scribble a note and give it to him. Leaving the hotel, their group still in silence, Charlotte was surprised to see the carriage set out not towards the station, but towards the jute mill, but she was still not concerned. Oliver's father always had many things to do at his mills and many people to speak to. As they rode further into the town the thickening smoke from the mill chimneys gave the air a tang of soot, the red sandstone buildings as grimed with black deposits as if they had been burned in a great fire.

They arrived at the mill as a shift was ending. Droves of girls, with shawls wrapped around hard, fleshless faces, streamed past the carriage in a loud chattering of female voices and wooden clogs on cobbles. The mill girls ruled Dundee since they were cheaper to hire than the men, who were left jobless and stayed at home with the children, while the women swore and swaggered and catcalled at the boys who stood unemployed on street corners or who shepherded children to play on Magdalen Green.

Telling Oliver and Louisa to wait in the carriage, Aunt Sylvia ordered Charlotte and Mary to follow her. She headed across the cobbled courtyard, the thump of the steam pistons and clattering of looms echoing out across the courtyard from the great iron doors of the mill.

In the gloom of the foreman's office, Mrs Gillan took Mary by the arm and steered her towards him. 'This is the girl I sent a message about. You'll know her aunt, lives in a tenement in Shepherd's Loan. Please be so good as to call the woman from the mill floor and inform her that from now on her niece works here. She'll need to have the girl lodge with her. Say goodbye to Mary, Charlotte.'

Charlotte felt her legs sag, no longer brave and defiant. She burst into tears, ran and held tight to Mary, whose pretty, round face was also washed with tears, her eyes wide with disbelief.

'I'll come and get you,' said Charlotte. 'Soon as I can.'

Mary nodded but the foreman pulled her away. Charlotte watched her disappear through a door in the back of the office.

Charlotte rode back to Kelly in stunned silence. She took off her beret and left it on her knee, let the cold wind play over her stubbled hair. Oliver sat pale and rigid in unspoken support. Louisa had sunk back in her seat, a deep frown between her eyebrows.

Charlotte looked up at Aunt Sylvia, and seeing that small, satisfied smile as she gazed serenely through the window glass, Charlotte had to look away again quickly, afraid that she might fly at Mrs Gillan and kill her with her bare hands.

As soon as the carriage pulled up in front of the house, Charlotte threw herself out and ran to the Laundry Cottage. It was the last thing she wanted to do, but she knew she must tell Aunt Jean herself what she had done. And because of it, Mary would not be coming home any more.

CHAPTER 7

1949

Martha was in her studio, working on a painting of a jug filled with cobalt blue delphiniums and deep orange tiger lilies, but her mind was elsewhere, turning over some inexplicable developments.

When Alasdair had got married, Martha had vowed to herself with easy confidence that she would never be like Eugenia, that small and chilly woman with the strictest of rules. Martha would be far more welcoming to Alasdair's wife. And yet here she was, seemingly turning into exactly what she had feared – the dreaded mother-in-law.

Admittedly, Caro wasn't making things any easier, so hard to reach and often more than a little prickly. Alasdair's wife was not one for sharing confidences.

Martha mixed some more of the blue oil paints on her palette. Of course, it had been winter the first time she'd visited Duguld's parents in Kelly, snow on the ground, the sky almost as blue as the delphiniums, the colours of the castle stones sparkling under frost, pinks and ochres and soft greys. Inside, she'd been shocked by the cold. The tiny fires in the grates. But she'd just read *Waverley* and saw everything through the most romantic of lenses, in love with the Jacobean rooms redolent with history.

In a rather avant-garde bohemian-style dress that she had made herself on a Singer machine in the art-faculty building, and a headband that she had embroidered with poppies, Duguld said she looked just the thing, and she thought so too. An ironic and yet appropriate dress for a week in a castle.

Martha had been touched when later that week Eugenia in her dark tweed suit had worried that Martha hadn't packed enough warm clothes. Eugenia had had the driver take them to St Andrews to pick out lengths of tweed to make skirts. A fabric that scratched against the skin, but with wonderful subtle colours in the weave, greens like the hills, the pinks and yellows of the flowers in the grass. And with good sateen lining and the thick cotton lisle tights from Liberty that Eugenia introduced her to, it was warm and comfortable. Eugenia bought an armful of sweaters and cardigans, a pair of stout leather brogues for walking on damp grass. It was only when Martha caught sight of Duguld's mother across the room in a mirror, and realized that it was herself she was seeing, that she had understood what had happened.

It didn't stop there. Over the months, once she and Duguld became engaged, Eugenia was anxious to share recipes, how to manage a linen cupboard, gardening advice. Because one day – and I'm sorry we will pass this burden on to you, Martha – this old place will be yours and it won't be easy. How to write a thank-you letter. The implication was that this training was all done out of solicitousness and love. How could she object?

Martha did object. Her own mother had done a very thorough job of raising her and she did not need raising all over again – this time correctly. She felt shamed and unmade to have to be put through the refiner's fire of Eugenia's dressmaker and recipe book. This new Martha, ironed and neatly folded and squashed flat, felt doubly hurt, for herself and her mother.

The truth was, Martha had arrived at Kelly quite pleased with who she was, expecting to be appreciated as she was, for all she brought to Duguld's life, for Eugenia to see what Duguld had found to love in her.

The transformation project had made her silent and mutinous, as Martha withdrew and staked out her own space. When she and Duguld moved into the castle, silent hostilities broke out between her and Eugenia, that diminutive and dour presence always with a worry or a suggestion on how one might do things better. It was a painful and lonely time, cast about with self-doubts. Embarrassed at her lack of *savoir faire* when it came to Eugenia, with no words to express her confusion to anyone, Martha had retreated to a makeshift studio in one of the stable blocks that had fallen out of usage since the advent of motor cars.

Duguld had been no help at all. At the first mention of friction between Martha and Eugenia he would take the dogs out for a long walk, or disappear into the lavatory to sit on its burnished mahogany plank and read the pile of dog-eared *Country Life* magazines, for hours on end. Martha had had some very dark thoughts about their marriage. Her helpmeet, the person she had expected to listen to her worries, when it came to Eugenia seemed to be deaf.

'That's just Mama,' Duguld would say, caught like a rabbit in headlights, squirming to get away. She'd begun to see what a lonely situation the castle was in, stranded in miles of fields, a distant view of the North Sea.

So Martha had promised herself that she was never going to make that kind of mistake with Alasdair's wife. She would accept whomsoever Alasdair chose for himself with open arms. And with Caro, she could see that Alasdair had found someone he could be proud of, such an independent girl, one of the first women to get a degree at Cambridge, who came from such practical, successful stock. Martha did not share Pippa's silly reservations around class and education, pointless putting Pippa right on the matter yet again – how had she raised such a daughter? Martha celebrated Caro's qualities, in fact.

When it came to Caro, Martha approved of the larger picture wholeheartedly, unreservedly, but it was the details. Always the details that tripped one up day to day, as when Caro turned up on her first visit in that unexpectedly revealing dress with the rayon fabric that clung so. Every feeling writ large on the girl's face. That friendly confidence that Martha found a little unnerving – because she could see that there were certain subtleties of etiquette about which Caro had no idea.

Time would teach the girl all that was needed, Martha had told herself. She would work it out just by being with them – and yes, Eugenia had done her work too well. Martha did mind about these matters of etiquette now, as if Eugenia were watching still.

But here was the thing. What Martha had not reckoned with was how little she would figure in Caro's plans. Little good it would do Martha to accept the girl as she was – dear as she was. As far as Caro was concerned, she and Alasdair weren't going to be at Kelly long enough for Martha to express an opinion either way. What Martha might feel about their future plans was a consideration that hadn't crossed Caro's mind.

In Caro's eyes, Martha realized with dismay, the young couple's real lives were hundreds of miles away in London. They would make the journey from London twice a year, Caro had said, as if it would please Martha, the idea that they'd remember to come and see her just two times a year.

When Caro and Alasdair had gone on the train back to London after that first visit and the usual solitary quiet settled over the castle, Martha had stood for a long time in the drawing room, her reflection in one of the old mirrors fading in the evening light. An ache in her heart, as Alasdair travelled away on his train. Had she lost him?

Enough. Martha had gone down to the kitchen, switched on all the lights and made a strong cup of tea. Then she did what she always did when she missed Duguld horribly. She went into the old stables and began to paint, pictures of the garden in summer, just out of view, the children small again, running towards her through the summer air.

So when they had said they would like to live in the Laundry Cottage, Martha had been delighted, her intention to be welcoming, chums even with dear Caro. So why was Caro increasingly distant and prickly, as if all their communication were being carried out through some muffled telephone wire, jumbled with misunderstandings? What on earth was going wrong?

CHAPTER 8

1949

That odd moment on the stairs when Caro had overheard a conversation she was not supposed to hear had stayed with her like a bruise she couldn't resist poking. Sometimes she blamed herself, for not being up to the mark in some way she didn't entirely understand, and sometimes she blamed Martha and Pippa for being so unfair and quite frankly snobbish. It made her feel wobbly about a lot of things she had never needed to consider before. Was this blouse too suburban? Was her hairstyle too suburban? Should she make more effort to iron out the South London twang to her speech that had seemed perfectly respectable before she came to Kelly?

As she and Alasdair lay in the dark that night she'd finally told him what Pippa had said. 'But too grammar school and suburban. What does that mean?'

He'd half-huffed, half-laughed. 'That's Pippa. Honestly, take no notice. None of us come up to Pippa's standards, believe me.'

'And how could she say I pushed you into marrying me?'

'Well, she's wide off the mark there. Just silly. I seem to remember chasing someone across Cambridge, engineering bumping into her here and there.'

He shifted closer, put a comforting arm over her, nuzzled her neck, but irritable at having her feelings dismissed, she moved away. They lay apart in the dark, both feeling hurt. She hadn't even mentioned what had been said about Diana. Refused to dignify it by repeating it.

So the matter was closed, and apart from Felicity, there was no one else Caro could talk to about it. She thought about calling her sister, but Phoebe had just written to say she was engaged and was full of the joys of married life to come. It was no time to depress one's little sister with Caro's failures on the in-law front. Besides, everyone knew that phone calls were expensive, only for important and briefly imparted news.

She woke feeling defeated the next morning, due over at Kelly in the afternoon to start putting the old files in order, though she was no longer feeling so excited about the prospect. The first time she'd be leaving the baby with Barbara. It rained all morning, the lawns behind the cottage sodden, dark fir trees at the edge of the wood dripping into rapidly accruing pools. Washing was draped round the kitchen, permeating the cottage with an atmosphere of damp and soap. Risking a lull between downpours, Caro headed for the castle, steering the pram round water-filled potholes along the muddy path. She was relieved to see Felicity soon asleep. She should wake in a good mood to play happily with Barbara or lie out in the pram.

Coming out of the woods, Caro noticed a petite figure ahead on the path, dark hair, a mac over her arm. Wasn't that Diana? Hearing someone behind her, the woman turned and waved. Waited for Caro to catch up. The woman held out her hand.

'You must be Caro. How d'you do? Diana Stokes. Just moved into the house over on the other side of the woods. I expect Alasdair's told you our family estates share a border.'

'He mentioned you, yes.'

'I've been away for ages but honestly there's nowhere as lovely as Fife in the summer, is there? Even in the rain. I love it. Though I must say I've had to banish myself to the lodge to get out of Mother's hair. She swears she loves having me back, but you know how it is. Oh, and this is. . .'

Diana peered into the pram. Caro found herself gripping the pram handle, steering it away a little under the guise of rocking the sleeping baby.

'Felicity.'

'How lovely, but then you'd expect nothing less with two such stunning specimens for parents. And they say you're doing great things with the family records. Must be fascinating. Just your thing I hear.'

'I didn't realize Alasdair had told you so much.'

Diana straightened up. She wore a perfume that was not unpleasant, hints of orange and sandalwood.

'Gosh no, not him. Alasdair's always hopeless at giving you the important facts. It was Martha who told me about your project. I'm going to be in and out of the castle too, giving her a hand with some of the antiques to see if there's anything of great value hiding among all the bric-a-brac. An effort to raise some funds, as you know. I work for Curtis and Malloy in Edinburgh, mostly in the art department but we also value furniture and so on. So I expect we'll be seeing quite a lot of one another.'

'Oh well, splendid.' They started to walk on.

'Anyway, so lovely to meet you finally, and I'm sure we're going to become the best of friends. Won't we, Felicity?' She addressed this into the pram in a higher voice.

'Look forward to it.'

'Oh. You're going in the kitchen door. I'll carry on. Meeting Martha in the library. Till later.'

Caro pushed the pram into the kitchen corridor and parked it there, a niggle of disappointment in her chest. Alasdair, if he knew, had said nothing about their new neighbour.

★

Duguld's study was in the North-West Tower, overlooking the front lawns and the distant view of the sea. It was filled with a calm light, the cream walls painted with delicate green vines. In a green metal filing cabinet with worn brass handles she found well-ordered files dated from 1780 up to 1860. The files and ledgers relating to the Gillans' more recent family's history, however, had been left in jumbled piles in a mahogany cupboard next to the desk. According to Martha there were more documents stacked in the old linen press in the housekeeper's room downstairs, not to mention boxes in the attic rooms that had been untouched for years. Those would have to wait. She only had a couple of hours at the most. She settled at Duguld's satinwood desk.

The walls of the room were thick, the only sounds the wind coming in from the sea gently rattling the window frame, and sometimes she could hear the chirping of sparrows in the ivy, but she couldn't hear a peep from Felicity two floors below. It was disconcerting to be so cut off, but she wasn't, she promised herself, going to be the sort of mother who ran down every five minutes to check on her child. Barbara was clearly wonderful with children. Martha trusted her implicitly. Half an hour later she ran down to the kitchen, on the excuse of making coffee, and found Felicity playing happily with a rattle.

For her research at Cambridge Caro had loved truffling out lost nuggets of information in the library basement. She could almost feel her fingertips tingling now as she carefully untied the string on a crumbly manila folder that looked as though it had lain unopened for centuries. She began a new box of file cards to note the references for each family member, and started to sort the folders and documents by date. For the missing woman, however, she found not a single document, even in folders that mentioned Oliver or his daughter Eugenia. Someone really had gone to a lot of effort to wipe Oliver's wife, Eugenia's mother, from the record, she thought, leaning back on her heels and surveying the piles of folders and papers she had placed on the carpet.

Running back down the stairs at the end of her two hours, sure she'd been gone too long, Caro was relieved to hear that Felicity wasn't crying.

Martha was sitting at the table pouring tea. Across the table, Diana sat smoking a cigarette, Felicity on her lap playing with her silky scarf, smoke curling around the baby's wispy hair. The baby was wearing an elderly woollen cardigan that Caro had never seen before. A wooden chest lay open on the table, several silver spoons lined up in a row. As Caro came in, the women broke off their conversation. Felicity began to cry as soon as she saw her mother.

'There you are,' said Martha. 'We've just made a pot of tea. Barbara was rather busy in the end so I've been giving her a hand. Come and join us. And clever old Diana's been looking at the silver apostle spoons that my father used to collect.'

'Question is,' Diana said, 'whether they're the real thing, lovely old medieval silver that would be worth a small fortune, or –' and here she pulled a face – 'Victorian copies which would be valuable but in a much smaller way. Worth just the price of the silver really. I'll need to take them with me to Curtis and Malloy for a second opinion, but if I'm honest, I think we are looking at Victorian copies.'

'Oh well, of course,' said Martha, sounding deflated. 'We can continue to hope but I'm sure you're right. Duguld was always so proud of his collection so I thought. . .'

'We'll keep looking,' said Diana. 'We might even find something in the attics or various old cupboards. Sometimes small, overlooked things can turn out to be rather special.'

'And talking of forgotten cupboards, I thought Flissy looked a little chilly so I dug out some of the children's old woollies,' said Martha, turning to Caro.

'I wondered where Felicity's jumper came from.'

'Isn't it darling? And there's more in the box there. Have a look through and see if there's anything else you can use. I so loved knitting for the children when they were small. They'll need airing out a bit, of course. But we don't want this little one to catch a chill.'

A powerful smell of mildew came from the box as Caro took out a pile of small cardigans and jumpers. She picked out a small Fair Isle beret to be polite. It was a beautiful pattern in blues and greens, matching the jumper the baby was wearing. Perhaps the smell would wash out. After making apologies for not being able to stay and chat, she tucked Felicity into the pram, relieved to be back out in the garden again. She'd felt unnervingly displaced after walking in on the little scene, Felicity so content with Diana, she and Martha chatting away like old friends – as if Caro were some ghost watching a future to come. Which was a ridiculous idea. She breathed in cool air, the weak sun raising mist from the sodden ground.

Halfway home the rain started pattering down through the branches, the wild garlic flowers that ran rampant among the trees giving off an unexpectedly foreign odour in the damp air. Felicity began to cry, her cheeks bright red as if she were too warm. Caro removed the cardigan, though the baby's klaxon calls continued all the way back.

She found Alasdair washing potatoes for supper. 'Wasn't sure what we were eating, but potatoes are always a good thing, I thought. And I'll make an omelette?' His sleeves were rolled up, his tie on the kitchen table and the top couple of buttons of his shirt undone. He looked tired.

Felicity settled to feed. Caro finally felt herself relaxing. A baby's cry was worse than an ambulance siren for stirring up nameless panic.

'I'd have got supper on earlier, now you're a working woman, but the bus was so slow today. Good news is, though, I won't have to put up with the old jalopy for much longer. Managed to get hold of a motorbike. Ex-army job. Needs a bit of work but should be just the thing for nipping into university and back.'

'Really? You didn't mention that you were going to get a bike.'

'Oh darling, should I have? You don't mind?'

'I never trust motorbikes, especially when the roads are so wet.' She found herself bursting into tears.

'Whatever's the matter, darling?'

'There won't be any room for a baby on a motorbike. You'll be going all over the place on your own, and Felicity and I will just be here stuck inside with all the rain, without you.'

'Hey, hey, what is this?' He enveloped her in his arms. 'It's only to get into the department. For boring work. And we can use Mother's car when we need to. She's always saying we can. Or we can get a sidecar for the bike.'

She shook off his arms abruptly, went to the kitchen window, her back to him.

'Caro?'

'Did you know this Diana person has moved in next door?'

'Mother mentioned it.'

'Oh. So you did know. And she's going to be around the castle, valuing stuff. It's just. . . Alasdair, have you told me everything about Diana?'

'Is that what's upsetting you? Are you talking about that time she dragged me into the Balmoral for lunch? Because I told you, if we'd known you were in town we could have all eaten together.'

'No. I mean before us. When you were younger. Was there something between you and Diana?'

'Honestly, Caro, perhaps in a rather piffling teenage sort of way, for a while, but that sort of thing hardly counts. We were always at the same dreary tea parties organized by the dowagers of the county set so their young could meet the right people; all horribly boring. Diana was the only one who was ever any fun. There was perhaps a bit of a crush, more on Diana's side, but never anything serious. I think the mothers talked. But you know how it is, gossip makes gossip. There was nothing to it. And I'm sure you must have had crushes when you were little more than a child, that you've never bothered to mention to me.'

She shuddered. 'Thomas Markham. Spotty chin and sweaty palms. Thought he was wonderful at the time.'

'There, you see. There's absolutely nothing to be upset about. And before you know it, you and Diana will be the best of friends.'

'She seems very, I don't know, highly strung? As if she might suddenly do anything.'

'Oh well, that's Diana. Always was a law unto herself.' He chuckled. 'When we were about thirteen or fourteen, her boarding school in St Andrews broke up for term later than everyone else's. So she jumped out of the dorm window one night and walked here in the rain. She knocked on my window, climbed in dripping wet. I had to go and find her bread and cheese and blankets until it was a decent enough hour for her to walk over to her own house and pretend that her term had ended – until the school rang and told her parents otherwise.'

'She came to you. So you were close then.'

'Oh Caro, don't let's go round in circles. We were pals. A childish thing. And more to the point, I've got a surprise for you. Something I think you're going to like very much.'

'Is this more about the motorbike? A horrible helmet and goggles?'

He disappeared into the sitting room and came back with a large brown envelope, handed it to her. 'Anyway, I think you'd look very fetching in goggles and a helmet. I'll look into it.'

Caro narrowed her eyes at him as she slid a cardboard-mounted photograph from the envelope, a misty brown picture of a group of older children in Victorian clothes artfully staged on the lawns of Kelly.

'Goodness, this is lovely. Who is this?'

She took it to the kitchen window where the light was better. Two teenage girls in long print dresses stood facing each other on the lawns behind the castle, hands entwined, one with dark hair, a direct almost mutinous gaze to the camera, the other with blonde ringlets, gazing towards where a boy of around the same height stood with one arm leaning on a sundial. Slightly behind them stood a maid, a sweet-faced girl of around thirteen or fourteen perhaps in a white apron and cap. The arm of the girl with dark curls was blurred, as if she couldn't bear to be still any longer.

'D'you see?' Alasdair said excitedly. 'It's a photograph of Oliver at Kelly. He's younger than in the portrait we have, but that's him all right.'

'This is wonderful. And from the clothes I'd say the time fits for it to be Oliver. So who are the girls? They look like characters, especially the dark-haired one. The blonde girl's quite a beauty.'

'Turn it over.'

Caro read out the faded brown cursive on the back.

'Dear Oliver, a picture of your sweetheart for you to keep. Keep practising the dark arts. Fox Talbot.'

Caro's eyes were wide as she looked up. 'Oliver's sweetheart? So do you think one of these might be our missing girl? If she and Oliver had grown up and married perhaps?'

'Don't forget the maid. There's the maid too.'

'Yes, of course. It would certainly explain why his wife was *persona non grata* if Oliver married a servant. I wish we had more to go on. But this is utterly wonderful. Where did you find it?'

'It's from the archives in the university library. I knew they had a collection of early photos, many of them taken in the large country houses around St Andrews. Photography was a great fashion here among the big families and professors quite early on. So I made a few enquiries, and the very nice girl in the archives did some searching for pictures taken at Kelly, came up with this. Said I could borrow it for a while since it's of family.'

'You mean you used your charm to get her to part with it.'

'Who could resist? We'll have to be careful with it, of course, and return it quite soon.'

'I wish we had names for the girls. Fox Talbot, though, wasn't he someone famous in the history of photography?'

'He was, an early pioneer and a professor here. And it looks like he was a friend of the family, though all the big county families would have known each other.'

'So there could be more photos?'

'Exactly. The archivist's promised to have a look, let us know if she finds anything else. So you see, I do think about you. All the time. And darling, am I forgiven? About the motorbike?'

'I'm sorry. Just me being silly. The motorbike is a very practical and splendid idea. Of course it is. Oh, but this is so exciting.' She held up the photo next to his face, looked from one to the other. 'Could we be looking at your great-grandmother, as a girl? Can you see a resemblance?'

'Perhaps. But you have to remember that most teenage crushes evaporate with time. And I'm sorry you were upset about the silly Diana thing.'

'I don't know why I get so worked up when I'm the luckiest woman in the world – you, Felicity, our life here.'

He wrapped his arms round her shoulders, she resting her chin on his warm forearms as they both gazed out of the window in a moment of contentment, cocooned safely inside the solid walls of their home. It was starting to get dark, the ground so saturated that pools of water glimmered in the last of the light.

★

Caro sat up late on the prickly old horsehair sofa in the sitting room that evening, letting the fire burn down low, examining the photo for every last detail, the room quiet except for the rain coursing down the gutter pipe by the window. Every so often the lamp dimmed. The old generator always struggled to cope in damp weather.

That night the rain drumming on the roof permeated her dreams, calling out to three girls moving away across the flooded lawns of Kelly, the hems of their long dresses dark with water, never once turning or looking back.

Early the next morning, Caro woke to silence. There was an odd smell, like dank pond water. And listening out, she could hear an odd noise every now and again, something knocking against a wall downstairs. Frowning, she pulled on her dressing gown. At the top of the stairs she stopped in horror.

The narrow hallway below had been turned into a canal of murky brown water, everything it touched ruined. The baby's shoes and a hand brush were bobbing on the surface, tapping against the wall. Reaching the bottom of the stairs, she took a deep breath, hoisted the hem of her nightdress, and sloshed through the cold water. The kitchen was also flooded, the tables and chairs marooned in muddy water. A strange, diffuse, upside-down light came from the window, illuminating the low ceiling. The back door was swollen in its frame but she managed to pull it open. The back garden gone under a gleaming sheet of white sky, the iron laundry posts the masts of drowned ships.

Sloshing back through the cottage, she found Alasdair in the sitting room, ankle deep in water, pyjama trousers rolled up to the knee. In his arms, Felicity was looking down at the new arrangement with interest.

'I'm sure we can save something,' said Alasdair, sounding not a bit sure. The room's familiar tang of woodsmoke with its memories of cosy evenings had been ousted by a smell of wet horsehair from the sodden sofa. Ash eddied out from the drowned fireplace. A book floated face down in the water. Caro waded across to rescue the photo of Oliver and the girls that she'd left on the side table. The edges were buckled with the damp, the faces of the children staring out at her. She shivered.

Alasdair was rarely defeated or glum, but now he sighed as he held up a book, the wet pages falling away.

'What a mess, and just after we'd got everything so snug.'

With a swishing of water, the old jeep drove up outside, Martha wading across the front garden in wellies.

'Well, that's it,' she exclaimed. 'There's no question of you staying here, evicted as you are by this horrid water. Oh darlings, such rotten luck. At least it will be no trouble to make you up some beds in Kelly, but I have to say, in all the years we've lived here I've never known the Laundry Cottage to flood like this.'

They spent all day moving their things out of the downstairs rooms, the wet furniture removed to the castle storerooms to dry out.

'Well, thanks for saving us, Ma,' said Alasdair as they sat by the fire in Kelly that evening. 'There are worse places to have to take refuge.'

In front of the fireplace, the high-backed Jacobean chairs had been drawn up around a small oak table dark with age and past lives. The mellow firelight reflected in the oil-painted scenes of woods and pastures on the wooden panelling. Martha served out plates of mutton stew with suet dumplings. But even with two jumpers, nothing could drive the cold out from Caro's bones.

'At least the flooding hasn't spread any further,' Martha said. 'Some kind of drainage problem localized around the cottage, Terry thinks. Problem is, though, that we've no map of the old cottage's drains, so goodness knows how long it will take to find where the blockage is.'

They were put in the Blue Room on the second floor of the North-West Tower. Alasdair sank onto the deep mattress of the four-poster.

Caro unpacked their things and ran the hottest water she could get in the deep roll-top bath in the adjoining room. They were both aching all over from carrying boxes and furniture. They sat one each end, steam making Alasdair's auburn hair curl in the way that she loved. The toile wallpaper of shepherds and shepherdesses was watermarked, with past condensation on the cold walls like the contours of a map.

'Don't you wonder who used to be in our room, who used to come in here and wash at that old marble stand, with hot water brought up by the maid? In the time when Oliver was alive,' said Caro.

'Possibly, though it would have been more of a dressing room in Oliver's time. I think the bath was added in the twenties.'

'Just wish the room was a bit smaller so it would keep warm. One of the good things about living in a cottage. But at least we'll be home soon.'

'I've had a letter from the archivist at the university library,' said Alasdair as he sat reading it at breakfast a few days later. 'Such a nice girl.'

'Does she want the photograph back yet?' asked Caro. 'I was hoping to keep it for a while, do more research around it.'

'Quite the opposite. Says she's found another two pictures that she thinks might be connected to Oliver.'

'Really? Does she say when we can go and see them?'

'As soon as you like.'

'Might as well go in today then,' said Caro.

'How interesting,' said Martha, taking the letter. 'Why don't I come with you? We can take the car.'

★

'I hope you don't mind us rushing over as soon as we got your letter,' said Caro as she shook hands with the archivist in the subdued atmosphere of the library.

'I'm glad you did,' she said. 'But Mr Gillan didn't come with you?'

It wasn't that Alasdair used his charm on purpose, thought Caro, but it was there. 'Mr Gillan's awfully busy, I'm afraid. But he really appreciates you helping us like this.'

The girl nodded, led them to a basement room lined with rows of metal shelves stacked with books, folders and manila boxes. She took a box down, placed it on a table, and undid the string. Inside was a photograph of a ship, pasted onto a cardboard mount. This was not what Caro had been expecting. She and Martha peered at it, made out the name on the bow, the *Narwhal*.

'I think Oliver was supposed to have sailed on an Arctic whaling ship one summer,' said Martha. 'I wonder if this might have been the one?'

'Quite possibly. I wouldn't have connected the picture with him if not for this other one stored with it,' said the archivist.

She placed a second photograph on the table. It showed Oliver, in a white tie and formal kilt dress. Either side of him, a young woman in a slim, hourglass-shaped ballgown, one fair-haired, one dark. The darker girl shorter and slighter.

Caro gave a gasp of delight.

The archivist smiled. 'Yes. The same girls as in the Kelly picture, but older. And note the writing.'

Gold, fancy lettering at the bottom of the mount gave the name of the photographers, Valentine & Sons. Beneath it, three names had been added in faded black ink. Caro read out, 'Miss Louisa Strachan, Oliver Gillan Esquire, Miss Charlotte Strachan. Their names. At last, we know their names. Louisa and Charlotte. Thank you so much.'

'Louisa and Charlotte Strachan,' repeated Martha thoughtfully. 'Not names I recognize. But such lovely young women. Would it be possible to take this to show Mr Gillan?'

'Of course.' The archivist tucked a strand of her pale brown hair behind an ear. 'And if he could return in person to sign it back in.'

'Oh dear, another fan for Alasdair, I think,' said Martha as they went down the steps outside. 'He really is impossible. Now why don't I take my favourite daughter-in-law for coffee at Kerracher's?'

Later that afternoon, Caro and Alasdair sat on the bed in their room, examining the picture.

'So could our missing bride be one of these girls, do you think?' said Alasdair.

'It feels like it,' said Caro, 'though we don't have any real proof. Oliver could have married someone we don't even know about.'

'But look at the way he seems to be standing slightly turned towards Louisa, how his eyes gaze towards her. I'd say his attention is definitely on her.'

'I see what you mean. But we need more. I've been hoping to find letters or something written by Oliver somewhere among all the papers I've been going through, where he muses about his love life, but I've found nothing personal of his. What I need to do now is start looking through those stacks of boxes in the attics that no one's opened for years. There could be something there that might give us a clue.'

'Don't rush off yet. I was thinking perhaps I might do a little research myself, into my own missing wife. See if I can remember who she is.' He nuzzled the back of her neck. Caro sighed and leaned against Alasdair's chest, her eyes closed.

A voice called from the bottom of their stairs. 'Darlings, I've a pot of tea made.' Footsteps climbing.

Alasdair and Caro sat up straight, exchanged a rueful smile. 'Oh, for the days when we could wander around the cottage undisturbed,' whispered Caro. 'Dressed or not. And no one to comment if you get up late after a bad night with Felicity and stay in your dressing gown till lunchtime.'

'I know, darling.'

Caro stood the photo on the bedroom mantelpiece, next to the one of the children in the garden, and followed Alasdair downstairs.

CHAPTER 9

EDINBURGH, 1882

After that summer when Mary was sent away, Oliver's mother found difficulties with any future visit from Charlotte and Louisa, citing her nerves. And when they did come to Kelly, it was only for a brief visit, afternoon tea in the Long Room with Oliver's mama and the girls' aunt always there, listening in. And an increasing awkwardness had begun to develop between Oliver and the girls as they grew and changed, a self-conscious new hat for Louisa here, a fluffy moustache for Oliver there, Charlotte always scowling at being kept indoors. Finally, there was a summer when the girls did not come at all.

'Oh, they won't want to stay with us these days,' said his mother when Oliver asked. 'They'll have far more exciting invitations now Louisa's almost seventeen. I hear she's been staying with Lucy Glenconner and her family. We must be very dull here for them compared to Dornoch Castle.'

Oliver sometimes wrote to Louisa and Charlotte, leaving the letters on the tray in the hall to be taken to the post, but over the weeks not a single reply came back. Seeing Oliver searching through the post yet again, his mother told him firmly that a gentleman must accept when a lady did not wish to be in touch. Oliver stood with his head against the cool glass of the library window, looking over the lawns and rhododendron banks, torturing himself with the view of the very places where he and Louisa had exchanged promises and a kiss.

He buried himself in study, preparing for exams to enter the Edinburgh medical school. He could not wait to be wandering through the bustling streets of the town, and since everyone went to Edinburgh, one day – as he saw it – his and Louisa's paths would cross again. He had a natural talent for the sciences, his school teachers said, could go far. His mother saw him as a professor of medicine in the future, a position of gravitas and respectability, and combined with the considerable money from the mill and a title from a match with someone like Lucy Lochinver, the family would be able to hold their heads up in any drawing room from Fife to Angus.

His father was less happy. 'You'll still need to know how to manage the mill when we're gone. Keeping the castle in good repair will not be cheap,' he told Oliver. Once a month his father insisted he accompany him to the Scourieburn Mill, to sit in on long meetings and learn about jute manufacturing and whale oil prices, always whale oil. Or interminable afternoons in the gloomy office, trapped inside the manager's cubicle with its screens of mahogany and yellow glass killing the light, trying to stay awake while one of the clerks explained the orders ledger. Oliver took every opportunity to volunteer to go down to the docks, ostensibly to help oversee deliveries of jute from India or shipments of hessian sacking for America, seeking out tales from the whaler men of green night skies and white bears taller than a man.

Once a month Oliver would accompany Father on his tour of the factory floors through the deafening din of shuttles and looms, Father striding ahead, shouting out all the information that Oliver should know, about the teasing out of the jute plant fibres, the washing and crushing, the oiling and the spinning – a process that spun their wealth. The red stone jute mill with its lofty skeleton of iron pillars holding up the two floors of heavy machinery, the black steam engine thumping like the beating heart of a great beast, this was the original of which their own elegant home was a palimpsest.

When he passed by the looms that Mary now oversaw, he'd stop and talk with her, glad to see her pretty, freckled face and her ready smile again, the mill girls looking sideways at them and waiting to tease Mary later. One afternoon, as Father talked with the foreman, Mary darted up to Oliver and placed a letter into his hands. Said she'd kept it in her apron pocket among the scissors and needles for days, waiting for him to come by. Miss Strachan, she'd whispered to him, was sure Oliver's mother stole the letters they'd written to him.

He'd kissed her hands, the mill girls whistling and shouting bold things that made him blush.

The letter was from Charlotte, not Louisa as he had hoped, but the news could not have been more wonderful. Charlotte and Louisa were moving to Edinburgh with the aunt. By the time Oliver arrived in Edinburgh to begin his degree, she and Louisa would already be living there. She had written down the address for him and he was to come and visit them the very day he arrived. Louisa insisted on it. How they had missed him.

He hurried back to his cubicle in the office, sent away the accountant, closed the door and immediately wrote a letter in reply.

He had never studied so hard, never been so wildly happy. In a few months' time he would be in Edinburgh, near to the girls. Louisa had not forgotten him.

The very first day that Oliver arrived in Edinburgh, he called at the address Charlotte had given him, the last number in a crescent of imposing Georgian town houses. He was shown into a spacious drawing room, its windows overlooking a park enclosed by iron railings. It had been almost two years since he had seen Louisa and he barely recognized the swan-necked creature who stood before him now. She wore a narrow, blue gown, her pale hair held in a topknot with a fringe of golden curls. Her face had been sculpted and refined by time, but she was even more beautiful for it, though her ivory skin was bruised by greyish shadows under her eyes and the little lines between her brows were a fraction deeper.

The girls' aunt was seated near the fire, more shrunken and bent than ever, swathed in a shawl.

'Who's this?' she asked tetchily.

'Oliver, Aunt. You remember, Oliver Gillan from Kelly?'

'Why hasn't he brought the tea, Louisa?'

'It's coming momentarily, Aunt.' Louisa steered Oliver away towards the window seat.

'I'm sorry. She does get confused. One has to think of all sorts of things now that she doesn't manage very well.'

'I'm so sorry. That must be very difficult. Is there no one to help you?'

'Oh, we get by. One has to. But please, I'd rather you didn't say anything to anyone. It's another year or so until I am twenty-one and attain my majority. I'd hate the lawyers and trustees to interfere because they think our aunt is frail. Insist that she go into a nursing home, even. We see very few people and so manage quite well. But now you are here. Dearest Oliver, how we have missed you.'

He saw tears welling in her eyes.

'I'm only sorry that you did not get my letters,' he said. 'I don't want to speak ill of Mother but she did a very hurtful thing.'

'I always knew that Aunt Sylvia only suffered us for your father's sake. But our times with you at Kelly were still some of the happiest of our childhood.'

'And of mine. You know I intend to confront Mother, make her apologize.'

'Please don't. She wouldn't like us any the better for it. You can't make someone like you if they are set against it. Let's not talk of it any more. But a doctor. I always knew you must do something good in this world. Sweetest boy, our own dear Oliver, it's such a comfort to have you near. One feels so vulnerable at times. There was a nasty incident last month when I had to dismiss the housekeeper. She tried to bully me, stole jewellery from Aunt.'

He noticed how the lines between her brows had deepened again.

'Dear Louisa, if you need money, I have my allowance and—'

She gave a little, surprised laugh. 'Oh, then you don't know. We have become wealthy. A distant cousin in the colonies, it seems we were his only family. My worries now are almost about us having too much. There's Charlotte wanting to go away to Paris when she finishes school to study art. And she can. We have the means. But now she's eighteen, I have so little time to help her find her way before she may do as she likes. And one does worry.'

'And who will help you, Louisa, with all your burdens?'

'Oh Oliver, if only someone would.' She placed her hand on his.

The doors flew open and a slender young woman bounded in, dark hair held back in a net, a practical style more like the aunt's than Louisa's, a worsted dress and jacket, ink on her fingers. The unmistakable wide smile and dark eyes.

'We were heartbroken, thinking you had forgotten us,' Charlotte said, examining his face. 'Though we guessed that witch of an Aunt Sylvia was at the bottom of it. How could she? I feel like dashing straight over to Kelly and demanding our letters back.'

'We won't do that,' murmured Louisa.

'We should.' Charlotte piled a plate with some of the bread and butter that had been brought in with the tea and sat between them on the window seat, eating as she talked.

'It was Louisa who said we should move here, after the cousin left us his estate, which was jolly splendid of him, but honestly, takes a lot of getting used to, realizing one can almost do anything on reaching one's majority. Is that how a man feels? Then Louisa said we should come here to meet people, the right people apparently, which I thought was poppycock, but now you're here. So clever old Louisa. We'll all be together again. I should ask Mary to stay. Why not? And did Louisa tell you I'm going to Paris? Though I hardly want to go now that you are here. I am so happy.'

'So am I, especially seeing that you have not changed one bit.'

'I have changed, though. I see things quite clearly now.' And he wondered why her eyes were sad though she smiled at him.

He floated back to his lodgings, the memory of Louisa's small, light hand on his, her perfume of blue hyacinths.

He visited Louisa at home every week, marvelling as she grew into a confident woman holding dinners and soirées. Charlotte left for Paris at the end of the year and Louisa relied even more on Oliver as he gave advice, listened, comforted – and hoped. Louisa had swerved the kiss he had tried to leave on her cheek once or twice. Said he was her dearest friend, there was no one else she cared for so much, but she could not think about such things until she reached her majority.

Mama, of course, had heard rumours but on her visits he managed to avoid any definite answers as they dined together in Princes Street. She asked him whom he would invite to accompany him to the ball she was holding at Kelly in a few weeks' time. Miss Lochinver, who remembered him very fondly, was still unattached. Still in possession of a title.

But Oliver dodged the issue by claiming he had to hurry away to a lecture. He already knew whom he would ask. And in a few weeks' time, Louisa would be twenty-one.

CHAPTER 10

Oliver sprawled his long limbs across the leather bench, a tweed waistcoat over a crumpled woollen shirt, loose tweed trousers bagged at the knees, his unlaced boots placed to one side, staring into the peat fire. Around him, the saloon bar of the Clachan Inn smelled of worsted wool thawing out from a day up in snow-covered hills, of whiffs of stout and ale, and steak in gravy. Ice picks and ropes hung from pegs around the dark brown panelling. A sharp click of billiards and a fug of tobacco smoke. But Oliver was unaware of his surroundings, thinking only of the little red leather box back in his rooms in Edinburgh, inside it a sapphire set between two diamonds. Was it best to give the ring to Louisa at the Kelly ball? Or should he ask her in the privacy of her home? But Kelly was so much part of their story. She would feel the same way, he knew it. He would propose to Louisa at the Kelly ball.

Adam Carruthers, stouter and shorter, in similar sturdy walking clothes, sat next to him on the bench, leaning forward to warm his hands.

'Ye gods, I'll never understand why we choose to go hiking when there's still snow on the tops of the hills, even this late in April.'

'Builds character,' said Oliver, coming back to the room and picking up his mug of hot toddy.

'Builds chilblains,' said Glenconner, his thin and mournful face pained as he rubbed his feet. Lord Glenconner was the most recent member of the club, not yet aware of the code of no complaining. So far, no one had been invited to use his first name, though he addressed the others as Oliver and Adam.

'Speaking of chilly substances,' chipped in Adam, furrows on his large and earnest forehead. 'About your mother's ball, Oliver. It has left me with a problem, you see. Who to invite? Could have consequences.'

'My advice is steer clear of all females for as long as you can,' said Glenconner. 'Running around after a woman's a full-time job, with long hours and bad terms.'

'You may say that, but it's the women of one's family who won't leave a man in peace, not until he's safely tied down, don't you know,' Adam replied, staring into the fire. 'If only such things were as simple as rugby, with rules one could understand.'

Glenconner took his pipe from beneath his wide moustache. 'There's really no mystery to it. You want a good bet that will bring in the money, but check her teeth and fetlocks to make sure you get the creature she's sold as.'

'So speaks the great romantic,' said Oliver. 'I shall marry for love and only love.'

'How is Louisa?' said Adam. 'Has she agreed to accompany you?'

'She has,' said Oliver, unable to suppress a smile.

'Now there's a pretty girl,' said Glenconner, pointing his pipe at Oliver. 'She came and stayed with my sister last year. Charmed Mama very much. Shame the father left no money on her.'

'Oh, but haven't you heard? They've been named as inheritors to a distant relative who snuffed it in the tropics,' chipped in Adam. 'They're very comfortably off now. Anyway, I've always found the younger sister the most handsome,' he added, blushing. 'And such fire to her. She's back from Paris. I saw Charlotte coming out of Mr Murchison's art school the other day, clutching her drawings.'

'Heard they do life drawing at that new school,' said Glenconner. 'Models in the natural. So have you plucked up the courage to speak to Charlotte, then, Adam?'

Adam's blush deepened. 'Once or twice. Problem is I don't know her well enough to ask her to the Kelly ball. I say, Oliver, won't you invite me to tea with her one afternoon so I can have an opportunity to ask her? Be a sport.'

'Now didn't the Strachan girls used to stay with your family after their father's expedition was lost?' said Glenconner. 'At least there was no shadow cast over Strachan's daughters in the way that there was over Franklin's men, eating their boots and then each other and all that. I say, Adam, why are you winking at me so horribly?' He glanced over to where Oliver sat staring doggedly into his beer. 'Oh, what a fool I am,' exclaimed Glenconner. 'Of course, your relative was one of those men trying to march home across the ice, wasn't he? Well, as I've said, I've never believed any of those stories. Lady Franklin was right. If there was any butchery by cannibals, then it will have been at the hands of those savages.'

'I think you did know,' muttered Adam.

Oliver shrugged. 'Don't trouble yourself. I can assure you that my uncle would have behaved like a true son of Empire.'

When Oliver went up to his room some hours later, Adam caught up with him on the landing. 'You won't forget about inviting me to meet Charlotte?'

'Delighted to. But you know Charlotte will do as she will, and I can't promise anything on her behalf.'

'Oh, I understand. That's what makes me like her so. And you know, Oliver, I never have once had the slightest doubt about your uncle. The things they said. . . No wonder it made your mother so ill.

As for Glenconner, he's an idiot whose money and title have failed to make him a gentleman.'

'Don't worry, old friend. Let's not speak of it.'

Adam clapped him on the back, wheeled away towards his room. Oliver gave a deep sigh. Would the world never let them forget the stain of the Franklin expedition after all these years? It seemed not. In the meantime, his mother grew ever more nervy, reading slights into the most innocent comments. And once Sylvia detected an insult, she never forgave it. Never forgave Charlotte for leading a game called cannibals in the Kelly woods when the girls first came to Kelly, as if Charlotte had devised it solely to insult Mama. Just as she seemed to have never forgiven them, Charlotte in particular, for the time she had so shamed Sylvia in front of the Lochinvers at the Castle Hotel.

So over the past year, he had been forced to keep his visits to Louisa a secret from his mother. But now he urgently needed to tell his parents, before proposing to Louisa at the Kelly ball.

But how to broach the matter? He went into his room and began pulling his braces off his shoulders. Then stopped, arrested by an idea. What if he did not tell them? What if he were to simply appear at the ball with Louisa on his arm? Mama would be too busy with the many distractions of a hostess to make any objections. She would have the whole evening to absorb the fact that it was Louisa, and only Louisa, whom he loved. And once she had accepted it as inevitable, then Mama would come to love Louisa as much as he did. After all, Mama loved him. He loved Louisa. How could it not all work out well?

And Charlotte would be there with Adam, the first to hear their news, directly from her sister. But even with this happy thought, niggles of worry followed him through the following days, tapping on his shoulder as he sat in lectures. Anxious sweat on his palms.

CHAPTER 11

There was a time when Charlotte would have braved the horse fair in Edinburgh's Grassmarket in her day dress and boots, drawing as she pleased, confident that she could shrug off any unpleasant attention. But not any longer. Instead she chose to engulf her slight figure in the anonymity of loose-fitting trousers and jacket, a scarf at her neck, her long hair hidden beneath a pie-shaped cap. Once, she'd even earned a shilling for holding a man's horse. The man had thrown the coin at her in payment. She'd always been more handsome than pretty, a boyish figure, wide mouth and dark eyes. In her working man's uniform, no one gave a second glance to the shabby young artist who came morning after morning to make notes on the great shires, carthorses, and the farriers who brought them to market. No detail was too small to be sketched, notes and comments in the margins.

Now the horse market was emptying. Appraising her work one last time, she packed up her sketches and pencils, stowed the folder under her arm and headed back to the studio.

Only draw what you see with the eye. And above all, draw from nature. That was the mantra from the young bloods in London. The same ideals that were echoed in the art-student cafés of Paris where Charlotte had studied the previous summer. But how could a woman paint if she were not allowed access to everything? She'd burned to paint with such truth when she had first come across such ideas in the Paris atelier of Mr Dupuis, throwing herself into the hours of observation and sketches. Attention was all-important when it came to art, Mr Dupuis said, his breath in her ear.

She shuddered, a memory of standing in the Paris atelier one evening, no one there but Mr Dupuis, his hand on her shoulder, how it had moved suddenly and she had had to fight him away, no shred of dignity left for her when he finally gave up.

If only all men could be like Oliver, nothing false in the way he talked with you, no underlying, oily motives.

For a long time she'd thought she had no wish to marry any man, until she returned to Edinburgh and began to spend time with Oliver again. With Louisa too, of course, because wherever Louisa went, Oliver would always be close by, hoping for Louisa's attention. Which made the rush of feeling that Charlotte had experienced towards this new, adult Oliver, his tall frame, his open, green-grey eyes and the smile that she thought about so much, all the more painful. It was not going to do Charlotte any good to realize that she loved Oliver, because while she was away in Paris, Oliver had fallen even more deeply in love with Louisa.

She liked turning in through the doors of Mr Murchison's art school. Most of Edinburgh's interiors were thick with heavy furniture and dark wallpaper. Here the rooms were bare as a chapel, tall white walls scuffed with paint marks like faded remains of ancient frescoes. The only furniture, easels, desks or cupboards, stippled with paint flecks. The air smelled of turpentine and of the paraffin in the round cast-iron stoves at each end of the room that gave off a little heat if you stood near enough. It wasn't Paris, and it still hurt to think of the giddy freedom of those first few months, flaunting her bravery at being one of the few female students in Dupuis's studio. She had lived with a family recommended by a friend of her elderly guardian, a lady who did very little supervising, which suited Charlotte very well as she set off to cafés or theatres with the other students from the art school.

She had thought that since she was blessed with an income and blessed with the freedom it allowed, then she could ignore her female state. Now she knew differently. The scandal caused by her complaints about Monsieur Dupuis had driven her from Paris, her art-school teachers closing ranks to defend him, a thin man with long greasy curls and bad breath. '*Mademoiselle*, are you not ashamed of yourself, making such sordid accusations?' the head of the school barked as she stood in his office. It was a bitter truth to learn, that men may wade through all kinds of muddy waters and come out smelling if not sweet, then at least acceptable. Not so for a woman.

She had told no one at home why she'd returned so suddenly, wanting to draw a line under the sorry business. Edinburgh was plainer, greyer, but she had come to appreciate the monk-like simplicity of the quiet spaces in the drawing school where she could work without the eddies of drama that had swirled around the Paris studios.

Edinburgh was also colder. She was reluctant to change out of her protective disguise of warm jacket and trousers, but her woollen dress, a linen apron, fingerless gloves would do almost as well. She tucked her hair inside a net. On the canvas in front of her, a rearing horse, a farrier pulling on the rope attached to its bridle. The horse's eyes were rolled back in fear. Absorbed in her work, she did not hear steps crossing the room until the floorboard behind creaked. She startled, turned swiftly.

'It's you.' Delight lit up her face.

'I'm sorry. I didn't mean to make you jump,' said Oliver. 'Goodness. That horse looks as though it could gallop from the painting, it's so well done. What a memory you have for how a thing looks.'

Charlotte put down her brush, wiped her hands on a cloth. 'Let me make tea. I know how to do it on the stove and I have everything I need. How lovely to have a visit from you.'

She was aware of him watching her as she carried out her little domestic ritual.

She poured the tea into two enamel mugs, realizing that his was smudged with green paint. The milk was questionable. Did it have a whiff of turpentine? Oliver would never mind. She watched as his eyes travelled around the studio, trying to see what he saw. If she had known he would visit, she would have chosen a nicer dress, tried to find something Louisa might have worn. Really, was it so strange that he preferred Louisa?

'I admire you, Charlotte. You always take on life on your own terms. I know of no other woman who paints like you, life as it really is, not some idealized drawing-room sketch. You never change.'

She sighed. 'Oh, but we have changed. We're not the wild little gang who used to race around the grounds at Kelly.' She closed her eyes and held her face up. 'Charging around the fields and the gardens behind the house.'

'My Charlotte. You'll always be that same wild little soul.'

She refilled their cups. 'Sadly, life has a way of changing one, of pushing one into a box. Think of Mary, who was faster than all of us, leading the charge. And now.'

'I see her from time to time when I'm in Dundee. She still works in Father's jute factory.'

'Mary was the cleverest of us, you know.' Charlotte gestured around the room at the canvases and benches of paints and brushes. 'I suppose someone like me – I like to think I'm being progressive, standing on my own two feet, but the truth is people like us stand on money. Louisa gets cross with me when I talk about giving everything away, says I'm an anarchist. Says it would do nothing to change things.'

'Well, you can certainly paint.' Oliver had moved to stand in front of a canvas of three shire horses in a field, stayed examining it for a while. Watching the back of his neck, the familiar curve of his head, the way he held his hands loosely behind his back, made her feel like an exile longing for home. When he turned, she saw clearly that particular colour his eyes had, a greenish grey with flecks of brown, so difficult to get right, his pale red hair. She stared too long.

He didn't notice.

'By the way, I wanted to ask you something. It's about this ball. I know it's not really your thing, but I wondered if you might like to go?'

Her heart skipped. Was she hearing correctly? She had a mad moment of giddy happiness.

'Of course I'll come with you,' she blurted out.

He looked cornered. 'Gosh, I see I'm being confusing. I'm so sorry. No, I wouldn't inflict that on you. No, you see, I was wondering if you might like to meet a friend of mine for tea, Adam Carruthers. You know him slightly and he's awfully keen and would love to ask you to accompany him. Louisa has kindly said she'll come with me.'

'Of course. Louisa is perfect for you. She's always known how to do all the grown-up things like dinner parties, how to be in society. All the things I hate and make me a hopeless companion.'

'You're far too harsh on yourself. I, for one, think you are a splendid girl. And Adam's smitten, I'd say.'

'He doesn't even know me. And you know how dreary I find all that.'

'For my sake.'

'I'll come to make up the numbers, and to laugh at everyone making fools of themselves. And to annoy your mama. But if you're taking Louisa, then beware, she's very serious about these things.'

'Charlotte, I wanted to confide in you. Something I've spoken to no one else about. With your parents no longer here, I wanted to ask if you would give me your permission, your blessing, to ask Louisa to be my wife at the ball.'

'You want my permission to marry Louisa?' she said brightly. 'Of course. And you have my blessing. With all my heart. The two people dearest to me. But what does Louisa say? She does expect this?'

'She will be expecting this, of course. We are deeply in love.'

'So you haven't broached the subject at all with her. Dropped a hint?'

'This is not a matter that needs words. I only hope that you too will find such a deep bond one day, Charlotte. When you see that we men are not all poor stuff, when you finally fall in love.'

Charlotte stood and began to busy herself with cleaning paintbrushes. 'Oh, I've no need of a male companion. And as for your plan, it all sounds very good, yes, very well thought out. I congratulate you. You both. And now I am going to have to rush, another appointment, if you'll excuse me.'

Oliver jumped up from the stool. 'I've taken too much of your time already. But you'll meet Adam? For my sake.'

Dazed, and longing for Oliver to leave, she agreed to meet him. He left. She dried the tea mugs with the cloth she'd used to wipe her paintbrush, and which left little smudges of green paint where she'd wiped her eyes.

She had found someone she loved, deeply and for ever. And he had not the slightest inkling.

CHAPTER 12

1949

If they were going to be living with Martha for so many weeks then Caro was determined to make the best of it. A chance for her and Martha to really become friends. After all, there was so much she admired in Martha as a person. And no matter what had been said in that silly conversation she'd overheard, Caro had a stubborn confidence, borne out she felt by past experience, that once Martha and Pippa really got to know her then she would suffice – more than suffice. Admittedly, the more she got to know Alasdair's family, the more she found odd little differences in approach that left her feeling like a tourist in need of a phrasebook, which was surprisingly tiring, like having to speak French all day – but Caro was optimistic that with a little more work, she could get on much better with Martha. After all, she'd made some warm friendships with the women of Martha's age that she'd worked with during the war.

Hard work had never bothered Caro. She thrived on it. And goodness, who wouldn't consider themselves lucky living in a castle, she thought, as she opened the shutters of the bedroom window early the next morning, the old glass panes casting an underwater aspect over the brilliant yellows and greens of the morning landscape. Alasdair was already up, hoping to get some work done on his book, he said, before the department grew busy with students. He came out of the bathroom, tying his tie. His cheek smelled of shaving soap as he gave her a kiss.

'Here, let me help,' he said, seeing that she was struggling to fold back the second shutter. 'There's a knack.' He gave it a lift, folded the wooden panel in half and pushed it into its case.

'Everything seems to need a special knack at Kelly,' she said. 'Is there a secret manual somewhere? You do realize half the taps have no letters left on their enamel discs so you've no idea which is hot and which is cold. And the way the light suddenly goes out in the downstairs loo.'

'Just have to keep pulling on the light cord till it clicks back on.'

'Super. Does anyone mean to do something about that one day?'

'I know, darling. I'm sorry. Actually, Mother keeps asking if I can set a day aside so I can help with fixing a few things. It's got too much for Terry now with the grounds as well. Anyway, better get off.'

'Aren't you coming down for breakfast?'

'I'll have coffee when I get there.'

After he'd gone, Caro went down to the kitchen, sat Felicity in the highchair. She was hunting round for her coffee pot, without which she couldn't begin the morning and which she was sure she had left on the shelf the day before, when a noise behind her made her jump. She almost didn't recognize Martha for a moment, her hair down in a long grey mane, a blue silk dressing gown giving a bat-like effect as she reached up to the shelf above the Aga. She took down a storage jar marked *Sucre*.

'Darling, are you looking for this? I know it says sugar but the coffee's kept in here. Tea's in the jar marked *Sel*. Inaccurate, I know, but they're such pretty jars, from a French flea market years ago.'

'I was actually looking for my coffee pot. The red one.'

'I thought we'd better put a few things away so the kitchen doesn't get too crowded. You can use my one any time. I know you make your coffee like me, with a proper filter. None of that horrid powdered stuff, or from a bottle.'

Surprised at how much she minded the disappearance of her own pot, Caro watched Martha pour the water into a plastic sieve on top of a battered silver vessel. The coffee certainly smelled good.

Martha settled in the Windsor chair next to the range with a contented sigh. She reached up for the photo of Oliver and the two young women that Caro had brought down the night before.

'I still can't decide which of these girls Oliver must have had his crush on,' said Martha, narrowing her eyes. Louisa looks the obvious one, undeniably pretty, but Charlotte looks like a bit of a dark horse. Fiery and full of vim.'

'Now we've found out their names, perhaps we could discover some more about them. I thought I might have found letters from Oliver somewhere in the files by now, mentioning the girls perhaps. I've found several letters for other family members among the papers, but nothing for Oliver.'

'There should be some, according to Duguld, though I've never seen any. And he always said there should be a diary written by Oliver somewhere, but we never saw that either. A shame, because it was supposedly written on an Arctic whaling ship, which would have been fascinating to read.'

'So Oliver sailed to the Arctic. Probably on the *Narwhal*, as in the photograph that the archivist found.'

'Yes, a lot of student medics travelled to the Arctic back then with the Dundee whaling ships, partly for the extra cash, partly for the adventure. Duguld was sure we'd find the diary when Eugenia passed away and we had the sad task of sorting through her papers. We searched everywhere, every corner of the old bureau where she used to do her correspondence, but never found a single letter of

Oliver's and certainly not the diary. Duguld thought Eugenia must have hidden them, or even destroyed them for some reason. But then she always was such a secretive person. I can see her now, locking the desk drawers when she'd finished her accounts. Once, she noticed me watching her and was quite sharp, asked if one didn't have something more constructive to do than spy on people.'

'Alasdair's grandmother sounds as though she was rather fierce.'

'Not fierce exactly, but very anxious and reserved. Wouldn't be countermanded when she'd decided something must be done in a certain way. A great worrier. And very Victorian and proper in her etiquette. She had a horror of doing things incorrectly. She was a tiny little thing, always in black.' Martha shook her head and smiled sadly. 'There was little joy in poor Eugenia. One could understand it, never knowing where her mother went or why she left her own child. One could hardly blame her, raised in this big place without parents, though Eugenia loved her nanny, I believe. Yet she never kept in touch with her nanny as an adult, which was strange. Whatever happened to that child took the joy and spontaneity out of her soul and replaced it with a consuming watchfulness.'

'Poor Eugenia. One can hardly imagine how it must have been.'

'You know, Eugenia's old desk is the one you've been working at, in Duguld's study.'

'Really? Would you mind if I had a good look through it?'

'By all means. As far as I know there's nothing of interest in there now, apart from the castle accounts with their own sad tale. Just make sure you put them back in the order Pippa's husband left them in, last time he did the books for me.'

Before Caro began work on the archives that afternoon she took a moment to stand in front of Eugenia's honey-coloured desk and consider it. She pushed up the roll-top cover to reveal the rows of pigeonholes and tiny drawers. Two stacks of drawers lay beneath a tooled leather top, a knee space in between with a shallow central drawer. Feeling like an interloper, Caro went through every drawer, finding dull bills and receipts mostly from the last few years, several account books, but no sign of a stash of letters. She stood back, mentally picturing the shapes of the drawers that she had pulled out against the outer dimensions of the desk. Frowning, she took out the middle drawer under the desktop again, measured it against the side of the desk. It was shorter. She put her hand into the drawer space. The back definitely stopped well short of the actual back of the desk. There must be an empty space behind it. She tapped on the wooden back, pressed along it, poked it with a wooden ruler, but nothing gave, the joins solid. Disappointed, she stood back again. Most likely there was nothing but a structural space at the back of the desk.

Later that afternoon, Caro took Felicity for a walk along the path to the cottage to see how things were progressing. She pushed the pram around to the back lawns. The water had receded. She found Terry and the other two men standing around a large trench dug along the lawn, doing nothing but stare down into it, concern on their faces. Her heart sank.

'How's it going?' she called out.

Head down, Terry strode over to meet her. 'Not well, Mrs Gillan. We've come across a bad problem.'

'How do you mean?'

'I thought it must be the roots of some trees nearby getting into the drains, but it wasn't just that.' He hesitated. 'Seems someone's buried something down there and over time the drain walls have collapsed into the disturbed ground.'

'But at least you've found the problem.'

'I'm afraid all we've done is dig up more problems. I've been in the cottage to ring Martha, asked her to get in touch with the police.'

'The police?'

'There's no nice way to say this but we've uncovered bones. Looks like some poor person's been buried there in an unmarked grave.'

'You mean you've found a body?'

'The remains of a body, I should say. And the police insist we must leave everything as it is until they arrive.'

Caro put the brake on the pram and started across the grass.

'I wouldn't go and look, Mrs Gillan,' Terry called out.

Her heart beating fast, she approached the edge of the long gash in the lawn. Halfway along was a wider pit of around two feet by six feet, wet, sandy soil piled up around two sides. Reddish water had pooled at the bottom, stones protruding, washed clean by the water. A long one, and the top of a large, smooth spherical stone. No, not stones. She realized with a jolt that she was looking at the top of a skull. Stepped back so quickly that she almost slipped. Terry caught hold of her arm.

'So this was lying here all the time we were in the cottage? Oh no. Terry, do you think it could be a woman?'

'We've no way of knowing, but the police will have experts who can tell things like that.'

They could hear a door slamming in front of the cottage. Martha came hurrying towards them, her face grey and strained, her hair pulled from its bun by the wind.

She stared down into the trench. Covered her mouth with her hand. 'Oh my dear Lord, how perfectly, perfectly ghastly. I was hoping there'd been a mistake, the bones of some ancient stag poached on the estate perhaps. But even I can see this is no stag. But who? And why on earth bury them here?'

'Not for any good reason,' murmured Caro. She glanced sideways, her eyes meeting Martha's. Martha shuddered and shook her head.

'Let's stop looking at it. We'll start imagining all sorts of dreadful things. I think we should go back to the house. Nothing we can do until the police arrive.'

'I can wait on here for them,' said Terry.

'Thank you. And I must get in touch with Alasdair and Pippa before they hear it from someone else. This sort of news will travel like wildfire.'

'I'll follow you over with the pram in a minute,' said Caro. 'Just popping inside the cottage, see how it is.'

After Martha had driven off, Caro went into the cottage kitchen, intending to run up to the bedroom and get a few things she hadn't had time to pack. The thick smell of mildew and sour dishcloths was overpowering. The water had receded but the floor was swirled with mud. The line of damp had moved down the walls an inch or two, like a slowly emptying bath of dirty water, but the plaster was still sodden to the touch.

She heard Terry coming in.

'Six months to dry this lot out, I'm afraid,' he said. 'But at least all your things from upstairs have been taken over to the old dairy where it's nice and dry. Mrs Gillan said to, since the cottage will be damp and empty for so long.'

'Oh? I see. That's good. Thank you.'

Caro turned the pram back towards the castle, wishing she hadn't seen the ruined rooms, wishing she could forget the sight of the open pit in the garden. She felt homesick for their life in the cottage, so warm and filled with noise and the scents of cooking.

It was lovely to be at Kelly, of course, Martha so kind in so many ways, and yet life felt oddly hemmed in. The rooms on each floor led from one to another. You could never be sure if someone might walk through the room you were sitting in. A feeling of being on one's best behaviour. She missed their old, relaxed Saturday mornings, free to wander around in dressing gowns till ten without comment if she'd had a bad night with the baby, evenings snuggling by the fire in the little sitting room, or simply the freedom to have a row and make up, with no one listening in.

By the time she was back at the castle, she'd given herself a talking-to. Moping was not going to help. And besides, the discovery that afternoon had given a vital urgency now to finding a name for their missing girl. Martha was right to say that they shouldn't jump to conclusions, of course, and they couldn't assume the body was the woman who went missing, but Caro felt sure there had to be a connection. And she was going to find it.

Reaching the castle, through the trees she caught sight of the police car heading towards the Laundry Cottage, felt a tightening apprehension in her stomach. The truth was, she wasn't sure she'd want to return to the cottage now, not after what had happened.

What she dreamed of, one day, when they could afford the rent, was to live in one of the little houses on the cliff at St Andrews' overlooking the sea, Alasdair able to pop home for lunch, she with her own research post in the history department, part-time perhaps.

But right now, that all seemed a very long way off.

The rest of the day was about waiting. Waiting to hear from the police, waiting for Alasdair to come home. Caro was relieved to hear the sound of his motorbike earlier than usual that afternoon. She stood at the door with Felicity in her arms as he jumped off the bike.

'I got away as soon as I could,' he said, taking off his leather gloves and his helmet. 'Have the police said anything yet?'

'They're still over at the cottage. They're going to come and update us before they leave.'

'Think I might go over, see what's happening.'

'Do,' said Caro. 'I'll stay here. Don't really want to go back to

the cottage right now. It doesn't even feel like our home any more.'
After being rational about everything all day, she burst into tears. Let
Alasdair enfold her and Felicity in one of his warm hugs, his jacket
smelling of wool and fresh air.

'I'm so sorry, darling. Our poor cottage. But we're here and it's
you, me and Flissy that make up our home. Yes? Nothing changes that.'

Late that afternoon, Caro, Martha and Alasdair stood in the
kitchen with Detective Cameron, a tall man with dark grey hair
and narrow eyes that seemed to appraise everyone. Making his
own judgements.

'I'm afraid we'll have to keep the site open,' he told them. 'It will
be a while before we can let you get back to normal.'

'Can there be a normal after this?' said Martha with a sigh.
'Detective Cameron, be honest with us, do you think something
horrid happened at the cottage?'

'Finding an old grave doesn't necessarily mean there's been foul
play. It's not unheard of to have had an irregular burial back in the
day, and it does appear as though this body has been there for a while,
somewhere between fifty and a hundred years. We should know more
precisely later.'

'There was a woman in the Gillan family who went missing, about
seventy years ago,' Caro blurted out.

'We can't know if it's the same person,' said Martha.

'Do we even know if it is the body of a woman yet?' asked Alasdair.

'The coroner was able to drop by briefly to advise us with the
removal. He thinks it's a woman. There's a distinct difference in the
pelvis. But that's an interesting timeline for your relative to go missing.
Do you have any more details?'

'She was my great-grandmother,' said Alasdair. 'But I'm afraid all
that we know about her is that she disappeared, leaving a child behind.'

'Though we think we might have found some possible clues,' added Caro. 'Shall I get the photographs?'

She ran and fetched them from the shelf and handed them to Detective Cameron.

'You see in this one, there's a reference to one of the girls being Oliver's sweetheart. And then in this one where the same girls are older, Oliver looks very taken by Louisa. Their names are there at the bottom of the picture. Louisa and Charlotte Strachan. We were wondering if Louisa might possibly be the missing woman.'

'I see. So the blonde lady, Louisa, you think might have married Oliver Gillan and then disappeared?' asked Detective Cameron, still examining the photos.

'Yes. Louisa Strachan. But it's little more than a guess really.'

'We'll see what else we can find out about her. And we'll be looking through old police records for any reports of someone missing in the area.'

'There's also a maid in the first picture, of course,' added Caro. 'We don't know who she is, but she must have been about the same age as the other girls. Perhaps she was still living at Kelly at the time of the burial.'

'The census should tell us that. Do you have a register in the house of the servants living in the castle and the cottage going back that far?'

'There must be one in the study, I believe. We'll look it out,' said Martha.

'I think this calls for a stiff drink,' said Martha after Detective Cameron had left. 'Things have taken a rather dark turn. Perhaps we should stop trying to find our missing woman for a while. Leave the police to their investigations. Concentrate on the task in hand and just transpose something for the National Trust application.'

'But we must keep on trying to find our missing wife,' said Caro. 'I think she would want us to.'

'Sweetheart, whoever that woman was, I'm sure she has no opinion about it now.'

A knock on the kitchen door. Diana appeared. She wore a short car coat and red chiffon scarf.

'Ooh, whisky in the afternoon. Are we celebrating something? Saw there was a bit of a hoo-ha going on at the cottage. Handsome men in uniform and so on.'

Alasdair fetched another glass, sloshed in a measure of whisky, handed it to Diana before telling her what had happened.

'I can't believe it,' she said when he'd finished. 'What rotten luck. First the flood and now this. You seem to be cursed in some way. And so sorry to barge in. I was bringing these back.'

She placed a box on the table, carefully unwrapping eight silver wine cups from linen cloths, checking them to make sure nothing had been damaged.

'What did the valuers think?' asked Martha, hope in her voice. 'Are they, as you suspected, priceless medieval treasure that will keep us rattling on as we are?'

'They're good Victorian reproductions, but hardly priceless. I am sorry,' Diana replied with an apologetic pout.

'Oh dear,' said Martha, her shoulders visibly slumping. 'Here, perhaps you could fill my glass again, Alasdair, after such an unremittingly difficult day.' Martha took a sip. 'At least the hotel chain are not going to pester us to buy Kelly any more, not with something like this.'

'Americans love a castle with a ghost, don't you know,' said Diana. 'They'll probably dash round offering to buy the ghost as well.'

'Diana, you say the most ridiculous things,' said Martha, shaking her head. 'But you certainly know how to make people smile, even in the worst of times.'

CHAPTER 13

A small leather box tucked safely inside the inner pocket of his jacket, Oliver stood in front of the mirror trying to tie the two black strips of silk hanging from his wing collar into a bow tie. Fumbled it again.

'May I?' said his father's elderly valet. Oliver held up his chin. The valet swiftly turned out a sharp bow. 'All it takes is a little calm.'

'Thank you, MacAulay. So many items to assemble for formal kilt dress. Couple of them seem to have gone missing after the last college dinner – the kilt pin, the flashes.'

'I mentioned it to your father. He sent some of his. After all, Mrs Gillan will want everything to be shipshape tonight. But you may have your own reasons to look so well turned out?'

'It's no good, MacAulay. I'm not going to say anything.'

'You have us all guessing downstairs whom it is you may have invited, and as for your poor mother, I believe the expression is "on tenterhooks".'

'As you know there are several fellows coming from Edinburgh at my invitation.'

'And a particular lady?'

'A group of dear friends.'

Straightening his waistcoat, Oliver studied his reflection in the mirror. The Bonnie Prince Charlie jacket with its silver buttons fitted his slim form and wide shoulders exactly, a new kilt that swung when he turned, the amber jewel of the requisite dagger shining from the top of his sock, a black silk cummerbund and a grey sealskin sporran. Green sock flashes and a kilt pin borrowed from Father.

'Your mother will be most happy when she sees you.'

'Thank you,' said Oliver, feeling queasy at the mention of his mother. In the end he had decided that it was best and kindest to tell her nothing of his plans, yet. He would simply appear with Louisa at the ball, and later, he would present the news of their engagement as a fait accompli.

And in time, he was sure of it, it, Mother would come to love Louisa like a daughter. How could she not? It was a failing of Mother's that she longed for a title and for Lucy Lochinver as a daughter, but with Louisa's fortune one could hardly say she was of any less standing now, surely. He wiped the sweat from his palms with a handkerchief, the anticipation of the evening to come feeling half like excitement and half like the beginnings of a chill.

When should he propose? He and Louisa would dance, of course. Oliver loved the traditional Scottish dances but Louisa preferred a waltz. It was Charlotte who'd loved the wildness of the fast reels as children. He would wait until the waltzes then, holding Louisa delicately in his arms. Then they would move apart from the crowd, the music fading as they walked out in the gardens together, Chinese lanterns glowing among the flowers, the scent of jasmine and night stocks on the air. He would go down on one knee.

MacAulay had finished brushing down his jacket. Oliver took a deep breath and with a swirl of the kilt turned for the door, a man about to face battle.

'Good luck, sir,' said MacAulay with a bow of his head. MacAulay had never had the money to own a kilt, nor had anyone ever worried that he should.

Oliver found his parents at the top of the staircase, positioned ready to welcome guests as they arrived in the hall below, Mother upholstered in white silk, a tartan sash across her chest and a tiara in her hair, its little diamonds sparking in the light of so many candles. Father was magnificent in a heather-and-green kilt and a sporran of long Highland cow hair. His tailcoat jacket was crossed over with leather straps military style, on his shoulder a wide tartan sash held by a silver brooch. Argyle socks, laced ghillie brogues and a feather from his own pheasants in his bonnet completed his evening dress.

Sylvia drew her tall son into the welcome party. 'Have you ever looked more handsome? If only you'd let me invite dear Lucy Lochinver as your guest. But you are right, it is polite to keep one's dance card open, and she will be here with her parents. She has always been so fond of you.'

'Dear boy, do stand still,' said his father, staring out majestically over the hall below as the first guests began arriving. 'One would think you were on the brink of some ordeal, not a Highland ball.'

As soon as he was able, Oliver made his way outside. A piper played by the front door as the line of carriages stopped to let out men in full Highland dress and ladies in elegant columns of silk with little bustles, high shawl collars, ruffles at the bottoms of narrow skirts. Some wore tartan sashes over one shoulder.

A large circular marquee stood in the middle of the lawns, glowing against the bluish evening from the scores of lanterns and the two large candelabra inside. The workmen had spent a week erecting the tent, laying down boards, hanging greenery and flowers around the posts. The evening was cooling fast, a smell of damp grass and dew rising in the air with a tender nostalgia of past summer evenings and with the anticipation of hours to come. Oliver saw the Lochinvers with their plump and cheerful daughter going inside the house. He decided to walk through the trees along the drive, looking out for a certain face in the windows of the arriving carriages.

An hour after the time on the invitation, long after the piper had stopped playing the guests inside, the dance music from the band starting to drift across the lawn, Oliver began to fear that they would not come. He saw his mother hurrying from the house.

'There you are. I told Lucy that she should keep a dance for you, and that you'd take her in to the cold banquet. And the most extraordinary thing. Did you know the Strachan girls are here? I saw them in the gardens with a short man. Who on earth invited them?'

Oliver hurried around the castle and into the walled gardens. The dusk had thickened, the white flowers and the Chinese lanterns and the dresses of the girls standing out against the evening shadows. They were standing by the photographic booth. It had been decked out in blue-and-red stripes like a medieval knight's tent.

'There you are!' cried Charlotte.

'We were thinking we would like to have a photograph taken. But now we can have a picture of the old gang, here together at Kelly again,' said Louisa, taking his hands.

'Though not the old gang really,' muttered Charlotte, as they stood either side of Oliver. 'Since Mary isn't here.'

'Besides, dear Charlotte, goodness knows when we shall see you so well turned out again,' added Louisa as the photographer moved Louisa a little forward, Charlotte's chin a little up.

Earlier that day, Louisa had insisted Charlotte succumb to hours of fittings and hairstyling. And part of Charlotte had been ready to go along with the transformation. Was this the sort of thing that Oliver cared for? Like Louisa, her hair was pulled high in a narrow confection, her fringe curled and frizzed like a poodle. A velvet choker at the throat, bare shoulders and a silk corset affair that exaggerated her torso into a small bust and narrow waist, a great deal of whalebone and stuffing hidden under the pale pink silk. Narrow tulle skirts fell in layers, caught up at the back in a bustle shape. She very much doubted than anyone could dance in such a dress. Louisa was a dainty hourglass vase in lilac-and-silver silk, the narrow skirt tied behind in a great bow like a gift. She looked elegant and flirtatious and utterly charming.

Oliver, in the middle, beamed at the camera, though he found it hard to take his eyes off Louisa. It was a good omen, he felt, that Louisa wanted a memento of the evening.

Outside, Adam waited for Charlotte to insist he join the party in the tent being photographed, but no such request came.

Amongst the crush in the dancing marquee Charlotte found it hard to keep track of Oliver and Louisa, the boards quaking with the pounding of portly men and young bucks in Highland dress, swirling and skirling and shouting out blood-curdling cries, the ladies dancing with less abandon in narrow skirts and dainty heeled shoes.

'I prefer not to,' she said when Adam suggested joining an eightsome reel, miserably waiting for the moment when Oliver and Louisa would rush to her with the news of their engagement – though the crush was convenient for avoiding Adam. He was hardly going to miss such a glum companion.

Outside the marquee she found that the rest of Oliver's party had arrived, Glenconner and Gillespie, smoking in the dark. She cadged one of Gillespie's cheroots and walked down to the stream alone, the music growing faint, the lights of the castle swimming in the black water. Adam appeared.

'They said you'd headed this way. There's a terrific spread. Shall we dine?'

'I have a better idea,' said Charlotte. 'How would you like a tour of the castle?'

The coldness that had grown between the girls and Sylvia had never dimmed Charlotte's love of Kelly. Now she felt a longing to walk through the rooms again, invited or not.

Adam followed her through the kitchens into a side passage and up a stone spiral staircase that came out unexpectedly on a study leading into a drawing room. By the time they had visited various rooms in turrets and were standing in the small chapel on the first floor, Adam was disorientated. He sat down on a small straight-backed chair to catch his breath. In front of him, the painting of Sylvia's brother.

'I say, wasn't he the one lost with Franklin's ill-fated expedition? All those rumours.'

'Indeed. The stories about what he was supposed to have done inspired the games of Eskimos and cannibals we used to play in the woods as children. Some say the men could never have committed such crimes, but if you were starving to death, don't you think you would be driven to it? They insisted sons of Empire could do no such thing, but really, most people know they probably did.'

A movement behind them made Charlotte turn. Sylvia was standing in the doorway.

'So that's why you invited yourself this evening. To come here and stir up foul rumours. Baseless lies. Sitting here, in the chapel, casting mud on all that is sacred to his memory.' Sylvia was almost shouting now. In the long drawing room behind her, a silence had fallen over the guests. 'I would like you to go now, Charlotte. Leave this house and never come back. And perhaps this gentleman, whoever he is, if he is a gentleman, would order his carriage and take you home. I never want to see you inside the walls of Kelly again. Not in this lifetime or the next.'

'It's Adam Carruthers, madam, a friend of Oliver's.'

'Take her and leave.'

It was impossible to find Louisa. Seeing Glenconner outside still, she told him she was feeling unwell and leaving with Adam.

'I understand. You must go then. I will undertake to make sure that Louisa gets home. And I hope you are soon recovered.'

Oliver felt as though he were moving through a dream. Just as he had imagined, he and Louisa danced together, sitting out the more boisterous reels, Louisa on a plush chair, he standing behind her, the vibration of the pounded boards thrumming under the soles of his ghillie brogues. When Glenconner or another gentleman asked Louisa if she might like to add them to her dance card, she declined, feeling tired, she claimed. The little folded dance card hanging on her wrist with its tiny pencil on a ribbon remained empty, even though politeness demanded that one should fill one's card with courtesy dances for friends of one's mother and for those less likely to receive invitations. This too Oliver saw as a good sign and it gave him courage. His own card remained tucked away in his pocket next to the small red box.

In the long marquee they ate cold cuts and drank champagne, Oliver serving as butler, holding her glass as she ate tiny mouthfuls of ham. When the waltzes started up they returned to the marquee and danced together again, twice, Louisa shimmering in her lilac-and-silver tulle, though in the crush of so many people Oliver had to steer with care. Then, as she said she felt over-warm in the crush, they had walked away from the music into the cool night air, her hand on his arm, Chinese lanterns glowing in the trees, just as he had imagined.

But not towards the gardens. Louisa had other ideas. 'Let's walk across the lawns to the woods,' she said. 'And look.' She held up her arm in its silvered tulle to the Milky Way rising in a delicate tracery of light. They were standing together only yards from glossy rhododendrons where they had first exchanged promises, though the flowers were all gone now.

'Such children we were,' Louisa said, shaking her head. 'Do you remember? Heads full of dreams.'

'I remember every moment I have spent with you, Louisa,' Oliver said, hardly able to believe that all his dearest dreams were coming true. With a feeling of destiny he fumbled in his jacket, went down on one knee and opened the red leather box.

Louisa had turned away to look into the dark banks of shrubs and perhaps into their past days. When she turned and saw Oliver kneeling on the grass, offering the tiny box, the ring glittering in the moonlight, she startled. She shook her head, hands clasped in front of her mouth, dismayed. But in the darkness, Oliver could not see her expression.

'Dearest, will you be my wife? We have loved each other for so long. There can never be anyone but you, my dear one.'

With a cry of distress she swooped forward, closing the box and pushing it back towards him.

'I had no idea. No idea at all,' she said, 'that you would do this. That you might think. . . You have always been my dearest friend, a beloved friend, but this. . .

'Oh, I must think. I am so very confused. I love you, of course, Oliver, but as a friend. I must think.'

'And this?' Standing, he drew her close, kissed her on the mouth. She kissed him softly back. Pulled away.

Out of the darkness, Oliver saw the white shape of his mother coming across the lawns like a comet. She seemed wild, unbalanced. And he saw immediately that there'd be no reasoning with her. 'So this is why you left poor Lucy waiting for you to come and take her into the dancing marquee. I might have known. But what is this? Something has happened.'

Seeing the box in Oliver's hand, she snatched it from him. She flipped it open, the ring winking up at her.

'I hope you're happy now, scheming minx that you are, Miss Strachan, finally managing to snare Oliver. But let me tell you it will be over my dead body if you think any wedding is going to take place. Oliver is not of age for another year. We won't allow it. Ever. And as for you, from this moment on, you are no more welcome at Kelly Castle than your sister. So I suggest you leave now. Now!' Sylvia screamed, making Louisa jump.

A crowd had drifted towards them, listening to the entertainment. Louisa pushed through them, ran without looking, and sobbing, bumped straight into Glenconner who had been standing at the edge of the lawn.

By the time Oliver had disentangled himself from Sylvia's grip and finally caught up with her, Glenconner had helped Louisa into his carriage. She sat like a white spectre against the black silk interior. In the space of a few moments Oliver had gone from holding the world in his hands to having nothing, Louisa slipping away from him as he watched.

'I cannot speak, Oliver,' she told him. 'I cannot bear such hatred. Your mother... I don't have the strength.'

'But dearest—'

'I will write to you.'

'When? When will you tell me your answer?'

'In the morning. I will try and write. I am sorry.'

Glenconner climbed in and sat opposite Louisa. He called out sharply and the carriage pulled away.

Collapsed against the padded seat, rocked in the carriage and watched over by Glenconner, Louisa felt rescued, safe. With tears in her eyes, she reflected that no one, not even Sylvia, would feel she could scream publicly at a Lady Glenconner. She was tired, so tired, of being alone and undefended, of having to think for both herself and Charlotte and for poor, dear Aunt. Memories came back to her of Glenconner's mother in her silk morning dress, always a small dog in her arms, always a kind word, always gracious – in the way that one may be from the height of unassailable privilege. The house that seemed to run itself, with a host of servants moving along hidden passages to remove every care.

As soon as Charlotte arrived home in Edinburgh, depressed, glum, she went straight to bed, with no wish to wait up for Louisa and hear her gush about her happiness. She did not rise until late the next morning. Found Louisa already at her writing desk, staring out of the window. She was surprised to see that Louisa was still in her dressing robe, pale hair tied up tightly in a topknot, the dark smudges under her eyes marring her pale, waxy skin. Their aunt was eating a boiled egg and drinking tea from a saucer at the breakfast table nearby.

'At last,' said Louisa. 'You are up. I have been awake since five o'clock. Writing a letter that I needed Greenlaw to deliver first thing.'

'I see. You cannot wait to share your news with the world and now you wish to tell me?'

Louisa's frown deepened. 'Which news do you speak of?'

'Oliver,' snapped Charlotte. 'I know he proposed to you last night. He told me he would. So you will be Mrs Oliver Gillan. I am happy for you.'

Louisa closed her eyes. Shook her head. 'Dear Charlotte, I have to tell you. . .'

She paused. Someone was hammering furiously on the front door. Louisa grasped Charlotte's hand and held tight.

'Whatever is going on?' grumbled the aunt.

Oliver had reached his lodgings in Edinburgh in the small hours of the morning. He had not slept a wink. All he could think was that she had said that she would write that morning. He sat waiting, unable to eat the porridge that had been put before him in the cold room where the sun failed to reach. When Mrs MacInsh came in with a pot of tea and took a letter from her apron pocket, he tore it from her hands. She went out, tutting at the manners of young men today. Standing, he unfolded the sheet of linen paper, his eyes scanning the words. By the foot of the page his world had crashed in ruins.

Louisa was so very sorry, and she blamed only herself for allowing what she now saw was a misunderstanding to have arisen between them, and it had never been her intention to mislead, wanting only to make those around her happy; nevertheless it was the case that, lately, an assumption on Oliver's part seemed to have crept in between dear friends. And it had cost her a long night of agony and soul-searching to know how it had happened, but once she had realized the misunderstanding then she knew it was her duty to disabuse him of any such notions.

For the news that she wished to share, and she was sure that one day Oliver would be glad for her, was that last Tuesday Paul Glenconner had proposed and although she had declined, with much thought and considering of what would be best for all concerned, that very morning she had written to him and agreed to become his wife after all.

Oliver felt as though he could no longer understand the written word. This had to be a mistake. Still in his shirtsleeves, he ran to Louisa's house.

He found the aunt and the two girls in the breakfast room, Charlotte's eyes cast down, her cheeks red – Louisa calm and composed.

'Why is he here? It's very early,' the aunt was complaining, but Louisa rose with a sad smile. Tears shining in her blue eyes, she took Oliver's hand in both of hers.

'I knew you would understand and wish us well,' she said as she led him back into the hall.

'If you would hear me out. . .' he began.

She lowered her head. 'I am sorry,' she whispered. She retreated back into the room and closed the door.

As he walked away along the street feeling stunned and numb, he heard footsteps running behind him. Turned to see Charlotte, her hair flying out in the breeze.

'I'm so sorry,' she began, holding fast to his arm, her face filled with pity. 'If I'd known. . .'

'Not now, Charlotte,' he said, brushing her hand gently from his arm. 'This, I must bear alone.' And with a formal bow of his head, he walked on.

He sat all morning at a desk in the anatomy library. In front of him a glass case filled with fossilized teeth and skeletons. The bones of a monstrous extinct beast strung up above his head. His books were open but his eyes were on the glass, dazzled by the light reflected from the tall windows, seeing again Louisa in her lilac-and-silver gown, a white-gloved hand on his shoulder as they danced. He rubbed his eyes, focused on the arrangement of fossil bones beyond the glass. Tried again to read the words that made no sense.

By two that afternoon Oliver had abandoned his books and was sitting in the World's End Inn, a beer and a whisky before him, three more inside, the room distancing itself in a welter of noise as students and working men came in singly or in groups. At some point, Oliver saw Duncan Patterson loom up and squeeze in beside him. The table filled with rowdy medics bringing their songs and bawdy jokes, and some two hazy hours later Oliver had come to an arrangement. Since Duncan could no longer take his place as ship's surgeon on a whaler out of Dundee the next day for urgent family reasons, Oliver had offered to stand in for him.

And why not? He'd always longed to set sail with the ships that set out for the Arctic each summer. He nodded his way through

Duncan's précis of the details in a happy haze. He would be away for the long summer vacation, far from any female with eyes the colour of hyacinths. And surely, he thought – and this was his plan – by his return Louisa would have missed him and had a change of heart. More whisky was fetched. It was an excellent plan. Duncan had all the equipment ready, warm boots, tweed trousers and jacket, balaclava, mittens, a stone bottle to warm chilly sheets. Duncan had even donated the empty journal that was to be his diary, to record Oliver's exciting new adventures, he said.

'God, but you are a lucky beggar, Gillan. How I've longed to follow in the steps of Franklin.'

'The explorer who perished.'

'Not Franklin exactly, but think of it, to step off the edge of the world into the unknown. To tread on ice where no man has trod before.'

All Oliver needed to do was go with him to the lawyer's house, sign the necessary papers, then there would be plenty of time to collect his things from Mrs MacInsh's before the train left for Dundee harbour.

The best of friends, arm in arm, singing, a bottle of brandy between them, they went along to the lawyer's home, dogs barking in their wake. Duncan knocked the lawyer up who came down in his nightclothes, a velvet dressing gown tightly belted, none too pleased as he listened while Duncan explained the problem – to which a smiling Oliver was the solution. Money exchanged hands to encourage the lawyer's best efforts. Oliver signed the papers.

They took a cab to collect Oliver's new possessions from Duncan's lodgings, the two of them still full of hilarity, then went to collect Oliver's things from Mrs MacInsh's.

As soon as he was on the train amid bags and boxes, Oliver fell sound asleep.

CHAPTER 14

Caro was alone in the house when the phone rang. It was Detective Cameron from St Andrews police.

'Is that Mrs Gillan?'

'Caro Gillan. I'm afraid my mother-in-law is out if you wanted to speak to her.'

'I was ringing to confirm that the body is definitely that of a woman.'

'I see. Gosh. So it really could be our missing bride.'

'It's a theory we will be following up. And if you could let Mrs Gillan senior know that we've heard back from the records office about the Strachan sisters.'

'Did you find that Louisa went missing?'

'No, not at all. Louisa Strachan married a Lord Glenconner and lived to middle age. In fact, her one surviving granddaughter passed away quite recently, though without heirs. Charlotte, however, is a different story. The only record we found regarding Charlotte was a birth certificate. No death or marriage certificate seem to exist. So as far as the records go, Charlotte did, it appears, vanish into thin air.'

'Goodness. So could it be Charlotte buried in the garden then, for some reason?'

'It's a possibility, but it may be that she moved abroad somewhere, which would explain the lack of records. The solicitors who manage Louisa's granddaughter's estate are searching family records, trying to find a legal inheritor. They'll let us know if they find anything about Charlotte, but so far it does seem that Charlotte Strachan disappeared without a trace. And the timelines do fit.'

'Poor Charlotte. Having spent so much time looking at her picture, I almost feel I know her.'

'We have to remember it's still a theory at the moment, not proven.'

'I understand.'

'There's one other thing that you may find of interest. We found the name for the little servant girl in the photograph. A Mary MacGrievy. Lived in the Laundry Cottage at the time the photo would have been taken, left shortly after.'

'You mean she also disappeared?'

'Not disappeared. She went to work in the jute mill owned by the Gillan family. Seems to have stayed there for several years.'

'I'm relieved to hear that. Mary MacGrievy. Thank you.'

Caro put down the phone. She'd been so sure Louisa was the missing bride, the inscription on the first photo, the way Oliver's attention rested on her in the second one, and she'd wondered if it might be her body even. But Louisa had married and had children. Charlotte was the one who had gone missing.

Studying the photo of the ball again, however, Caro could see no hints that Charlotte might like Oliver from that mulish, unimpressed expression she directed towards the camera. No hints that Oliver might have been in love with her. Though it was only one photo, of course. She needed to see what Alasdair thought, and Martha, if they ever got back from St Andrews.

She took Felicity through to the library where Martha had brought down the old rocking horse and some little books that Oliver and

Pippa had liked. Stopped dead outside the door to the North Tower, skin prickling along her arms. Was that footsteps coming down the spiral staircase? But she was alone in the house.

Diana burst out of the tower door, surprise on her face.

'Goodness, you made me jump,' said Diana.

'I had no idea you were here,' said Caro. 'Thought we had a burglar.'

'So sorry. Just popped in to get a couple of things I need to take to Edinburgh with me this week, for valuations. Forget I ought to warn people when I'm charging around the building. My fault entirely. Anyway, better dash.'

And blowing a kiss from her red lips with her red nails, Diana hurried away with a small box under her arm.

But Caro still felt unsettled, glad to see Alasdair and Martha coming back in the car. She ran down to give them Detective Cameron's news.

That night, after being kept awake by a teething baby for hours, Caro finally fell asleep. Immediately, someone shook her shoulder. She pulled herself up in the semi-dark.

'Hello, sleepy-head.' A warm kiss from Alasdair. He opened the shutters.

'Isn't it very early?' she said, squinting at the light.

'Nine o'clock. We all had our breakfast ages ago. Felicity's had porridge. Mummy's looking after her. She said we should let you sleep on a bit longer.'

'You should have woken me sooner. I'll be down in a sec.'

Caro dragged on some clothes, pulled a comb through her hair and ran down the three flights.

In the kitchen, breakfast had been cleared from the long wooden table in the middle of the room, a single setting left at the end for Caro. Felicity was playing on the rug, Martha pushing a toy duck towards her while Felicity laughed.

'Here's Mummy. And we've all been out to feed the chickens and walk the dog.'

'I'll take her now if you like.'

'No need. No need. We're fine, aren't we, darling? Get yourself something to eat while you have a moment for yourself. And you know, if you wanted to get on in the study for a while – I know how keen you are to – then I can look after this little one this morning.'

'It would be good to make an early – well, earlyish – start. I thought I'd go up to the attics to have a look round.'

Martha did not reply for a moment. Then said almost too brightly, 'Well, if you think so dear. Very good.'

'Would you rather I didn't?' asked Caro. 'I don't want to intrude.'

'You're not intruding, dear. It's silly of me, but after Duguld died I put a lot of his things up there, golf clubs, suits. I haven't been able to face going up to sort it out. And there's so much stuff that's been left there for decades, anyway, by goodness knows whom. One doesn't know where to begin.'

'It must have been so very difficult, losing Duguld so early.'

'He was barely fifty. Far too soon to lose him. But I'm so lucky to have my children. And it would be a great help for someone to go up there and have a little look at things. Thank you, dear.'

'I'll run up and make a start then. And thank you for helping with Felicity. She loves playing with her granny.'

The West Tower staircase led off the cold back lobby at the back of the kitchens. Caro climbed the narrow steps, and dizzy after spiralling up four floors, came out into a narrow corridor, a row of doors each side, once servants' rooms but now unused and unheated. The first rooms were empty and swept clean, just a single iron bedstead and washstand left in one. But at the far end the two rooms were used for storage, filled with things that had been useful once. A baby's crib, a battered cello case, cardboard boxes and rusty travel trunks covered in a fine layer of dust. At the back stood a narrow wardrobe with a cracked mirror in the door. A dusty window looked out over the grounds. She peered through, expecting a view of the sea, but saw a forest of dark pines moving in the wind. In front of them she could see their cottage and the gouges in the lawns.

She found nothing of any interest in the boxes she opened: old skates, a box full of ledgers for groceries, menus. A broken train set. She was about to call it a day but out of curiosity she creaked open the wardrobe. It was filled with fusty old coats and suits, a moth-eaten fur. But crouching down to open the drawer along the bottom she saw that something had been pushed to the back underneath the coats, a small parcel tied up with string. She pulled it out, brushed off the dust.

She unpicked the knots and unfolded the brown paper. Inside she found a bundle of cream material, silky, folded neatly. Something inside it. The material gave off a strong smell of mothballs as she carefully began to unfold it. It was a long dress, cream silk and lace, but it hadn't been finished, the cuffs unhemmed and trailing threads. A wedding dress, surely. As she opened out the last fold something fell onto the floor. She bet down to retrieve it. It was a notebook, a faded inscription on the cover: *Oliver Gillan, diary of the "Narwhal"*. With rising excitement, Caro began to flick through the pages, unable to believe that she'd finally found Oliver's diary. It felt too thin for its spine, however. Opening it at the back, she found that almost half the pages had been pulled out. She began reading the entries. The cursive writing was beautiful but hard to make out. Giving up for a while she set it aside and shook out the dress, holding it against her in front of the wardrobe's tarnished mirror. A beautiful wedding dress, a web of lace over white satin. It had been made for someone slighter than Caro, but as the hems were unfinished it was hard to know how tall the person would have been. But who on earth would make such a lovely wedding dress and not wear it? From the style, fitted waist and narrow skirt, Caro guessed it must have been made somewhere around the end of the Victorian period, the 1880s perhaps. A date that would fit in with their missing bride.

But Alasdair's great-grandmother had, as far as Caro knew, been officially married. So what was the story behind the dress?

She shivered. This part of the house hadn't had any sun yet. She carefully folded the dress back inside its paper and perching on a trunk tried to read more of the passages from the diary, getting used to the old-fashioned way Oliver formed his letters. A wind was blowing in through the sash window, giving impatient rattles and thumps, leaving goosebumps along her arms, but Caro kept on reading.

After a while, she couldn't keep it to herself any longer and with the dress folded carefully in her arms, the diary on top, she ran down to find Martha.

They decided that they had to wait for Alasdair to come home and share what they had found. Now that summer was ending, the evenings were already getting cold. After supper that evening, sitting around a fire in the snug, Caro, Alasdair and Martha took it in turns to read aloud from Oliver's diary, following his journey with amazement.

CHAPTER 15

Oliver was dreaming of ships on wintry seas. He woke to find a train guard shaking his shoulder.

'Gentleman told me to make sure you got off when we reached Dundee.'

Blinking in the bitter April wind, Oliver was left standing on the platform surrounded by piles of mysterious luggage. Disjointed memories of last night's events came back to him. A vague memory of signing a document – or was that a dream? With mounting horror he scrambled through his pockets and pulled out a vellum envelope, inside it the notary's document. He stared at it in disbelief. This could not be. He had to get back to Edinburgh and to Louisa. If he could only speak with her again, he was sure she would change her mind.

Leaving the bags with a porter, Oliver hurried towards the docks. He had to find the captain of the *Narwhal*, get him to release him from whatever document this was that he'd signed. A pale yellow light rose over the far hills on the other side of the Tay Estuary, the masts and buildings of the docks etched black against the light. Even at this hour, the docks were a cacophony of noise and bustle, a rumbling of wheels on cobbles, men cursing and shouting, the ringing of hammers on steel, the screech of gulls, a steam whistle. The ever-present stink of whale oil, acrid and sweet, and the sootier smells of tar and smoke.

Oliver had been dockside in Dundee many times but the Arctic sailors' tales of polar bears and icebergs had always seemed to exist in a world apart, fabled, violent and endlessly exciting. He'd never stood on the docks as someone who could cross over from land to ship and set sail with the fleet. In spite of his desperation to get back to his beloved, he could feel the undercurrent's pull of unknown adventures.

The ships of the whaling fleet were moored along the Earl Grey docks, the quaysides already thick with families making their last goodbyes. He threaded through the crowds in the wake of a trio of cheerfully unsteady sailors. Catching up with them, he explained that he was looking for the *Narwhal*.

They put arms round his shoulders and bore him towards a ship's walkway in a cloud of alcohol breath.

'Here's your *Narwhal*,' one of them said. 'And Captain Grant is a lucky master. Brings all his men home and with pay in their pockets.'

'Though I wouldn't like to sail with his brother, the other Captain Grant,' said his companion, spitting on the quayside.

'How do you mean?'

'His brother lost his ship last year. Claims it was pinched in the ice and went down by an act of God.' The sailor tapped his nose. 'Others may give a different version of his story. Let's just say there was a handsome insurance payout for the owners for their leaky old vessel.'

He shielded his eyes, scanning the decks. Pointed out a stocky figure standing alone on the quarterdeck. 'There's your captain.'

Pushing onto the crowded boat, Oliver picked his way past the knots of families, weeping wives saying their goodbyes, past barrels and hen coops and rope coils, the wind whipping northwards as if willing the boat to leave. On the quarterdeck, he found the captain deep in conversation with one of the crew. They were studying a list and looking none too pleased.

'Three men missing. Won't do at all,' Captain Grant said, a short, thickset man of late middle age, long plump cheeks and a boyish face that contrasted oddly with white hair cut straight across in a thick fringe. He wore a navy pea coat with brass buttons.

'Never heard of you,' he said as Oliver showed him his papers. 'I thought the agent had signed up a solid man, name of Dr Patterson of Edinburgh. How'm I to know you're not a quack or a nincompoop? Have you ever done a day's work in your life, lad? Because there'll be no time to tend to shirkers or ninnies once we set sail.'

'I can assure you that I am as able as any medical student in my year. However, sir, I agree that I am not meant to come on this voyage. If you could replace me with another man then I would be most grateful. In fact, I hereby resign as the ship's surgeon for it never was my intention to sign that document.'

'But sign it you did. Much as I'd like to have you replaced, this ship sails today, and since we cannot legally leave port without a ship's doctor on board, then I ask you, whose name is on this document, Mr Gillan?'

'Mine, sir.'

'Yes. Mr Oliver Gillan. That will be you. Then, Mr Gillan, you sail with us, or face jail. Unless you have a spare ten thousand pounds so we can recover the costs for the entire trip should you prevent us sailing?'

'No, sir, but if I may point out —'

'You may not. Stow your belongings in the cabin marked "Ship's Surgeon". In two hours this ship leaves port.'

He turned away. Oliver stared open-mouthed at his back. The captain called over his shoulder. 'Wait. Your first task as ship's surgeon. You can accompany Nicolson to the Overgate to round up any fools still spending the last of their pay on drink. Bandage up any who've been brawling and get them back to the ship. Welcome on board, Mr Gillan.'

Nicolson was a lad of around seventeen, a woollen cap with ear flaps tied up across his head, wide nankeen trousers short above his ankles. With dawning horror at what he had signed up to, Oliver followed the rattle of Nicolson's clogs along the Overgate.

'But where to look?' Oliver asked, thinking of the many pubs and drinking dens along the Overgate, all the while still trying to think of a plan to escape and coming up with nothing.

'Only one place,' Nicolson called back. 'And aye, there'll be some broken bones to strap up if they've taken the drink all day.'

'No point taking seamen on board for an arduous voyage if they've a broken limb,' Oliver called back.

'It's not our men who will have the broken bones,' he replied.

The Arctic Inn was a one-roomed cottage at the bottom of a gulley of sandstone tenements blackened by soot. Greasy windows let out a yellowish light as if the evening gloaming had already set in. The din was deafening, men in the last stages of inebriation, shouting over rowdy games of cards, singing. Other men slumped in deep sleep or possibly an alcoholic coma, Oliver judged. A thick fug of smoke and alcohol. Around the walls he caught sight of metal harpoons and thick, wooden harpoon guns. He peered at the etching of a sailing ship held fast in ice, small stick-like figures crossing the white expanses around it.

A woman, a lady of the night, no doubt – respectably dressed but who can tell, thought Oliver – was rifling through the pockets of a seaman as he dozed against a wall.

'Madam,' he said. 'Have you no shame? Taking money from a sleeping man, even if he does owe you money.'

She turned on him.

'What d'you tak' me for, you whelp? I'll have you know I'm the wife of this useless lump and I'll ha' what's left of the pay he's left afore he's drunk the lot. When I think of aye the good husbands who hand their whaling advance straight to their wives before they sail, and I've this useless lump.' She rabbited out a small leather pouch, and with a satisfied but grim smile, left the man to his snoring.

Nicolson had gone to speak to the bartender, a woman not much taller than the prow of the bar, behind her rows of whisky bottles lit up by the lamplight like a stained-glass window in shades of amber. She nodded towards a figure slumped over a table in an alcove so dark that the lamplight spreading in a circle over the table might have been in a ship's cabin in a dark Arctic winter.

'Ah yes, our blacksmith,' said Nicolson. The spindly blacksmith sniggered.

Later Oliver would find the two men had changed places, taking up roles suited to their size, since the blacksmith had no documents, and a cook needed none.

The blacksmith was a small, wizened man of perhaps sixty with sparse yellow-and-grey hair, a complexion like kippered leather. He stood unsteadily when Nicolson shouted in his ear, not helped, Oliver realized, by his wooden foot. It was only when they had him standing, arms hoisted over their shoulders, that Oliver heard a growl and turned to see a second figure in the darkness of the alcove, more a bear than a man. He rose to some six feet, heavy with both muscle and fat, narrow eyes under a shaggy cap, a beard covering most of his lower face. He shook Oliver's hand, crushingly, in his own meaty one.

'MacIver,' he said, 'ship's cook.'

The spindly blacksmith sniggered. A cunning gleam in the cook's eyes made Oliver feel he was missing some private joke.

Back through the Overgate, the docksides now a solid mass of people. Oliver was astonished to find Charlotte standing by the *Narwhal*'s walkway.

'Thank goodness! There you are,' she said, hurrying towards him. 'I was so afraid I'd miss you. So is it really true then? Is there nothing I can do to stop you? I heard the news from your landlady when I called to see if you were quite well after Louisa's news. Only to find that you were gone. And on a whaling ship. I got myself to Waverley station as fast I could. Oliver, you must make them release you.'

'Believe me, I've tried. The deed is done, signed for and irrefutable. We sail in an hour or so. I cannot believe you have come all the way here.'

'But what does your mother say?' She saw his face. 'Oh. She doesn't know.'

'That will be a favour I have to ask of you. Can you be the one to deliver a note to my parents that I must write now, explaining what has happened.'

'Your mother will have a fit of hysterics.'

'If only she had been more welcoming to Louisa, then perhaps things might have been different,' he said bitterly.

'Perhaps. But in the end, Louisa and your mother have the same outlook on the world, an eye for what is fashionable and well received.'

'Like Glenconner with his title.'

'Don't be too hard on Louisa. She simply wants to be secure and safe. To never feel like an orphan again.'

He took Charlotte's hands in his, examined the paint-rimmed nails and the knuckles chapped by hours of cold studio work with oil and turpentine. A wisp of red paint on the strand of hair that fell over her cheek.

'At least you, Charlotte, are never other than yourself. You always see true, speak true.'

She opened her mouth as if to reply, her cheeks deep pink, but Nicolson interrupted. 'Better give me your sweetheart's ribbon, sir. You must have a ribbon for luck.' He held up a garlanded wreath streaming with ribbons of all colours and lengths, three or four knots along each one.

'Oh, but I . . .'

'Here,' said Charlotte, taking off her hat and pulling a russet ribbon from round the crown.

'Don't let him see you make the knots, miss, or the luck will be gone,' said Nicolson. She turned her back to make her knots, passed the ribbon to Nicolson to tie in with the rest.

'Thank you,' Oliver said after Nicolson was gone. 'I believe these little superstitions are important to whaling men, a connection to the wives they will not see for many months.'

'And to those who wait on shore.'

'Charlotte, can you spare the time to wait while I write the letter?'

'Of course.'

'Let's find my cabin. My writing things are there. You won't mind a bit of confusion, things not yet sorted and stowed away?'

Past pigs in pens and tea chests. Down into the confines of the lower deck. Inside a cabin marked 'Ship's Surgeon' they found Oliver's trunk and a welter of boxes that had been heaped up inside.

'Well, it's cosy,' said Charlotte as he hunted through his bag for his writing box, found paper and ink. 'I'm glad to have seen this. Now I can picture you during the months that you are away, sleeping here each night while the Arctic sun never sets.' She turned away. 'Just as my love for you will never set,' she said to the wall, almost angrily.

'I'm sorry?' Oliver stopped writing. Had he misunderstood?

She turned. He saw the tears in her eyes.

'You must know that I have always loved you, can never stop loving you,' she told him angrily.

'Oh Charlotte. What a pickle we are, me with my hopeless affection for Louisa, and you with your fancy that you care for me. I am but a pale stand-in for the real one who will come along one day. And then you won't even notice me there.'

'And so will you stop loving Louisa?'

He shook his head. 'No one has yet told my heart that things have changed. I cannot stop how I feel. And I am sorry for you if that is how it is for you also. So let us put our foreheads together, as old and faithful friends, and take some strength from each other. Time will show us what is meant to be.'

'Do you really believe that?'

'I can try to.'

The steam whistle blew. The first mate calling out for all not sailing to leave the ship.

'Will you do something for me?' Charlotte said. In that already confined space, she moved an iota closer. 'Would you hold me for a moment? Just once.'

Oliver put both arms around her in a brotherly hug and she stayed very still, head on his shoulder. Then she stepped back and gathered her gloves, and he handed her up the companion ladder, though Charlotte had never been one to want any delicate treatment.

They stood on the windblown deck, people streaming from the ship. He grasped both her hands. 'The best of friends, just as we have always been. There never was a braver or truer girl than you, Charlotte.'

Nicolson appeared at her elbow. 'Miss, you should go now,' he said. And she was led away, lost from view in the huddle of people being ushered towards the gangway.

The men lined up along the rails to wave goodbye to those they were leaving behind, be it gladly or in sorrow. No sign of Charlotte. It seemed the entire city had turned out to see the whaling fleet off. Oliver had never seen such a crowd and it was a wonder that a few people didn't fall off the quayside from the press of the throng. A minister was holding prayers for the safety of those about to set out on the perils of the sea. Songs and hymns and a pelter of good-luck tokens, pennies and oranges, shoes, and smoked red herrings as a joke that smoked fish were the only fish they were likely to get. Women and children weeping to see their men go, for the whaler men spent the summer months from April to October trawling the icy seas of Greenland and the Davis Strait and many had not seen summer corn growing or a harvest brought home for years, all in the hopes of catching the bowhead whale – the right whale, as the men called it, for its plentiful yield of oil and bone.

He finally caught sight of Charlotte one last time. She had pushed through to the end point on the pier, waving her hat with wide movements, her dark curls streaming out from their fastening. Oliver waved back, blew her kisses, until the men each side began to rib him about having such a fine sweetheart. And for a moment it felt as though his heart had been peeled open, a vista of a life in which he loved Charlotte, so brave and fine and loyal.

But Louisa was the one true faith upon which all his theology of the world had rested. His faith was in ruins, a vast part of the sky had been torn away, but Louisa was still the fixed star by which he would navigate home.

He watched Charlotte until she became a blur among the crowd, growing smaller and more distant until she disappeared and the sea rose and fell against a far view of the town.

And then a thought occurred to Oliver. But what of the fifteen or so men on a ship that would normally have a crew of thirty? He smiled in relief. Of course, they would call in at Lerwick to take on some of the Shetland whaler men. Oliver had heard his father talk of visiting Lerwick on business, and the scrum of crofters turned sailors hoping to make a living on one of the whalers. All manner of men gathered in Lerwick, he'd said, seeking work on the boats, or to make a profit from the whalers. Surely there must be a medical man waiting in the town who would welcome the chance to take Oliver's place, earn a decent few shillings over the summer.

Soon he would be back in Edinburgh, and have cleared up the

misunderstanding. His heart insisted it could not be otherwise.

Behind him, a scuffle was taking place. Two of the sailors were pulling a group of three boys from inside a boat up on the davits, the captain clattering down from the bridge.

'I've got three of them, Captain Grant,' said John Mackay, pushing the boys in front of him, each shivering in the sharp wind cutting across the Tay.

'If you men hadn't hammered your brains with whisky the night before we sailed we'd not have stowaways, making a nuisance of themselves.' The captain leaned in towards the tallest one, a skinny lad of around thirteen. 'Like being eaten by bears, do you? Swallowed by a whale like Noah himself?' The boy shrank away, pushed forward again by MacKay.

'Set them down at Stonehaven, MacKay, with a loaf of bread and let them find their own way home to their mothers. That's the last call we'll make ashore before Hudson Strait.'

'I'm sorry,' Oliver said, following the captain along the deck. 'Did you say we are not calling in at Lerwick to make up the crew, as the whalers always do? I have a matter to attend to. A letter to post.'

The captain gave him a shrewd look. 'A matter to attend to, eh? You are still hoping no doubt to find a legal way to jump ship. I thought I made it clear to you, Mr Gillan, that we are not bound for Greenland and the North Water, too many boats after too few fish. We're set for fresh seas in Hudson Bay and will make up our crew on Baffin Island, from the natives.'

'Baffin Island?'

He shook his head. 'Go and consult the map on the chart desk.'

'And how long before we reach Baffin Island, Captain Grant?'

'A month, six weeks if we have to push through any ice. Another two or three after that until we reach the far side of Hudson Bay. That's where we'll winter come September. By then we should have our tanks half-filled with whale blubber and be ready to hunt more whales the moment the ice begins to melt next spring, and weeks before the ships in Dundee have even set sail. Now, if you give me your mail, I can send it off at Stonehaven. Your last chance for a year or so.'

'You mean to say that we don't return to port in six months' time? The whalers always come home by the autumn.'

'Not this ship. It'll be more than a year and a half before you see Dundee again, boy, maybe two, so take a good last look.'

Gripping the side of the boat, feeling dizzy, Oliver stared down at the swirling sea. Could he jump? And then? He was trapped, and more than a year before he'd be home again. But what might have happened in a year?

He ran down to his cabin and dashed off a new note to Louisa, begging her not to forget him, a note to Charlotte with his thanks for her kindness, and a short note to his parents apologizing and asking them to explain to the provost that he would be absent from the school of medicine, not for the summer but for some two years – if the provost would allow him to return to finish his degree after such a long absence, he thought to himself grimly. He tried not to imagine the screams from his mother when she read the note, the anger in his father's eyes. He handed his letters to the captain and stayed on deck to watch the town retreating into the distance.

They were barely three miles off Dundee when the captain ordered the ship to drop anchor while the crew sobered up. Some of the men had considerable difficulty standing; others had given up and were sprawled on the deck. Even the captain, Oliver had noted, was thick-voiced and red-eyed.

Oliver helped roll a couple of inert bodies into the bunks that ran around the low-ceilinged forecastle like wide shelves. Names had been chalked up on the sliding partitions that were pulled across each night but they would have to sort that out themselves when sober. Then he went through the boat dispensing paregoric for sick stomachs, and strong coffee with molasses for thick heads. It did not take long to work his way from prow to stern. This wooden fortress of around one hundred and twenty feet by thirty, hung about with ropes and pulleys and crammed to the rafters with provisioning, would be his entire world for the next two years. Reaching his cabin, he took off his jacket, lay down to consider the enormity of what he had so rashly committed to. He found a folded note in the breast pocket, opened it in a hurry. It was, as he should have known, from Charlotte:

Remember, you always have one true friend wherever you travel. And when you return, your truest friend will be waiting to welcome you home.

He put it gently back in his pocket, feeling her comfort and care emanating from that place.

Being ship's surgeon he had a small cabin of two bunks to himself, although it was hard to imagine sharing it. He could touch the wooden partitions each side with arms outstretched. The only light came from a small porthole at head height. He arranged the box of medicines and instruments on the small desk, next to the oil lamp. A wash bowl and pitcher on the shelf beneath. The lower bunk he used to store his belongings, the upper he would sleep on. He could hear the muffled voices of the engineer and second mate who shared the cabin next door. The rest of the upper crew, the first mate, and two harpooners, made up the occupants of the other cabins around the central mess table, a narrow through-passage running between the mess table and the cabin doors. The largest cabin, nearest to the warmth of the kitchen, belonged to the captain.

Oliver looked through the books packed in his inherited luggage, took one out and wondered how he was going to fill his time once the books were read. In a crew of fifteen men there would not be enough work to keep a surgeon occupied each day. After a surprisingly good supper of steak and onions and plum duff with wine and coffee, he slept soundly as the boat moved ever north.

He soon realized why the captain had not wanted to venture out into the open water with a drunken crew. The North Sea threw everything she had at them. To which his stomach responded by throwing everything he had into a bucket, the surgeon the sickest man on the ship. After a couple of dark days the cook sent down a dish of beef broth; he drank it doubtfully but it stayed in his stomach long enough for him to begin to mend. Clinging on to the companion rail, he ventured up on deck and regretted it immediately, the ship's bow rising from grey mountains only to crash down, sea pouring in cataracts over its front. He saw the men hanging on in peril of their lives. He was yelled at to go back down – too dangerous for a green man to be on deck.

He returned to his cabin to accept that this was how his life would end, in the cold waters of the North Sea.

After two weeks of storms, he awoke one morning to an unusual calm, something bumping against the cabin wall outside that sounded like pieces of wood. He went shakily up the stairs, his head still spinning with the past motion of the boat.

The wind had gone. From a curving horizon, a dark green sea spread out covered in brilliant islands of snow, some standing proud, their sculpted bases a glassy turquoise. Among them floated small icebergs white as plaster of Paris, with various ledges of dazzling aquamarine beneath the surface. Above them, the sky was a sizzling blue. He breathed in air that was cold and pure with the sting of salt. Folding his hands under his armpits, for the first time Oliver felt more excitement than anger.

'You'll need to wear a few more clothes, sir,' said the first mate, MacCree, eyeing Oliver's vest and long johns and his paisley dressing gown. 'Frostbite's a powerful enemy.'

'I had no idea how near we were to the ice fields,' Oliver said. 'That we could reach them in just two weeks.'

'In better weather you can reach the ice in ten days.'

'And I hadn't expected such beauty.'

'Oh, she can dazzle. But the Arctic is fiercer and more filled with humbling wonders than you can imagine. Changes boys into men. Seen it before with cabin boys and with green student quacks.'

But it was said good-humouredly. Reaching the floe's edge, where the whales might be found, had put all the crew in good spirits. A tall barrel was hoisted to the top of the mainmast, a man with a telescope standing inside on constant watch for the telltale fountain of a whale's spume. The rowing boats were brought down from the davits. Men sat on deck coiling the harpoon ropes, straightening the harpoon shafts where the soft Swedish metal had been bent into fantastical shapes by past catches.

'Better it bends than it should snap off and we lose our catch,' explained Menzies, the engineer, a tall, bony man with dark grey hair and an affable manner.

Days passed. No whales showed themselves. As they crossed the Labrador Sea a low fog came down, seeming to settle on the mast top, the water a sluggish sheet of continual ice pans moving together like cold scales. Then the ice thickened, became a field of white pieces pushed together into one mass, stretching perfectly flat to the horizon. The ship nosed forward, sometimes having to stop for hours or overnight while the lookout searched for a jagged black path of open water through the frozen white plains. A smell of coal smoke in the freezing air as the engines worked to full capacity each time they pushed on through the floe.

What seemed tiresome at first, as they inched forward, Oliver soon realized was in fact highly dangerous. Not only might they become trapped, but the longer they lingered in the currents of ice floes swirling down from the Greenland coasts, the longer they risked crossing the path of one of the great icebergs calved from the Greenland glaciers. In the long days and short nights, the crew watched the ice and the ship's progress like men at a tense cricket match, silent and breathless.

Early one morning, Oliver was woken by hurried footsteps, running up and down the companion stairs. Pulling on his clothes, he saw men carrying chests of possessions, the cook ordering bags of supplies to be taken up. They were, he realized, getting ready to abandon ship. He found the captain and the crew motionless on the port side of the ship, watching an iceberg the size of Kelly Castle moving swiftly towards them in a creaking flow of ice slabs. It was pure white, sculpted into flowing pinnacles on one side, a sheer cliff on the other, growing.

'My God, will she hit us?'

Every man stiffened, watching as the fantastical white vessel came towards them. With a grinding noise the vast cliff of ice came alongside, its frozen atmosphere spilling over the decks, a groaning and rumbling below the waterline. Men praying aloud. One jagged spar of the berg reached in across the decks, pulling out rigging as the men fled from its path. Within moments the iceberg had passed by.

Then suddenly all was movement again, whaleboats being set to launch, supplies thrown inside. The captain, shouting for men to come with him below, hurried down to the hold to see how bad the damage was. Oliver followed. Two planks had been stove in, water spurting through, but the carpenter was able to repair the damage before the pumps were overwhelmed.

'Three layers of six-inch oak, and steel reinforcing at the bow –

it's no' easy to sink a Dundee whaler,' the carpenter told Oliver later as Captain Grant ordered rum for the men.

'At least we'll be out of the ice stream coming down from Greenland soon, but we still won't be out of trouble,' said Menzies. 'There's a magnetic variation of up to fifty degrees some places in the Hudson Strait. Map's useless. And that's if the ice there doesn't get us. We'll be sailing on the skill of our captain – that and God's help.'

'Aye, but the captain here, he knows these waters as well as any man,' said MacCree. He lowered his voice, looked around to see if perhaps the captain was listening in. 'Captain's mother was an Inuit. He was born and brought up here on Baffin Island, over in Cumberland Sound where his father ran the wintering station. Nothing the captain doesn't know about Yaks, and nothing he doesn't know about the waters around here.'

'You mean to say the captain's father married a native? I had no idea.'

The first mate gave a small laugh. 'Aye, married in the way of an Arctic wife. Already had himself one wife in Dundee, and each woman with a son too. But of the two boys, it was the Inuit boy, our own captain here, who was the apple of his father's eye.'

'And did his wife in Dundee know about this Inuit family?'

'Pretended not to, for appearance's sake, but aye, she did. How could she not, when he brought the Inuit child back to Dundee for an education alongside his brother at the Harris Academy? Both followed their father into the whaling fleet, both rose to be captains. Though it's our captain I'd sail with, not the other.'

'Why do you say that?'

The engineer shrugged. 'Our captain can be a hard taskmaster, but he's fair. And he's a lucky captain who never takes home a clean boat. The men on his ships go back to port with pay. The other, now, he lost his ship to the ice last time he was captain. Works as a harpooner on the Nantucket boats these days. And I wouldn't like to cross him. Be thankful you'll never meet him.'

There was, Oliver realized, as he observed Captain Grant over the following days in the light of this new information, a reticence to the man's character, a holding back not only due to the loneliness of his rank, but also to a sense of otherness, a stoical isolation. His face revealed evident traces of his Inuit mother, Oliver realized. What must his life have been like as a child, being raised by Inuit with their ancient traditions? How different the captain's childhood must have been to his own. Yet he soon found that Captain Grant was a deeply educated man, who liked nothing better than to debate philosophical ideas from the books he read alone in his cabin late into the night. One of a surgeon's main duties, Oliver also quickly understood, was to be a companion to the captain, someone with whom a man of his rank could speak as an equal – although Oliver had yet to find the courage to ask about his Inuit childhood. And he wondered, too, about the lugubrious pessimism that seemed to form the bedrock of the captain's character; just what things the man had seen both in his childhood among the savages, and his time in the Arctic seas.

After a supper of stewed mutton and marmalade pudding one evening, Oliver sat on with Captain Grant over a bottle of port, discussing Darwin, atheism and then the writer of the famous book, *Frankenstein*. She had lived for a while in Dundee as a girl and was still spoken of by the grandmothers and grandfathers of the sailors and stevedores, who recalled her wandering along the docks in a green cloak, seeking out stories from the whaling men of icy deserts and strange Arctic beasts. 'And no doubt imagined her stories of a monster roaming the frozen Arctic from the tales she heard from the whaler men,' said the captain, filling his glass.

'You don't think we shall be meeting with any such ungodly monsters then, sir, roaming out on the icebound seas.'

'The Arctic has monsters enough already. No arguing with a charging polar bear, or the flipper of a rolling whale – or a man with the drink inside him and the long dark of an Arctic night in his soul. Our monsters, doctor, are closer than we think.'

The captain led prayers each Sunday morning. Now that the drunken revels of the night before sailing were forgotten, the Dundee men were proving a sober and dour crew, plain speaking, who worked hard in order to take their pay home to feed their families. The garland woven from the ribbons of their wives and sweethearts had been carefully taken down from the mainmast and placed in the small anteroom outside the galley where the air was dry and warm. Oliver saw men touch the garland as they passed, then kiss their fingers as if taking good luck. No ribbon there from Louisa, but seeing the russet velvet one that Charlotte had donated, he felt comforted by the thought of her friendship.

Some of the sailors had evident ambitions to improve themselves, studying by the smoky oil lamp in the forecastle for their seamen's certificate in hopes of moving up to first mate, or perhaps captain even. Some were devout. One of the rope coilers, Bible Tom, tried to waylay Oliver each Sunday with discussions about Oliver's soul, pressing him to accept religious tracts. 'For you know not when the deep may take you,' he added, showing, Oliver felt, a disconcerting lack of confidence in their ship and its crew.

As they entered a monotonous seascape of grey fog and slate-grey sea crowded with crazed pieces of luminous white ice, the mood on ship changed to a muted watchfulness, alert for the blow of a whale's spume, aware that they progressed through constant peril. With the charts outlining skerries and rocks so poorly and unreliably mapped, and with latitude readings fluctuating with the severe magnetic variance found in the Hudson Strait, they sailed in hope more than knowledge.

Overnight, the wind direction changed. The fog was gone, revealing a cobalt sky with a deeper cobalt sea, snow melting like suds across the polished blue surface. The south coast of Baffin Island came into view, barren rocks with a layer of rust-coloured grass, birds rising in a clear sky. Somewhere along this alien, uninhabited shore they were to call in for their native crew, though Oliver could see no differentiation in the scenery as they passed to show where one might be. Birds stirred the skies in constant flight, a pod of narwhals butted up among the ice slabs, silky grey heads marbled with flowing water, jousting their tusks together like jumbled spillikins, huffing up puffs of air before the shy creatures suddenly disappeared.

The men were debating whether it was worth the trouble of lowering a boat to chase them, their yield of oil being so poor, when a shout came from the crow's nest. Oliver followed where the men were pointing and made out something new on a bluff of broken cliffs, a triangular construction of stones somewhere between a gateway and the figure of a man. Tatters of cloth or skin streamed out from it. As they approached, Oliver saw figures running to gather round it, waving at the ship, creatures dressed in simple fur-skin clothes.

The anchor was dropped and two boats were lowered. A band of natives came down to the rocky shoreline to greet them, waving and calling out, the children jumping and dancing, ink-black hair blowing in the breeze. As Oliver's rowing boat came nearer, he saw how their animal skins of fawn, grey and white were at one with the colours of the flinty rocks and the snow on the ground, the natural taupe colours enhanced by the bluest of skies. The men wore square-cut parkas banded at the bottom and fringed, the hoods framed with thicker fur. Some wore shaggy breeches of yellowed polar-bear skin. The women wore more elaborate parkas, with strips of contrasting fawns and browns. At the back hung a long flap like a tailcoat. Some wore wide hoods that fell off the shoulder when left down. Other women wore their hood raised, with the face of a baby peering out from behind their shoulder, protected inside the hood's thick fur. Many of the women had decorated the fronts of their garments with patterns of beads, some with the bowls of spoons or rows of jingling pennies. All wore their hair in two bunches tied with ribbons.

Oliver struggled to read the faces at first, as if his eyes were adjusting to a new light, some long and flat-cheeked, recalling the long cheeks of the captain, others with finer-boned features with high cheekbones like apples and with rounder eyes. One girl had a delicate upper lip that protruded in the curve of a bird's wing, which Oliver would find himself recalling from time to time in the days that followed, trying to decide if this was beautiful or odd. The children in their thick fur clothes, with red cheeks and dark eyes, ran up to Oliver, shyly touching his clothes.

The gruff first mate, MacCree, scattered sweets from his pocket, which he must have brought with him for this purpose, suggesting a softer heart than Oliver had suspected.

Captain Grant spoke with one of the men in the Inuit tongue, the halting matter-of-fact sounds streaming from his lips like an incantation. Enu, the leader of the tribes, had dark, straight hair down to his shoulders with a thick fringe, and a lined, shrewd face with deep brown eyes. He turned and called out to the others. There was nodding and agreement and smiles all round.

The same impenetrable language was shouted out between the natives, now in a frenzy of activity, as they loaded into the boats bundles of fur, spears, harpoons, guns and an entire sled made of wood and ivory lashed together with strips of leather. A team of half-wild dogs was waiting to be shipped out in the next boat.

'Don't even think of trying to touch one,' MacCree said as Oliver approached them. 'They will eat whatever they can get hold of, your hand included.'

In all, twenty adults, eight children and the six dogs were to be added to the crew. Oliver stayed on land as the village was dismantled, watching with fascination as poles and what looked like narwhal tusks were wrapped in skins. Oliver saw that one tent was left intact, the old skins tattered. The Inuit seemed to avoid it, skirting around it in a wide circle. Was there someone contagiously sick inside, or a body, some taboo on entering?

The Inuit were loading the last of their possessions into the boats, ready to be ferried out to the ship, when Enu took the captain aside and delivered what looked like unwelcome news. Captain Grant glanced over angrily at the skin tent. Enu walked over, pulled aside the flap and called out to whoever lay inside. There was a cascade of English swear words in reply, a grumbling and stirring, and a bear of a man pushed his way out of the tent. He rose up, squinting at the sun, scratching a matted beard, a filthy fur coat, a face reddened by sun or frostbite. Or alcohol, thought Oliver with narrowed eyes. The man drew himself up to full height, towering above the natives who continued to ignore him.

'Well, blow me down,' said MacCree. 'If it isn't the captain's brother, back from the dead.'

CHAPTER 16

'Oh no,' said Alasdair when the diary entries ended and Caro stopped reading, the rest of the pages torn out. 'It can't possibly stop there.'

'I'm afraid it does though,' said Caro. 'But at least we know that Charlotte was hopelessly in love with Oliver. So could it be that her declaration of love opened Oliver's eyes? That he came back from his Arctic voyage finally realizing it was Charlotte he loved?'

'It's a good theory. Entirely possible,' mused Alasdair. 'But we desperately need the rest of that diary if we are ever to know the truth of it.'

'There's a faint chance the rest could still be hidden somewhere in the house,' said Martha. 'Though judging from the way those pages were ripped out so roughly, it doesn't look as though anyone meant for them to be found.' She pulled the blanket from the back of the sofa around her shoulders, leaned forward to poke the embers of the fire. 'Anyway, Duguld would have been so pleased to find this much of his grandfather's diary. Thank you, Caro. '

In the pool of lamplight, with the shifting embers adding a reddish hue, the three of them felt like co-conspirators, Caro thought to herself. It really did seem that she had made some progress with Martha of late. It was hard work at times, always being on one's best behaviour, trying to ignore those helpful little comments that blindsided her every so often – how to keep Felicity warm and well fed and so on – comments that made Caro doubt her instincts as a mother at times. But Caro had decided not to rise to them any more. And yes, it was trying, the way Martha might appear at any moment, full of plans and suggestions on child raising or domestic skills that, for all their merit, were often an interruption in what Caro was trying to do, and rather insulting really, but Caro would smile and be diplomatic, even if through gritted teeth, and simply carry on caring for Felicity in the way she felt her child needed. Politely ignoring Martha seemed the best way to get on in the end.

After all, she owed it to both of them. Martha was Felicity's only granny, they were family.

And as for all that silly stuff about being too suburban, well, she hoped she had shown Martha that that was far from the case, the two of them readily chatting together about books and ideas and so on.

Caro had been determined to succeed in winning Martha's good opinion, and so far, it had all gone rather well.

But glancing up from the circle of lamplight, Caro noticed the white silk dress of the exiled bride draped over the back of a *fauteuil*, seeming to float in the half-dark, posing its own questions, and she wondered just what on earth could have gone so badly wrong here at Kelly, all those years ago.

'You're sure you're not going to mind being on your own in Kelly?' Alasdair asked Caro as he gulped down the last of his coffee, standing at the table. He was wearing his grey jacket, his red hair brushed and shining, handsomer than ever in the morning light.

'I won't be on my own. I'll have Felicity with me. And of course I'll be fine. I used to drive all over the place solo in Gertie, remember, day and night.'

'But if you need something.'

'Then I'll use the telephone if, heaven forbid, Felicity should be unwell or a fire breaks out.'

'Now I don't feel like going.'

'Of course you must, darling. It's an honour to be presenting the main paper in London. And if you're to be put forward for a professorship one day. . . perhaps in London even. You must go.'

'I could always ask Mother to cancel her visit.'

'To an elderly cousin who's not well and who's been looking forward to your mother coming for weeks? I haven't suddenly become incapable just because I married you, darling.'

'I know. I know. It's just I hate being away for two whole nights.' He kissed Caro. Picked up Felicity from where she was playing with her toys on the rug to hug her and say goodbye, kissed Caro again.

'Go,' said Caro, taking the baby. 'You'll have fun, and so will we.'

And she honestly had looked forward to being on her own, sun-dappled on the driveway as she stood waving goodbye to Alasdair. Or to be more precise, she was looking forward to feeling that she could breathe a little. She and Martha had been getting on well, though it was tiring having to always be on one's best behaviour, never quite one's unvarnished self, and she could feel that Martha too was still in entertaining-guest mode, best foot forward. And it wasn't something Martha did deliberately, but it was strange how she seemed to fill every room that she entered in that way she had. Even the possibility that she might suddenly appear left Caro a little on edge all the time.

Yes, it would have been perfect if Alasdair were there too, just the two of them and the baby in the castle for a while, but his trip to London could lead to something in the future. Fife was lovely, but she missed the bustle of London, and she missed the life they had imagined with more opportunities for them both to work. There were few enough for a woman in academia, but certainly more in London than in St Andrews.

'We'll have a lovely time, won't we?' Caro said brightly to Felicity as she went back into the castle and shut the oak door behind her, the gloom of the hallway feeling chilly after the sun. And besides, she thought, Barbara would be in the next morning to give a hand. No, not the next morning but the day after. But that was fine. She tried not to think of the ground that had been dug up behind the Laundry Cottage three weeks earlier, what or who they had taken away. She felt her skin prickle. Was it ridiculous to feel so sure there was going to be a connection to the missing woman?

She made a supper of stewed mutton and potatoes – it had proved too complicated at Kelly to try and keep up a vegetarian diet – and mashed a small portion for Felicity while the wireless played the Third Programme, buoyed up by Beethoven's Pastoral. Humming a melody as she climbed the turret stairs, she looked forward to the huge four-poster with its lumpy mattress that was actually rather comfortable once you worked out how to manage it, fitting a hip here, a shoulder there in indentations left by generations of Gillans.

She filled the ancient claw-footed bath half-full since there was plenty of hot water with just her and the baby in the castle. She tested it with her elbow. She'd share it with Felicity who loved to play in water. The damp air misted the gold-framed mirror on the marble-topped washstand, condensing on the walls with their blue-and-white wallpaper of milkmaids and shepherdesses and adding a few more watermarks as the damp began to dry out.

After their bath, she wrapped them both in towels and singing a nursery rhyme lay Felicity down on the mat to finish drying her. Jumped. A sudden crash from somewhere in the castle. She listened out, but heard nothing further. Just a door slamming, she reasoned. Exactly the sort of bang a door would make if it had been caught by a draught, some window left open somewhere. Realizing she should have checked the doors and windows before the bath, she hurriedly finished dressing Felicity, swathed herself in a dressing gown, and with the baby in her arms did a tour of the downstairs to make sure the doors were locked, all the windows closed. The evening was falling fast, the light going. She found an open window above the kitchen sink, made a hot drink and headed back up the main stairs, turning off lights as she went. On the first floor, she decided to go the long way through the library and check the windows there too, but taking the winding back stairs from the kitchen, realized she'd come out on the wrong floor and had to backtrack. The house still had a way of confusing her like that, even after all this time. She found her way back to the library. The cumbersome wooden shutters that folded into casements each side of the windows were stiff to handle and so were usually left open at night – nothing out there but trees and cabbages anyway, Martha had said as a way of explaining why she never closed them. Looking out on the darkness now, Caro couldn't help but feel a shiver at the idea that there might be someone out there, standing and watching.

Really, she rebuked herself, she was being ridiculously foolish. Who on earth would do such a thing?

No one of good intent, her thoughts replied. And for some reason she thought again of the poor woman hidden away beneath the soil.

She made a mental picture of the floors, as she returned to their bedroom. And it had never bothered her before, but she felt annoyed now that the telephone was situated two floors below, a matter of moments to run down, but still a nuisance. Anyway, it didn't matter since there was no chance that Alasdair would call this late and risk waking Felicity. She thought about leaving the lights on outside her room, in case he did, but it felt profligate to let the electricity burn all night, just because she felt, what, nervous? She who used to drive all over the place on her own in the dark. She snapped the lights off on the stairs.

With Felicity asleep in the side room – it had once been the dressing room – she took one of the boxes of papers that she'd found in the attic and began to lay them out on the side table. She knew she wouldn't fall asleep very quickly if she went to bed now, so she might as well use the time. How silent the house felt, almost watchful.

She glanced at the photograph of the two girls and Oliver in evening dress that she had propped up on the mantelpiece. Their steady eyes looking out at her. After a while, she put it face down, a little unnerved by being so stared at. She took a bunch of old letters from the box, sat in bed and began to read.

Some time later, she was woken by the phone ringing. It had to be Alasdair. But why so late? Still half-asleep, she hurried down, hoping the ringing wouldn't wake the baby, enough moonlight through the windows to not bother with finding light switches, which were never where you expected them in Kelly. She picked up the receiver.

'Darling!'

There was no reply. Just silence.

'Is that you, Alasdair? Alasdair? Operator, can you put my call through, please, we seem to be cut off.'

Still a dead silence.

'Hello. Is someone there? I know you're there.'

She waited, a chill running up her back. The clock on the console said 2 a.m. Alasdair wouldn't call so late, unless there was a problem.

'Alasdair. Alasdair, has something happened? Who is this?'

An attentive, malevolent silence. Someone waiting on the other end. She crashed the receiver down and went silently up the stairs. The moon cast puzzling shadows from the window frames, leaning at angles around the walls. It must have been a wrong number. Nothing to worry about.

She had just gone bacck to sleep when she startled awake to realize the phone really was ringing again. It wasn't, as she'd hoped, a dream.

This time she turned on the poor electric light in the main hallway, shadows washing the far corners of the staircase, unshuttered windows black against the night. She picked up the receiver. No one spoke.

'Hello. You don't seem to be getting through.' Then she caught the sound of a breath, a ghost in the malevolent silence.

'Who is this?'

A second breath exhaled. Deliberately.

She put the receiver down, her heart beating fast.

She ran back up, closed the bedroom door and checked on Felicity. The rational explanation, she lectured herself, was still the best one, someone with a wrong number who'd been confused by her unexpected voice.

She was lying wide awake, the light on, when the third set of ringing started. This time Felicity woke too. Caro picked her up, took her down to the phone. The same wilful silence on the other end.

'I don't know why you are doing this, but I will wake my husband if this happens again.'

Shaking, she took Felicity back upstairs, fed her a little, settled her back down and then pulled the shutter aside a fraction and looked out over the front lawns, the lights of St Andrews and the far lights of Dundee twinkling faintly in the distance, the fields and the sea obliterated by darkness.

Had there been someone out there? Watching? Because it was as if they knew she'd be alone, as if they wanted to deliberately scare her. But who on earth would do that?

After the next set of ringing, she picked up the heavy receiver and slammed it down again. Then she made her own call.

It was almost dawn when she heard the police car drive across the gravel. She saw two men get out. Caro pulled on trousers and a jumper, picked up the baby who was already awake and went down to answer the door. They walked around the house and grounds but found nothing.

'It might put your mind at rest if your husband were home,' suggested the older of the two men.

'I'll be perfectly fine,' Caro insisted. 'I just wanted to report unacceptable behaviour. I mean, it's probably against the law to do that sort of thing, isn't it? Harassing people out of their beds in the middle of the night?'

'We'd see that as unacceptable. But are you sure you don't want us to call your husband, Mrs Gillan?'

'Now that you've checked and all is fine I'll be perfectly happy. He's back tomorrow. As is his mother.'

'Well, you have our number, Mrs Gillan.'

She waved them goodbye, feeling both drained and silly. Just one night on her own in Kelly and she'd proved to be your typical, hysterical woman. Which had never been her style. When she thought of what she used to cope with during the war years, helping out stranded servicemen with a lift back to base, never phased by rationing or coupons because she would always find a way to manage things competently.

Well, enough of being so feeble. It was a beautiful day with a dazzle of thin beams behind the trees, the sky gathering blue. She'd make breakfast, finish her chores, washing, lunch to make. Then she'd go out in the gardens with Felicity. According to Dr Spock, a child could never have enough fresh air.

But later, the house seemed so much larger and quieter than usual when she went back inside the gloomy hallway. Trying not to mind that it wasn't a day for Barbara to come in, she switched on the wireless again, began frying eggs – though Martha had tidied Caro's frying pan away somewhere strange again – and sang along to Felicity.

She jumped at a knock on the kitchen door, turned to see it opening. Caro found herself gripping the spatula like a weapon. 'Just me,' called a voice. And there was Diana.

'Hope you didn't mind me letting myself in. You did remember Martha gave me a key, coming and going as I have to? I was worried when I heard about last night.'

'You heard?'

'Yes. The police came by my cottage at first light. Couldn't think who it was, knocking at the door so early. Asking if I'd seen anything strange, anyone odd lurking around. They said you'd had a horrid night and so I thought you might need some company this morning.'

'That's so kind. Never been more glad of it.' Caro was surprised by how sincere she was. 'I've put the kettle on.'

'So whatever happened? Do tell. You must feel so tired.'

'Ridiculous really. Someone kept calling, but each time the phone rang and I answered there was nothing but silence on the other end. In the small hours of the night it felt very unnerving, I have to say. Probably nothing more than some rather confused person, you know, a bit gaga, calling a wrong number and not realizing what time it was. Shame I couldn't help them.'

'You're awfully brave. I would have been petrified. Good idea to call the police, I say. Can't be too careful.'

'Actually, I feel like a terrible time-waster. I'm sure they have better things to do. Do you take milk?'

'Oh, I say, you don't have coffee, do you? I'm not a tea person in the morning.'

'Now where would my coffee pot have got to again? Martha does like to tidy things away.'

Diana gave a little chuckle. 'I'd imagine Martha, lovely though she is, must be a bit of a nightmare. Nothing but the best for her blue-eyed boy.'

'Gosh no, she's such a help. So welcoming.'

'Don't worry. My lips are sealed. Now darling, I was thinking. Would you like me to stay over tonight, just till the others get back? I was going to come over today anyway to carry on with the Kelly inventory. And I am very good at cooking eggs if we were to share a bit of supper this evening. Have a bit of a gossip and a nightcap together and then I can bed myself down on the sofa. Really, I can sleep anywhere. Don't know how good I am at chasing burglars, but I'm happy to put in a bit of practice if needed.'

'I'll be fine. I couldn't put you to so much trouble.'

'Nonsense. I'm sure you'd do the same for me. Friends and neighbours and all that.'

'If you're sure.'

'Absolutely. Now where's that coffee?'

Caro found herself smiling as she hurried to make a pot of Kerracher's best, and glancing over at Diana, it was as if she saw her in a new light, no longer just Alasdair's old friend, but their friend.

After a hilarious supper – Diana had a fund of stories about Martha (and also about Alasdair, which stung a bit but that, Caro decided, was her own problem) – they shared one or two nightcaps from the whisky cupboard. Not a single peep from the telephone all night. Even Felicity slept straight through. Caro woke to daylight with a feeling of relief. And if it had not been for the whisky and the large gin and tonic, she might also have woken refreshed and clear-headed.

Down in the kitchen she found Diana drinking black coffee and smoking a cigarette. Diana nodded at the pot. 'Left you some. Nothing from our shady caller, whoever they were?'

'Not a peep.'

'I must have scared them away.'

'I'm sure it was a wrong number. And I've put you to so much trouble.'

Diana waved her hand as if shooing away smoke. 'It's been fun. Getting to know you. One's awfully isolated out here. I sometimes feel. . .' She stubbed out her cigarette in the saucer. 'Well, I'm glad you're around. Now, must love you and leave you. Bye, little one.' She waggled her fingers at Felicity. Kissed Caro on the cheek, in a waft of that warm, orangey perfume. But as she was leaving, she turned back, as if she'd just had a thought.

'Darling, what you really need is some time away from the baby, time for yourself. Come on, let's put our foot down and insist that Alasdair has the babe one afternoon. And time to stop dwelling on all these morbid thoughts about what happened here in the past. His mother can help Alasdair, and we girls will go into town and have a marvellous afternoon. Champagne and afternoon tea. And I won't take no for an answer.'

CHAPTER 17

Sitting opposite him as the rowing boat returned to the ship, Oliver had time to observe the captain's brother covertly – not a man one would want to offend by staring at him openly. He was a forbidding presence, silent, shaggy-haired, and with the bulky shoulders of a man used to heavy work, or fighting. He paid no attention to the crew other than to appraise them suspiciously, or turn his head and gaze morosely across the water, a man apart, consumed by inner troubles. He had a heavy sack by his side that he guarded closely. When the sack moved, it rattled like hollow stones.

'Gillan, take a look at harpooner Grant's hand, would you,' said the captain curtly as they went on board.

'Frostbite, that's all it is,' the harpooner grunted when Oliver took the large hand in his and unwrapped a dirty cloth from around rotting shreds of flesh, the dark, bloodshot eyes staring at him hard from beneath a long uncut fringe. His caribou coat smelled of old sweat and something foetid. His breath sour.

The captain came over and stayed to survey the damage. 'Do what you can, doctor. Mr Grant is a first-class harpooner, needs the use of his hand. And since we could make use of another good harpooner, he will be joining us for the voyage.'

No mention of them being brothers, Oliver noted.

'Will I now? Your harpooner,' the brother growled back. 'And you know full well I'd be captain of my own boat still, if it wasn't for an abominable run of bad luck last year. Harpooner be dammed. Soon as we get across Hudson Bay I'll take my chances at the trading post down at Churchill.'

His feet had been bound in rags inside skin boots, but had also suffered badly from frostbite. Oliver did what he could, explaining that they would have to wait while the dead skin peeled away, revealing what flesh would remain. Two fingers of his left hand were beyond help, however, and would have to be amputated. Oliver had never before attempted an amputation, but since it must be done, he went back to his cabin, sharpened his saw, read his medical textbook swiftly, and asked for the harpooner to be brought to the cabin table.

Oliver had to get the help of two men to chloroform him long enough to do the job. He had promised to take the fingers off only to the second joint, but since gangrene had set in badly he had to take both off right down to the stump.

When the harpooner came round he roared with the pain as he stared at his reduced hand, grabbed Oliver by his jacket. 'You'll pay for this, you butcher. You'll wake one morning and find half of your fingers gone. See how you like it.'

Oliver backed away, only praying that the wound would not fester and claim the rest of his hand.

'And my bag,' the harpooner said, trying to find it as he tossed his head from side to side. 'What have you done with my sack?'

'This what you mean?' asked one of the men, kicking at the dirty canvas sack with a stony thud. 'So what's the treasure you've got in there?'

'Give that to me!' he bellowed, gesturing so wildly that Oliver thought he'd fall. He hurriedly picked up the bag, a rattling sound from inside the canvas as he placed it on the harpooner's chest. Not as heavy as Oliver had expected. The harpooner lay clutching it even as he fell back into a deep sleep.

The harpooner improved his manners a little as the chloroform cleared, thanked Oliver gruffly for saving the rest of his hand. The captain afforded him his own cabin to wash and rest while the native women washed his clothes and dried them round the coal stove in the bunkroom. Harpooner Grant dined that evening in the mess, clean-shaven, his long, wiry hair tied back. Bloodshot eyes, thick shoulders that filled his jacket to almost bursting, meaty hands and face, eyes that darted around like a man on the watch for wolves.

He was full of tales. He'd been captain on an American ship, the *Neptune*, when it had been trapped by ice in the Davis Straits and began to sink. The crew were forced to abandon ship and remove everything they might need to survive a winter on the ice. But when the men had found the ship's liquor store, they had decided to drink it. Even he, he admitted, had had a tipple, seeing as there was no saving the ship. But then some madness had taken hold of the men. They made bonfires of chairs and boxes, dancing and cheering in a drunken frenzy as the boat was crushed and slid beneath the ice. When the fire died down, thirty men, most dead drunk, were sleeping on the ice as it split and carried them away, nothing to sustain them but the rest of the drink. They were never seen again. He, however, had been luckier, left alone on the ice that was still fastened to the land. He had walked through blizzards until he met with Inuit who had taken him in, fed him, and helped him find his way to South Baffin where he knew a ship would call in sooner or later to make up crew.

'You lost your ship, and every man on it but yourself?' said the captain.

'I suppose you'd have done better.'

'You will certainly not find me losing my ship to the ice. Or letting my men go wild with drink.'

'Always knew best, little brother. But you know full well, too, that there's a madness comes from sailing these seas through the Arctic nights. And when the madness comes down, there's no controlling it.'

'You control it by putting the stopper in the bottle,' said the captain.

Floating through the door came the sound of an accordion and fiddle. Oliver made his excuses and went to investigate, the music growing louder as he approached. The forecastle deck space was filled with several dancing pairs, native girls and Dundee sailors whirling together in old country dances. Both Inuit and Scotsmen seemed to know the same tunes and took turns in playing a small accordion. Oliver briefly saw the girl with the strangely pretty top lip, but she disappeared among the dancers. Another of the native women, tall with dark hair and amber eyes, captured Oliver to dance. He was only allowed to leave when he was sweating and his hair was plastered to his head.

The party ended at one in the morning, the long blue twilight finally changed to darkness. He stayed on deck, dazed by the thickness of the stars above, and saw on the poop deck the silhouettes of the captain and his brother; and from their gestures, it seemed their conversation was not a happy one.

CHAPTER 18

A few days later, Caro found herself flying through Fife's cornfields in Diana's little red sports car, the soft top folded back, the wind tangling her hair. Diana wore a headscarf and dark glasses and emerged with not a hair out of place.

Ensconced in the window of a grand Edinburgh hotel, waiters bringing trays of tiny sandwiches with the crusts removed as if for small children, and glasses of deliciously chilled yeasty champagne, Caro felt a wave of gratitude wash over her. Diana was right: just because you had a child, it didn't mean that you weren't still allowed the occasional sophisticated little indulgence.

Diana was leaning back in her chair in a pose that was becoming familiar, a cigarette in one hand. She waved the plate of cakes away when Caro offered them to her. Held up her glass.

'Happy with this,' she said, refilling it. Caro shook her head when she offered to refill her glass also. 'And I'm happy because I can see you needed this. Stranded out at Kelly with no girlfriends to talk to, no one to let off steam with about life. Unless you count Martha, and well. . .' Diana stubbed out her cigarette, raised an eyebrow.

'It's fine really. I have Alasdair.'

'Of course you do. But I for one am extremely glad you've come to Kelly. I feel as if I've known you for ages. And it's just good to have someone who's lived in other places, with more than the narrow view of life, in this neck of the woods. Don't you think?'

'It's certainly lovely to have a friend to talk to. And you're right, I have always been a bit of a town girl.'

'Me too. Probably the thing that finished my marriage off in New Zealand, being stuck out in the country with no one to talk to but thousands of sheep. You feel a certain loneliness creeping into your bones.' Diana gave a little sniff, then a rueful laugh. 'There's me feeling sorry for myself.'

'I'm so sorry. It must have been awfully hard, living so far from your home. I know how that feels.'

'Thank you. I never like to talk about Andrew, my husband. A bit painful. But it's good to feel I can. With you.'

Caro felt a flush of pleasure. 'I'm always here. If you want to chat. '

'Likewise. I mean, it can't be that easy, with the mother-in-law there all the time.' Diana leaned over, a naughty gleam in her eye. 'And don't you find, with Martha, it's not so much the things she does say as the things she doesn't. Still manages to let you know. A way of lowering over one.'

'Lowering. That's an interesting word. Oh, why not.' Diana filled up her glass.

'Yes, you know, sort of halfway between looming and disapproving.'

Caro gave a little laugh. It felt extremely naughty discussing Martha like this, but also a balm. The afternoon grew increasingly fuzzy and amusing as Caro unburdened herself. They drove home, still giggling when Diana dropped her off at the bottom of Kelly's drive. How beautiful the trees looked. The castle too. Goodness, was she tipsy? Well, so be it.

A sentimental and gushing Caro took Felicity from Alasdair, exclaiming how she'd missed her baby.

'And darling,' she told a bemused Alasdair as she nuzzled Felicity's neck. 'Sorry I made a silly fuss about Diana for no reason. She's a hoot. I think now she's going to be a good friend.'

'Super news, darling, but you do look awfully flushed. Are you sure you're happy there, with the baby? You don't want to lie down a moment?'

'Perhaps, just a moment. I do feel a little bit dizzy.'

Caro woke lying across the four-poster bed, her dress crumpled, evening falling. She hurried downstairs. In the kitchen, Martha was feeding Felicity soup. Alasdair nowhere to be seen.

'Thank you so much,' Caro said. 'For holding the fort with this little one.' And she meant it.

Over the next few days Caro floated through life. Anything Martha said seemed more bearable seen through a lens of humour. Ready to put out olive branches here, there and everywhere, this new, sophisticated Caro was not going to be offended by anything that Martha said.

Not that her mother-in-law was saying much. After a couple more days, it began to occur to Caro that something seemed to have sealed Martha's lips into a rather thin line. After a couple more days of her being withdrawn and cold, Caro could only conclude that she had done something to offend her. Was it about swanning off with Diana for the afternoon? Because if she wasn't allowed a little fun now and then. . .

Or could it be something worse? Was Martha upset because she'd called the police that night of the prank calls – the wrong number, rather? Or even worse still, had Caro said something to offend her? But what? Nothing intentional.

It took a few more days before Alasdair provided the key. Martha had let slip to him what the problem was.

'Something Diana mentioned. About how you'd told her that Martha seems to be in every room, hanging over you, so you can never relax.'

Caro was speechless for a moment. 'Diana said that? To Martha?'

'Diana was terribly sorry. She knew she was meant to keep it a secret, but Mother caught wind of something and being Mother she had to winkle the whole thing out. Diana came and told me what had happened, after Mother had been badgering her about it.'

'She told Martha.'

'And she's distraught, mortified. Hopes you can forgive her. As a friend.'

Caro contemplated with horror the yawning chasm now opening up between her and Martha. How was she going to bridge that? She screwed her eyes shut. Why had she thought she could spill out every last thought in front of Diana? She felt sick with shame at the thought of her words reaching Martha.

Somehow, she was going to have to make amends, and without ever directly mentioning what had happened in so many words. She owed it to poor Martha.

And then Caro felt a pulse of anger. Because if Martha wasn't so difficult, none of this would ever have happened. Wasn't there a teeny bit of her that was glad Martha knew how she felt? A little pull of power, marking out a boundary between her and Martha? Gosh, she realized, she really wasn't a nice person then. Because, honestly, truthfully, wasn't she a little bit glad that Diana was who she was, fun and charming but not one bit discreet?

In future, though, she would be much more careful about what she said in front of her new friend.

Caro was preparing supper for Alasdair and Martha that afternoon when the telephone rang in the hallway. She still felt a little pang of anxiety on picking up the receiver, even by day. It was the policeman who'd called by the night of the prank calls.

'I wanted to make sure you'd had no further problems after calling us out the other night, Mrs Gillan.'

'Absolutely not. Thank you for enquiring. I'm very grateful to you for coming to check on us when you're so busy. And it was most kind of you to let my neighbour know. She came round after you left and was very helpful.'

'We didn't visit any of your neighbours, Mrs Gillan. Unless someone called them from the station later. Perhaps that was it. Though I don't see how since we didn't report it until the next morning. Do you want me to enquire?'

'Oh. No, no. Please don't go to any more trouble. Probably my mistake.'

Caro put the phone down and stared at it, a deep frown on her face. But Diana said the police went to see her. Or did she say they'd called the next morning? They must have spoken to her at some point. Otherwise how could Diana have known?

Caro wrapped her cardigan across her chest. It was always so chilly in the hallway. Too little light. The thick stone walls deadening all noise beyond them. The deep quiet pooled above her head, giving a feeling of being underwater, a sense of things beyond her hearing.

Only one thing made sense, hard as it was to countenance, and Caro couldn't prove anything – but Diana, she realized, might well not be her friend. Quite the opposite, in fact.

She mentioned her fears about Diana to Alasdair that night.

'Diana, making prank phone calls in the middle of the night? You do hear how ridiculous that sounds?'

'But how did she know what had happened so quickly?'

'I don't know. Sweetest, I am sure it was a misunderstanding. Terry or someone else might have told her. I know it was horrid but you have to stop putting all your worries on to Diana.'

Caro lay feeling foolish and silenced. Perhaps it was a misunderstanding. Though she felt in her bones that it very much was not.

She stayed awake for ages. Finally, giving up on sleep, she wrapped herself in the woollen dressing gown, took Oliver's diary from the bedside table, and crept down the stone stairs into the bedroom one floor down in the tower. She switched on the lamp and sat on the bed with its counterpane made from blue-and-silver Indian saris. Pulling a blanket over herself, she settled down to read through the pages again – wishing once more that she had the rest of the story – crossing ice-covered oceans to the shores of Baffin Island, until her eyes began to close and she was dreaming of dancing in the hold of a ship, surrounded by men and women dressed in jackets and trousers made from the skins of caribou and seals.

CHAPTER 19

Listen, she told her, though Yarat didn't know why her mother was telling her the same horrible story again as the wind howled outside. Sedna, she told her, was the proud and beautiful daughter of a great hunter who hunted far out on the ice and could shoot an arrow further than any man. Sedna could have married any of the young hunters in her tribe, but she fell in love with the prince of the birds. She wouldn't listen to her mother, wouldn't give him up, for he had taken the form of the most beautiful of men with a chest like the curve of ice melt and hair as dark as the ravens. She ran away with him to the island of birds, this beautiful proud girl, leaving her father and all her family behind, filled as she was with a great love. Sedna ran towards her happiness. But the fulmar prince kept her in a tent made from ragged bird skins, where the wind whistled through the tears, and she often went hungry. Her prince turned back into a bird with hard little eyes and went hunting on the winds. For long hours she wept alone each day with nothing but the chattering, chattering of the birds around her whose language she did not understand. So she ran away, stole a boat and rowed home. But when her father saw her coming across the snow, he shook his head. He led her back to his walrus skin umiyak and he and the other men began to row her back to the island of the birds, for her fate was sealed. All the way, she begged him to let her come home to the place of her childhood, and he almost relented, his eyes filled with tears at her plight, but a storm rose up and swept her from the boat, carrying her back towards the island. She swam with all her might to her father, finally grasping the boat's side, but the men in the boat realized that the sea gods were angry with her for running away, and they crashed their paddles down on her hands every time she tried to hold on. Her thumbs and then her fingers came away, her hands pouring blood into the sea, and Sedna sank down to the ocean floor, waiting for death. And yet she did not die. She found herself changed, with a long, powerful fish tail, hair as long as a forest of sea kelp, and around her a host of seals and whales and other creatures that had formed from her body and from her bleeding.

And this, Yarat's mother said, as she held the baby to her breast in the lamplight, is the Sedna who gives us life and food. Just as you, one day, will no longer belong to me, but to your husband. To whom you have been promised since the day you were born.

But Yarat was disgusted by this story of a woman with bleeding hands with her strange offspring. She was disgusted by the injustice of it. This would not be her story, she raged in her heart. She would make her own story.

It was three years after the time of Yarat becoming a woman. Each month she must stay apart in the snow house chewing the skin for boots, longing to be out with the hunters, but it was taboo for women in flow to hunt.

Her mother told her that the time had come to go to the chief's brother as a second wife. He was old, almost forty years, with a face darkened by the glare of so many suns, and deep lines along his cheeks. He was a good hunter and listened to among the tribesmen, her mother told her, but Yarat saw that he had hard ways and had shown little care for his other wife when she became sick after giving him a child. Yarat begged and begged her mother to leave such talk until another summer had passed. So she agreed, thinking that by then Yarat would have come to her senses.

But Yarat had already decided that she would not come to her senses when a year had passed.

Each year, when the caribou hunting was done, the tribe travelled south until they reached the sea. There they would make a camp of turf houses, and hunt the seals and walruses, and wait for the Scotsmen, the Sikotsi, to come.

Yarat's father had told her tales of how he was a boy of just fifteen years when the whalers first came to their land. The Qallunaat came to us, he said, because they needed our help. Those whaler men did not know how to sew jackets and trousers from caribou to keep out the cold, or boots from sealskin to keep the water from their feet. They needed a shaman to help them find the whales since they did not know how to talk to the sea animals respectfully and ask them to let themselves be caught.

The Sikotsi would take the entire village on their ship and the people would travel with them all summer. The Sikotsi gave them food three times a day, even when the people were not hungry. They made sure all the children ate. Everyone would line up on deck with their tin cup for a drink called coffee. They gave the villagers iron pots and needles and knives, guns and sugar and beads, in return for their help with the whale hunting. And when the sailors played music from their accordions the children would dance for sweets.

For weeks after they reached their summer camp the men took it in turns to keep lookout up on the cliff where blueberries grew, their eyes sore with looking out across the shine of the water, waiting for a faint smudge of black smoke. The umiyaks came back one day and the men said they had seen ships sailing out in the bay, but that they had gone away again.

The men began to say in low voices that perhaps the Scots whalers would not come this time.

Then a shout came from up on the bluff, the lookout waving his arms, everyone running to the shore to watch a dark smudge on the sky at last. Soon they could smell the acrid coal smoke. The shadow grew, became a drawing made with a sooty stick, boats and kayaks readying to go out and meet the ship as it came in slowly, the afternoon light casting a copper shadow in the cusp of every wave. Its masts grew higher, higher even than the bluff, and there was the *Narwhal*, anchored against a blaze of light, kayaks paddling around her like beetles. On the shore, everyone chattering and smiling because the whalers were here again.

There was a wooden carving on the front of the ship, a woman with yellow hair and clothes that surely did not keep her warm when the ice arrived. Missiga was the ship's captain, or Mr Grant as the Qallunaat called him, and this is what Yarat called him when she spoke with the Qallunaat in their tongue. Even as a little child Yarat could speak to the whalers in their language, taught to her by her father who had once been to Dundee in Scotland and came back again with a jar of marmalade. She caught words as easily as a boy who knows how to make fish jump straight into his hands. She had the skill of words and stories from her father the shaman, though she was glad not to have his power to conjure up the spirits. As a child, she did not like to watch her father writhing by the light of the fire, bound in cords, his skin shining with sweat, and she feared that the evil spirits he called up to do battle with might linger on in the snow house and appear to her later while the adults slept.

Her familiar spirit, he told her, was a white fox, but only her father had seen it. Sometimes Yarat thought she caught glimpses of her in the shadows at the edge of the firelight but the little fox always slipped away before she could know her. Yarat could feel her now, watching from a hiding place as one of the small boats was lowered from the ship, the pairs of long paddles beating the water like crane-fly wings. Everyone ran to help pull the boat up the shingle. Mr Grant stepped out, his face more lined and his hair beginning to grow white. He squeezed her father's hand in his own in the Qallunaat way. Behind him, a younger man, with hair the colour of a fading sun. He did not look like the rest of the whaler men in their blue trousers and jackets. He wore a coat made of many flecks of colours, like the grasses on the tundra at the end of summer. Her father greeted him with warm respect. He was the ship's healer, she realized. And there were other men too, harpooners and boat steerers and iron workers and the man who prepares the food.

The captain wanted to know if the villagers had enough caribou skins to make winter suits for the crew, since their poor woollen jackets would let in the cold and the water once the long dark came. Then he counted how many village men would go in the little whaling boats and hunt for them. Yarat saw that the whaler men were too few to manage all the six small hunting boats on their big ship, and that they had counted on the Inuit being there.

Yarat could see also that they were not expecting the man they called Suquortaronik, the harpooner, to be waiting for them in the village. The captain's face stormy when he saw his brother appearing from the tent. Suquortaronik was once famous among the Inuit, respected as the greatest harpooner of all the Sikotsi ships. But after he became a captain and lost his own ship, he became angry to be only a harpooner again, and began to drink all he could of the Sikotsi whisky, even if he had to steal it. Which is why, they said in the village, he had been thrown off his last ship, for stealing the liquor, and had come to them to wait for the captain's ship.

Suquortaronik had asked for a girl to join him in his tent. They kept away from him. The harpooner, they knew, had left children all along the coasts of Baffin Island and Hudson Bay over the years. He took women who did not belong to him or want him, and it was no honour for a man to lend his wife to such a man.

He had arrived one night in their encampment stinking and half-starved, with a sack filled with something that made the dogs howl if they caught scent of it on the wind. But the village could not drive him away. For the Inuit to refuse food is a taboo that will be punished by one's own starvation in time, and so they left meat outside his tent, in the way that they left meat on the snow for the dogs, and no one went near him.

They were glad, now the ship was here, that the Sikotsi could have the harpooner. His being brother to the captain was another reason they had fed him.

The village was soon loaded up into umiyaks and boats, rowing out to the ship, as happy as though they had built a great snow house for a dance. And dance they did that evening in the ship's hold, as the sun above shone red in the sky and the sailors ambled and spun two at a time and the music came out of the squeezeboxes. Everyone in the village falling about with laughter when Sue Three Fingers was pulled up to dance with one of the men, hiding her face in her hands, her feet shuffling reluctantly as she giggled, then throwing out her arms to dance better than any of them. The villagers knew all their dances, and once the shyness was over even the children joined in.

The Inuit were given soup from a great pot, and coffee with molasses, and then made their sleeping places on the boards that lined the back of the boat like shelves, the women hanging up sealskins to give privacy.

In the morning Yarat awoke to the feeling of the world tipping slowly and deeply this way and that. She went up on deck, sniffing the air, the white sails of the boat filled with air like the wings of snow geese flying home for the summer. Fixed high up on the highest mast, a man with a spyglass was standing in the barrel, looking out over the sea for the shadow of a whale or the spray from its blowhole. Even down on deck she could feel this longing to catch sight of a whale, so the men could leap in their boats and give chase.

At the far end of the deck, in the shelter of the cabin wall, she saw the healer with red hair, sitting on the coils of ropes and writing in a book. And she wondered if she might learn the secret of reading one day, so that she could know what he had written in that book. She took her sewing on deck and sat on the far side of the cabin so she could watch him without him seeing her, close enough to listen in to try and catch what he might say.

Menzies, the engineer, crouched his tall, bony frame down next to him. 'Writing a diary? Thinking you'll go home and publish your wondrous discoveries in the Arctic and become a newspaper sensation? I've read many such accounts. Half of what they write is made up – how many polar bears I shot, a photograph of the great hunter in Arctic furs staring out into the snow. A tour of lecture halls with lantern slides. Is that it, doctor? Is that why you're here?'

'It's a far sorrier tale, and one which I do not wish to discuss at present. But I can tell you I have determined to keep a diary of everything I observe and learn of this curious Inuit people. How they survive in such harsh and isolated circumstances. Their diet and how they keep healthful. Their primitive beliefs and rituals.'

'Strange sensation though, isn't it,' said Menzies. 'Seeing human eyes peering out at you from all those animal pelts. I swear, you'd think you might be looking at half-animal, half-human creatures.'

The captain's brother, the harpooner as everyone called him, was standing a little way off, smoking, scratching at his belly. He came over to join in their conversation.

'Who's to say they are human,' he said. 'The Inuit don't have the intelligence of a person like you and me, though they are cunning hunters, I'll give you that. Like wolves or dogs.'

'I can assure you they are perfectly human,' said Oliver. 'I examined two of them yesterday, a man with a broken arm and a child with a fever – different physiognomy, yes, but entirely the same species as us. And they are, I suspect, of normal intelligence.'

Hidden behind the cabin wall, Yarat clenched her hands into fists, her English good enough to understand their insults. In her experience she had found the men on the whalers far less intelligent than any Inuit child when it came to knowing how to survive a winter on the ice.

'Some of the women have very sweet faces, I thought,' added Oliver. 'The girl with the colourful beading on her jacket, a pattern that looks like a white fox.'

The captain's brother laughed. 'Take her if you like. They have strange ways, the women, and the men will lend you a wife readily enough.'

'Mind out, there. The captain doesn't like any such fraternizing with the Yaks,' said Menzies. 'Keeps a tidy ship, prayers and Bible every Sunday.'

'What he doesn't know won't hurt him,' the brother mumbled back, stretching his arms up so that the cloth of his jacket pulled across his meaty shoulders. 'With half the country unmapped and unnamed, a man makes his own decisions up here, and like I said, they're not always intelligent, the natives. Our great captain, you have to remember – half Yak.'

Yarat pressed back against the cabin wall when the harpooner passed by her, raking her with his bloodshot eyes. She felt the white fox there at the corner of her vision, stiff, ears alert, sniffing danger.

Later, she lay on her bed in the hold, and thought of what the healer had said. A girl with a fox pattern on her jacket.

★

One afternoon, while the healer was up on deck pulling a tooth for one of the Sikotsi, Yarat took herself down to the small room where he slept. She slipped in, closed the door and examined the things he had arranged so neatly in the tiny space, a chest with bottles of potions, a cloth roll containing strange knives and tools, a metal tube, a clock, and so many books. She examined these with great curiosity, for it seemed to her that each had a little of the healer's spirit in them, precious in their strangeness. She found the book filled with the words he was writing about them. She sniffed its paper, licked the ink. But as she took her tongue away she noticed, pinned to the wooden wall, a little picture of a Qallunaat woman. She was all in grey colours, ashes in a cold fireplace, but Yarat could see that she had pale hair and pale eyes. She had a pointed face and wore a big amauti that came down to the floor with many decorations, so she was not poor, a chief's daughter perhaps. And as she held the picture, a sore pain in her heart, Yarat knew she was looking into the eyes of the woman who the healer loved.

She slipped out then and went to the bunks at the back of the ship. Let the curtain of sealskin fall so she could be alone there, and did not come out for the rest of the day. For the pain had told her that she had found the one who she loved, but his heart was already filled with a woman with pale hair and pale eyes.

After that, Yarat burned even more to read what the healer wrote about them. She told her father that she should learn how to read the white man's words so that they could understand the white man's thinking and protect themselves in case the Qallunaat should try to trick them one day with words on paper.

But for now all the women had much work to make the parkas and the trousers for the Sikotsi, ready for the winter that was to come, and she must stay with the women cutting and measuring, and sewing the seams with stitches with just the right tension, each one

CHAPTER 20

Martha had always felt sorry for that poor man in Kafka who woke up and found himself a cockroach. Imagine. She'd had nightmares about it. But that was nothing compared to waking up one morning and finding that you'd turned into your mother-in-law.

When Diana let slip what Caro thought about her, Martha was cut to the quick. Contrary to every effort, she seemed to be turning into that difficult, overbearing person that she'd so dreaded becoming – someone like poor Eugenia with her timid but iron-like advice.

And yet Martha had intended to love and support whoever Alasdair brought home. So she had welcomed Caro, liked and admired the girl with her open-faced lack of guile, and her not inconsiderable achievements.

There had always been times when Caro turned into a code she could not crack – try as she might. When everything Martha did seemed to be tolerated with silent irritation. She hadn't realized until then what a cold person Caro could be sometimes. Not to Alasdair or with the baby, of course. And she was warm and charming enough when talking on the phone to her friends and family in London. But with Martha she could become suddenly irritable and bristly. Short sentences. No conversation. And if Martha did try and open a topic, then goodness me, there was a fair chance that what she said might offend Caro and make her freeze Martha out even more.

Anyhow, there was Martha, going along in blissful ignorance, thinking Caro and she were mostly happy enough together of late. Then this bombshell from Diana, who happened to mention what Caro had been saying.

Tell Diana, tell the world. They all knew that.

What really hurt, though, was that Caro didn't have the courage to tell Martha herself what was upsetting her, leaving her to hear it as underhand gossip from Diana.

Diana at least would have blurted it all out, none of this creeping around. Impossible to clear the air now. Far too embarrassing for Caro and her to address what had been said, or even acknowledge that it had been said. Though they both knew. Was this the way Caro's family did things then, a soldiering on without addressing the issue? Instead of an open, honest row and apology, this increase in tetchy politeness and diplomatic stand-off.

So Martha was bossy. Never gave Caro any peace. And she lowered, apparently. Lowered? What did that mean? Martha still could not understand precisely what she'd done wrong. Felicity was her grandchild. How could she not mention what might be helpful?

And since yesterday things had been even worse between them. Possibly because of that book on baby rearing that Caro consulted like a Bible, by an American calling himself Dr Spock. Very new-fangled by all accounts.

Martha had merely said, 'But won't the child become quite wild if one panders to their every whim?' She didn't go so far as to approve of what Duguld had gone through with the nanny that Eugenia had foisted on him, of course, who had apparently insisted that a child should have an iron schedule for feeding and for sleep, screaming or not, who held that little boys should begin boarding school at eight.

But this idea Caro had that a parent followed the baby, feeding them when they felt like a snack, letting them sleep as they wished, was that right? Martha had wondered about it aloud, the long-term effects of being so permissive, but Caro was not, apparently, going to discuss it. Would rather wrap herself in an unreachable quiet. Whisking Felicity away for a walk or a nap when Martha came into the room.

Martha was going to have to more or less sneak time with her grandchild. When Barbara was babysitting.

And now this thing Caro had developed about mice in the castle. Can't have them scuttling over the baby's toys, she'd said, disapproving perhaps of the Gillans' more bohemian tendencies?

Martha had told her, 'But Caro dear, this is the country. One will always have mice and spiders and even rats out in the barn. And there's beauty to that. One has to get used to a few uninvited guests each autumn. We don't live in the town.'

'More's the pity,' Caro had muttered under her breath, but Martha had heard.

For the rest of the morning they settled into that exquisite, awkward politeness again.

Martha thought, just wait it out. We'll get over the Diana thing. It's a bit like walking on eggshells, but we'll manage. Caro will warm to our ways in the end.

Then she overheard Caro talking on the phone to her sister, Phoebe, in London, about how she longed to be home again. How she'd been asking Alasdair to apply for posts at King's or Imperial.

Her heart fluttering, a feeling of things falling away, Martha realized then that she couldn't afford a stand-off with Caro. There would be no winning there. So she redoubled her efforts, trying to be as considerate and thoughtful as possible. And all she got back was more spikiness.

Martha had never imagined that with so many good intentions, with a modern outlook that she considered to be more like Caro's than

Eugenia's, she could still crash the gears of her and Caro's relationship – raising the spectre of the worst kind of estrangement, a future in which she would be written out of Caro's plans, in which Felicity would hardly know her.

Sometimes Martha wondered whether it might be easier if she and Caro came from different cultures, say East Timor and Lapland. At least then the differences would be evident, and the work to understand each other more expected and visible. Because make no mistake, even if your son marries the girl next door, she thought, you'll surely find that she comes from a family with bizarre customs and ideas, with words trip-wired with *faux amis*. And one wonders, can one ever bridge such a gap?

Sometimes Martha sat and thought of Eugenia. Was there some way they could have got on better? Some way they could have understood each other? Understood what had made Eugenia such a timid and worried little woman, with such an iron view on how everything should be done?

CHAPTER 21

Though the Inuit lived by ancient ways, Oliver found them as cheerful and companionable as any fellow one might meet back in Scotland. Even their chief, with his wind-carved face and his long, shrewd eyes, might seem forbidding at first, but he was the most affable of fellows once one began to know him.

Wanting to record all he could of a rare way of life that was, he realized, being marred daily by contact with the whaler men's ways and customs, he took his notebook up to where the women were sitting on deck, patiently sewing caribou skins into garments for the crew. Such suits, the captain insisted, would be essential once the long dark winter began, temperatures falling below fifty degrees. For now the women made a picturesque scene under a pleasant morning sun. The Inuit wore their summer suits of sealskin, light and waterproof, with mottled patterns in grey and white like splashes of water on silk, some with a greenish tinge as if seen from the bottom of a pool. Oliver sought out the girl called Yarat, who spoke English so well, as his guide. She explained how it was important to catch the caribou at the right time, just after the moulting so that the hair shed less, but before the winter fur became too heavy. With two layers of fur, one facing the skin, the other facing the snow, the Inuit were able to survive in temperatures that would freeze flesh in seconds.

An old Inuit woman came close and began to place her hands along his chest and back. Oliver jumped. Yarat broke into laughter.

'She is measuring you for your jacket.'

Businesslike, scolding him in Inuktitut, the old woman skimmed her hands over his frame without ever touching him. She wrote nothing down, measuring only by handspan and eye. And later, when Oliver found out that his jacket and boots fitted to perfection, he would note down in his diary that perhaps the Western world had become too reliant on its pens and slide rules.

'I'll have the Yaks measure me for a new suit then,' said the captain's brother, striding into the middle of where the women were sewing. He let his filthy fur coat drop on the deck and held out his arms, revealing a wrinkled woollen shirt with dark stains under the armpits where the sweat had dried out many times. A drinker's sheen to his face.

'And don't be giving me any of your flea-ridden old skins. I want the best, mind you.'

The women looked up, scowling. None of them moved.

'Did you not hear me, you deaf crones?'

Shaking her head, the old woman stepped forward, but he lunged and caught Yarat by the arm.

'I'll have this one lay her hands on me.'

Yarat pulled back, her face showing disgust.

'Too good for me are you, you dirty Yak?' She made a yelping sound, struggling to get free as he forced her arm behind her back.

Oliver rushed to stop him, but Yarat had already twisted herself out of the harpooner's grip. She shot Oliver a forbidding look, shook her head. And pushing her dishevelled hair back in its place, she set to measuring the harpooner, her delicate face immobile as stone, her hands never touching the noisome body.

But as she finished, he snatched her again, planted a long kiss on her mouth. She pulled away, spat on the deck. He struck her across the face.

Before Oliver could move, the shaman was already there, standing in front of his daughter. The harpooner laughed.

'I'll give you my second-best hunting knife for your daughter for a night. It's a good offer.'

His face unreadable, the shaman led Yarat away.

'Nobody walks away from me,' the harpooner shouted after them. 'Especially dirty savages. And what are you all gaping at?' he yelled, spinning around and pointing his finger at the gathered crowd. The women bent their heads to their work. The crewmen melted away.

Over the following days, the captain's brother took every opportunity to talk loudly in the shaman's presence, about how stupid and dirty the Yak were, how loose in their ways.

The resentment building in the native crew was palpable, thrumming in the air like an approaching storm.

And still no whale had been sighted.

Yarat came to Oliver's cabin for her first reading lesson, as arranged. The lack of whales meant there was not much for the natives to do. Oliver asked her what her father thought about the whales hiding from them. Was it not the case that the shaman believed he knew how to find the whales?

She put her elbows on the desk, her chin on her hands, her dark eyes examining his face. 'He thinks the whales will not come because someone has broken a taboo. My father will ask the spirits tonight to tell us who it is.'

'How will he do that? May I be there?'

'You white men do not like these things. You would be afraid, I think. Sometimes even we are afraid when the spirits come.'

'But if you were with me, I wouldn't be afraid.'

She frowned and scanned his expression again, unsure if Oliver was making fun of her. But reading an honest eagerness in his eyes, she said, 'I will ask him for you. Though you must not tell the captain if you come for he does not like it.'

'Well then, let us begin our lesson. And you have a remarkable vocabulary, Miss Yarat. Better than many sailors.'

'I have sailed with the Sikotsi many times. I like your words. Though you do not have many of the words that we have. Only one word for snow.'

'Perhaps then you will teach me. But now we will begin with the alphabet and short words, and some day soon I think we might try a book.'

She picked a volume up from the shelf above the desk. 'What is this one?'

'*Great Expectations*,' he read out slowly, his finger under the letters. 'The story of a man who finds who truly loves him.'

She turned the pages.

'And there are pictures of the Qallunaat women,' she said, her finger on a drawing of a woman in a ballgown. 'So cold around their necks. And where do they carry their baby if it still needs its mother's breast?'

'They have another woman who will feed the baby.'

'But who makes them do that? When I have my own child, I will keep him on my back where he will be warm, and give him my own milk, as my mother did me. I would not like to live like those women.'

Oliver had often talked coarsely with men, listened to the swearing of the sailors, but no woman had ever spoken so openly about the mysteries of womanhood with him. None would admit that they had breasts let alone discuss their use with regards to the next generation. He found a beauty in her simple openness. Just as he found beautiful the way that a young Inuit woman with a baby on her back would answer the child's cries by sitting down in some quiet place, sliding the naked infant from her bare back and exposing a breast to feed the child.

'It must be a happy childhood to be cossetted by the mother, close to her all the time. I can't say I have ever seen many women at home hold their infant for long, at least not in the circles in which I have been raised.'

Yarat held the backs of her fingers on his cheek, stroked them down gently.

'Poor Oliver,' she said. 'Too much aloneness.'

He gently took her hand away. Coughed to control a feeling welling up from a deep place he had not known existed, a yearning for pure human contact. And there were, he realized, other feelings that could not be allowed. He was not, like the captain's brother, a coarse man, willing to take advantage of the simple native girls.

At the end of the lesson, half the alphabet mastered, a column of simple words read, Oliver told Yarat with some surprise in his voice, 'You really are the most intelligent of girls.'

'And you are not as stupid as most Qallunaat,' she replied, smiling at him. 'Come to the hold tonight, where my people sleep. Then you will see how a shaman talks with the spirits.'

CHAPTER 22

In her new green straw hat and her best dress, Mary had taken the train to Broughty Ferry, walking the last two miles to Charlotte's new house. It stood alone on a sand-strewn road overlooking the North Sea. Nothing in front of it but a long beach with marram-grass dunes and grey water, a faint horizon to show the grey sky.

Charlotte was at the door waving, ran out to greet her.

'Don't you think it's perfect?' she said. 'It belonged to a retired sea captain. Louisa doesn't think it grand enough to visit me here, but it has such large windows with northern light, overlooking the sea. The perfect place for me to paint.'

Mary took off her hat and sat on a chair in the window alcove, feeling the wind coming in through the frame. Around the disordered and dusty room were small canvases, paintings of arrangements of still-life objects, bowls and jugs and fruit.

'Aye, it's the perfect place to see no one,' she replied. 'So far away.'

'As long as I see you, dear Mary, that's all I need. And I am getting so much done.'

'Charlotte, do you have someone who comes to clean? And what are you eating? Because it looks very much to me as though you are spending your time just staring out over the empty sea waiting for him to come back.'

'I didn't invite you here to scold me, and I didn't tell you about my confession to Oliver so that you could use it against me so unkindly.'

'I am sorry. But a friend will tell the truth, and it seems that all you are doing until Oliver comes home is waiting, with all your life suspended. Charlotte, I can barely recognize you.'

'Women in my position, we do nothing but wait until we marry, until we have children. That is all we may do. I never understood that before, always despised such women. But now my heart won't let me do anything but hope, for the day when Oliver comes home. I understand now how a woman's happiness hangs upon a thread, on the word of a man. How little our sphere of action.'

'When is the last time you went out in your disguise as a boy and painted something real, with life and movement in it?'

'Oh Mary, I don't do that any more. It was always foolish. A woman can't be like a man.'

Mary bristled, her tone growing angry. 'And what do you think I have had to do, what most women of my class have to do in Dundee? We live like men. Since the mill owners won't pay a man a man's wage, it's we women who have to work at the mills, and it's the women who say what goes. I'll have no more of this self-pity, Charlotte. You'll come and see me in Dundee this next week. And I'll no' take no for an answer.'

Mary's tenement in Shepherd's Loan was halfway up a steep, cobbled lane that ran from the Tay river to the Perth Road, the building so filled with bairns that they spent half their lives out on the cobbles, shoeless and raggedly dressed. It was a far cry from the Laundry Cottage at Kelly, with its scent of clean linen airing over the range. The tenement was poky and rank-smelling – from the drains being so bad, Mary said. But she kept her room as sweet as she could. A jute-lace curtain with its yellowish light at the window above the stone sink and wooden drainer. It made Charlotte's heart sore to see the brave face on her friend's poverty. Why did she not help her more?

Mary had got out her good china and prepared a plate of home baking. Then when they were finished, she brought out two shawls, showed Charlotte how to wrap hers around her shoulders and hair.

'This evening,' Mary told her, 'we will be two mill girls, roving free around Dundee.'

They passed through the little bairns still playing on the cobbled street and went along the Perth Road where bands of mill girls were strolling towards the town, calling out saucy remarks to the men standing idle on the street corners and shrieking with laughter. They walked to the harbour, where the wind was pushing the boats to and fro, a flaming sunset going down behind the Tay hills. Then along the Overgate, where Charlotte led them to the Arctic Inn that was cramped between two tall rows of tenements. She went boldly inside, Mary behind her watchful for trouble, as Charlotte's eyes roved round every inch of the room, examining the harpoons and the ships' bells, the paintings and photographs of ships caught fast in the ice as though they might hold messages of Oliver.

'Oh Charlotte, I didn't bring you out just to end up here moping for Oliver,' began Mary.

'No, no. I'm glad you did. To be out among such life, and to stand here with men he might have sailed with, see things again. The feel of the wind, the smells, the life. I've been asleep, Mary.'

'What'll you girls be drinking?' asked the old woman behind the bar, a shawl crossed across her front, a wizened face and grey hair in a bun.

'Two mugs of porter.'

They found a small table and waited for their order.

'You are right, you know. There is much to see and do. Why should we wait for a man before we begin to live?'

'I agree. Of course I do. But please don't think I agree any less when I tell you my news. I have met a Mr Brown, and we are to be wed.'

'Mary, I've talked so much of myself. And you with this news.'

'But I'll still be working at the mill each day. My Jonny will have to mind the bairns when they come. And I'll carry on helping with the school for the girls in the mill so their lives aren't so hard. I'll stay on the committee for the union to try and get better conditions. There's so much to do, Charlotte. So many bairns in Dundee. It's no' enough for a woman to wait for her own bairn when we have so many already needing us. These bairns are all our children.'

The serving woman put down two mugs of porter.

'Are you looking for news of your man?' she asked.

'Not really,' said Charlotte, thickening her voice to a Dundee brogue. 'My friend here, her brother's gone on the *Narwhal*. We don't expect him back for another year.'

The old woman shook her head. 'That's the boat that's going to try and reach the far side of Hudson Bay, spend the winter there and come back with a full hold. It's a bold plan, but they say she's more likely to never come back at all, sailing in uncharted waters, risking a winter in the Arctic ice.'

A cold feeling lodged in Charlotte's stomach. She and Mary grasped each other's hands.

'He'll come back,' Mary said. 'He will come back.'

But the nub of cold fear stayed, even when Charlotte was painting in the harbour, dressed in her own clothes and in the sense of her right to be there, new pictures filled with life, capturing the smoke from the mill chimneys and the movement of the boats on the water. Or when she began campaigning to have the drains repaired in Mary's tenement. Or with her little class of mill children on Sundays as they crowded round to see her draw pictures and take the pencils that she carried in her pockets so that they might draw their own.

CHAPTER 23

After the embarrassing Diana debacle, it felt as though the varnish had been stripped away from the surface of Caro and Martha's relationship, revealing what really lay beneath. Though being far too embarrassed to ever mention such things directly, all she and Martha could do was to become even more polite than before, wary as diplomats trying to avoid a war. Martha being as demonstrably unobtrusive as possible, Caro doing her best not to feel angry at being treated like a china cup that would smash if it were dropped. It was exhausting. And the more considerate Martha was – I just wanted to say, but of course I wouldn't want to interfere – the more Caro wanted to scream, but I'm not that unreasonable.

And Caro had no idea how to change things.

It was also making her snappy around Alasdair. Especially when he suggested Caro should see the funny side of things as he breezed in and out of the castle, as handsome as ever in his new cords and grey jacket, his red hair like embers against ashes – and as impervious as ever to the nuances in the exchanges between Caro and Martha.

So Caro and Alasdair were having an argument at breakfast, yet again – or as much of an argument as you could have when Pippa was also there at the table with a coffee and a cigarette, apparently engrossed in turning the pages of an antiques magazine but listening to every word.

'Surely you can you pop out and get some bits from the haberdasher's in North Street in your lunch hour. Some new nappies, some bias binding, green silk so I can hem a little blanket jacket for Flissy.'

'Oh darling, may I do that another day? Problem is, Mummy's swinging by to take me for a spot of lunch at a place just along the coast in Crail, after she's done her errands in town. I could cancel. If you want me to.' She saw the exasperated look on his face, a man caught between a rock and a hard place.

'No, of course you must have lunch with Martha. At least we're going to Kingsbarns beach this Saturday. It will be nice to do something together, the two of us and Felicity, as a family.'

'Tomorrow? I told Mummy I'd look at the chimney in the Blue Room tomorrow. A pigeon's nest or something.'

'Oh Alasdair. No. You didn't forget, surely?'

'Darling, it was you who was pointing out how much needs to be fixed in this place. Look, do you want to come for lunch? If you don't mind taking two buses.'

'I have things to do, actually. And you know I won't take two buses with Felicity.'

When he was gone, Pippa looked up from the magazine. Gave Caro a sympathetic smile.

'Perhaps I shouldn't say this, but you have to remember that Ali was very young when Daddy died. Just twelve.'

'Yes, he told me,' said Caro.

'Of course, but you see, he'd just started boarding school, and he actually refused to go to school for a few weeks. He wanted to be here to make sure nothing happened to Mummy, I think. The school were very good about it. Very understanding. Of course, I was packed off back to boarding school. Good at coping, so they said. Thing is, there's always been a rather intense bond between Mummy and Ali since then. Teas in town when he's home, lunches where I'm not asked along, checking in with each other. I used to think, however will it be when Alasdair has a wife? So you shouldn't mind too much, you see – Mummy and Ali, it's nothing against you. Just how it's always been. I never minded. Not really. I was a daddy's girl.'

Caro kept her head down, embarrassed by Pippa's speech, but grateful that someone in the family had sympathy for how she might feel.

Then Pippa put her head on one side, watching Caro disentangling the baby from the highchair straps. 'I've actually felt thankful over the years, Ali taking on Mummy like that. It wasn't easy for her, and now one doesn't like to take away the support she's always relied on. You do see?'

Caro did a double-take. So this wasn't a friendly, how-are-you sort of chat? It was about not rocking the boat, about sharing Alasdair with his mother without minding.

But she did mind. Though she didn't like herself for it.

'Of course Alasdair should support Martha. We're both happy to spend time with her, but together. That's how we do things, Alasdair and I, as a team.'

Pippa gave a little huff. 'Gosh, you know if Ali wants to be so thick with Mummy, I'd enjoy being let off the hook. Anyway, I'm off now. Might swing by and say hello to Diana, then I'm back to Edinburgh. See you soon, darling,' and she blew a kiss to the baby.

Peace descended in the room with the cool light from the church-like windows, the fire crackling in the fireplace spreading a scent of coal smoke and warmth, Felicity contentedly eating the porridge that Caro spooned into her mouth while she sang the song about three little birds that the baby liked. Something caught Felicity's attention.

She leaned to one side, head bowed to the floor. Following her gaze, Caro caught sight of a grey object scuttling along the skirting board, disappearing into a small, gnawed hole. That was Kelly all over, tacked-up curtains and shaky doorknobs that came off in your hand – and now mice. Pretty as a theatre set, but not to be trusted. At home her father ran a plain but orderly home. He considered mice something shameful. Hated them with a passion for getting into the stocks of rice or flour.

As Felicity put both hands in her bowl, smearing the porridge across her face and hair, Martha came in, dressed in her coat, looking for her glasses.

'I'm sorry to mention this,' said Caro, wiping the baby's hair, 'but there's a mouse. Felicity noticed it.'

'Did you, darling?' Martha said to Felicity. 'Oh, the mice do come in this time of year. And we're certainly making our own fun with the porridge bowl. I always think a little creative muddle can be inspiring sometimes, don't you think?'

In spite of herself and her best intentions, Caro could feel an irritation rising. Was Martha implying some mania to tidy on Caro's part or a lack of imagination? Something to do with the class that Caro came from not being quite up to the mark? She began wiping Felicity down, Felicity objecting loudly to having no porridge bowl to play with.

'I wish all schools encouraged the arts more,' Martha mused. 'Did your school encourage the arts? Did you find it a happy place – Catford Grammar, was it?'

The answer – that school was so horrid that Caro tried never to think about it, how the girls flocked in cliques to bully the victim of the week – was not one she wished to talk about. Caro's family did not openly discuss their feelings at breakfast, or at any time. Realizing that her politeness was stretched pretty thinly, Caro picked up Felicity.

'Better get the baby out for some fresh air. Now, where did we leave your hat? In the lounge?'

'Oh, and Caro.'

Caro paused.

'It's silly, I know,' Martha said, her voice excessively cheerful. 'But there's no room one could call a lounge in Kelly. We have a drawing room, you see.'

Caro took a deep breath. Not the first time Martha had mentioned this. 'Thank you,' she said with a rather wooden smile, carrying the baby out. Honestly, this was 1950 almost. What did it matter if you brushed your hair in a mirror or a looking glass? Used a serviette or a napkin?

It mattered to Martha, clearly, since in spite of herself, Martha could not resist correcting Caro. And Caro would have risen above it but it was so tiring, the need to improve always there in the background. The truth was, Caro found it impossible to ignore Martha's opinions, be it on how Caro dressed Felicity or cooked onions or raised her voice to shout to Alasdair across a room – not done at Kelly, apparently.

As one of the first female students at Cambridge to be awarded a degree, Caro had always despised female stereotypes, laughed at the thought that she might live her life striving to be a perfect wife and mother. But through Martha's eyes, Caro judged herself harshly, by the gods of all things both female and traditional. Never good enough or completed in any area. It was so demoralizing and frustrating. Most of the time she felt like a pile of dropped dress patterns, the tissue-paper outlines all mixed up and sized for someone else. And ready to fly apart at any moment, suddenly ambushed and made angry by a comment from Martha.

What she felt like doing right now was using all the wrong words that Martha disliked. Preferably in one sentence. A small act of rebellion.

She'd been amazed when Alasdair had reeled off a whole list of forbidden words that were, it seemed, as welcome as the sight of drooping underwear. 'Horribly snobby but we don't really say "mirror",' Alasdair had explained when Caro objected to him about Martha's re-education project.

'You can't say "mirror"? Why ever not?'

'One uses the Anglo-Saxon word, "looking glass". "Sofa" not "settee".'

'The Anglo-Saxons had sofas?'

'Foolish, but there you are,' he smiled apologetically. 'Take no notice of Ma, darling. We don't.' And having given sound, practical advice he left. For work. For some errand for Martha. Always leaving.

A map of Alasdair would have clear lines, useful for going places. A map of herself, Caro realized, would be full of shaded liminal areas, still in the process of becoming, coastlines up for discussion.

But such conversations, around who Caro was now that she had a baby, only irritated and ultimately panicked Alasdair.

'Are you saying you want me to change nappies more?'

No, it wasn't that, but he could.

'Darling, what is it you want me to do?'

Which missed the point, and made Caro even more lonely and angry.

'I just want you to listen,' she said.

'And do what?'

She took the baby out into the garden to clear her head, the solace of hopeful birdsong. She found Barbara picking berries from the fruit cage for a summer pudding.

'You're still here, Caro? Thought you would have gone with Martha and Diana to meet Alasdair for lunch.'

'Decided not to,' she fibbed, her voice too cheerful.

Hurt, bursting with anger, Caro wheeled the pram into the sheltered herb gardens behind the kitchen, sat on the stone bench. Marigolds were still sprawled across the pea gravel and mint and lovage, thyme and tarragon mixed their scented oils in the warmth. She found her cheeks were hot, her blood thumping in her ears.

So Alasdair was having lunch not just with Martha, but with Diana too. Well, how very cosy. Wavering between misery and anger, Caro felt like picking up the baby and going home.

It had been months since Daddy had been up to see the new baby, staying with them at the cottage. Phoebe had yet to come up and visit. There were plans for her and Alasdair to go down and spend a week at her home, but they had been deferred for this reason and that.

What if she went now? That was how raw and upset she felt. Left a note and went to the station, just her and the baby. But if she did, would she ever come back?

'Good lunch?' said Caro to Alasdair in clipped tones as they went up to bed. She'd waited all evening for him to mention that Diana had been there with him.

It seemed he wasn't going to. He'd been noticeably quiet, in fact.

'Yes, thank you.'

No more details came.

In the bedroom, he took off his tie and threw it on the dressing table. Sat on the bed with his face in his hands.

'Everything all right?'

'What? Yes,' he replied, a tad irritable. 'Some marking to catch up with before I can get any sleep, that's all.'

'I'll leave you to it then.'

She was brushing her teeth in the bathroom, wondering what on earth was happening between them, wondering if she was beginning to understand why Charlotte or whoever it had been had left Kelly, when out of nowhere something struck her. Eugenia's desk. Why hadn't she tried the pigeonholes that sat along the back? What if there was a way to lift them off and get into the space beneath?

Hastily rinsing her mouth, she put the toothbrush back and ran down the tower steps. In the study, she flicked on the lamp and lifted the roll-top. In front of her a row of pigeonholes and small drawers. She pulled out the two little drawers that sat directly above the empty space, solid wood underneath. Then with a little jiggling, found that she could also pull out the frame that held the drawers. She leaned her hand on the wood beneath, did a little jump. One side gave way, the central panel tipping up like a see-saw. Her heart beating in excitement, as carefully as she could she levered out the piece of wood and felt inside the dusty space underneath. Something there. She reached out a roll of pages, unfurled them to reveal a tiny doll the size of her palm. It was made from animal skins, a stiff little figure in a fur parka and trousers, eyes and a mouth sewn onto the pale leather face with dark thread. The fur was worn away in places as if it had been played with or carried around by a child. But whatever was it doing hidden in the desk?

Carefully, she smoothed out the papers. She recognized the handwriting immediately, and with a gasp, realized they were the missing pages from Oliver's diary. But scanning through them, she saw that the last few pieces of paper were different. A letter, copied out several times. Sitting down on the chair, she began to read.

My darling,

I don't know where you are now or how the world is treating you. If I could only see your face one more time, know that you are well. How I long to hear your voice, speak to you, tell you that I will never stop loving you. All I know is that I will find you again one day. I promise.

Our child grows strong. How she loves to run in the grounds. Darling, she is like you in so many ways, looking deep into one's very soul.

I have been much impeded by my health in the chill damp of the castle but I try and keep up with her. Sing and play and count to one hundred as she runs and hides. Once, she stayed hidden away in some place I could not find. When she came back to me, she was, I could see, lost in her thoughts. You could not see me, but I was still here, she said. Just as we cannot see Mama, but she will come back to us one day. She tells me she sees you in her dreams, the kindest smile and the prettiest face.

Though I do not understand why you left us, I know that you love us. Those who say you left gladly and do not want to be found, we will never believe it. Come back to us, darling. There is nothing that cannot be forgiven. Or as soon as I am well again, I shall set out to find you, darling, but until then, we kiss you and embrace you in our hearts.

I will send copies of this letter, addressed to you, to anywhere I think you may be — for as long as it may take.

Your own, ever-loving

Oliver

The emotion was so vivid it felt as though Oliver had just put the letter down and left the room. She picked up the child's doll and turned it over, wondered who had made it. It must surely have been Eugenia's. But why had she hidden it away?

Gathering up the papers and doll, she hurried back up to the bedroom. Alasdair was sitting up in bed, marking.

'Where did you rush off to so suddenly?' He put his papers and pen on the side table, rubbing his cheeks in the way that he did when he was tired. 'What happened?'

'This,' she said, placing the papers and figurine on the bedcover. 'I found them in your grandmother's desk, in a hidden compartment. It's the rest of the diary. And that's not all. There's this.'

'Astonishing,' he said, reading the letter through twice. 'Oliver must have loved her so deeply, and then to lose her. . . And so this curious little toy was with the papers? Perhaps something Oliver brought back from the Arctic for my grandmother when she was small?'

'It might tell us more in the diary.'

'This is all incredible too,' he said, flicking through the pages. 'I think Ma is still up. Why don't we get a dram and read the rest of it with her? She'll be over the moon that you've found this.'

Martha was sitting in the drawing room, listening to Schubert on the wireless as she worked on a square of tapestry.

'Heartbreaking, isn't it?' said Caro when Martha had finished reading the letter. 'Do you think Oliver ever saw her again?'

'Sadly, judging by the date, I don't think he could have,' said Martha, a hand on her breastbone. 'I know that Oliver contracted TB, I think on his travels or as a medical student. I believe he would have died shortly after this letter was written so I doubt that he would have seen his beloved wife again, and she does sound beloved. And the child that he talks about, of course that would have been Eugenia. How alone and lost she must have been after he died, her mother gone. She had Sylvia, of course, though I think Sylvia had to go into a nursing home at some point, for nervous trouble – but that poor little girl. Let's hear what's in the rest of that diary.'

'Shall I?' said Caro.

'That would be lovely, dear. And I'm so pleased you came down to share this together.'

They took it in turns to read aloud, the other two listening, rapt. The clocks in the drawing room and hallway could be heard chiming in syncopated sequence, midnight and then one.

CHAPTER 24

The Inuit slept in the hold at the back of the ship, which had been left with enough space for them to stow their possessions and make bunks on the wide reinforcement planks that ran along the bulkheads. They had turned it into a kingdom of their own, some of the sleeping quarters hung with skins, their stone lamps giving off a candle-like light. Tonight there was no button accordion or cheerful chattering. They sat around the bunks and on the floor as solemnly as in a church, some of them nervous it seemed to Oliver, the children crowded together along the bulkhead, subdued, their eyes wide. Two women stood face to face and holding each other's elbows. They began to sing or grunt in a deep vibrating sound that seemed to pass from mouth to mouth.

The shaman, meanwhile, took off his over- and under-jackets and, dressed only in his skin breeches, let two of the older women tie his hands behind his back. Then they tied his feet together and bound them with a long cord to his waist so that he was trussed in a sitting position. He closed his eyes, the chanting stopped and a younger shaman began to circle him, beating a stick on a skin-covered paddle. The lamp guttered, went out. The shaman began to call out loudly as if arguing with someone. At times there seemed to be two voices as he thrashed around on the floor in the darkness and the drumbeat got faster. Some of the women wailed. A child started crying. The shaman began to make unintelligible animal noises, the drum quivering with a loud vibrato. A scream, and the drum fell silent. Someone hurried to light the lamp, the women to untie the shaman. Covered in red bruise marks and sweat, he lay as if unconscious. They wiped him with bird skins, gave him water to drink and watched him anxiously.

Finally, as if labouring under a great fatigue, the shaman sat up and gave a slow proclamation that Oliver could not understand. Then he was helped to his bunk, a man aged by years in the space of an hour, and the skin covering was let down so he could sleep.

The natives began conferring amongst themselves, apparently not agreeing.

'What was his verdict? What are they saying?' Oliver asked Yarat, who was following the discussion.

'It is the harpooner who has broken a taboo. He has something forbidden in the sack he guards. My father cannot see what is in it, but it is powerful enough to drive the whales away, and it is powerful enough to make Sedna take this ship down to the bottom of the sea.'

A few nights later, when Yarat came for her lesson – a moment in the day that Oliver now looked forward to – she told him what the natives had found in the harpooner's sack, one of them finding the courage to open it while he slept.

'He has stolen the bones of my people from their graves like a thieving fox. Many head bones. What do you call this bone?' She placed her hands either side of her head.

'Skulls? But why on earth would he collect skulls?'

He knew the answer even as he asked the question. Museums in America and London would pay well for examples of native craniums, attempting to show a Darwinian line of human evolution from primitive to modern man. He did not tell Yarat this. The implications were too insulting, as if it were possible that Yarat came from a less developed species of human than the brutish whaler men. The opposite, Oliver thought, was easier to believe, as the lamp caught the smoothness of her skin and the delicate lines of her features.

'So the harpooner must return the bones to Sedna, to whom all souls go when they die. If he does not, the harpooner will drown with his bones, and we will drown with him. We must make him give the bones back to Sedna.'

Oliver thought of the bear-like temper and meaty fists of the harpooner, a man often the worse for drink.

'I doubt anyone on this ship can make him throw his trophies overboard if he does not wish to.'

'You will see,' she told him.

Oliver had earned himself the reputation of being good at pulling teeth. MacMartin, the linesman, was sitting on a barrel in the forecastle, mouth wide open, while Oliver went at the rotten canine with pliers. A game of cards was in progress behind him. The shaman and the harpooner, playing for a fine knife and pair of white fox skins. The harpooner laughed as he scooped both into his pocket, the shaman out of luck. He sneered as the shaman begged for one more chance, desperate to win back the skins.

'You've nothing left to bet.'

'Enough of cards. I will hypnotize you. If I succeed, then you give me the knife and the skins. If I fail, I give you my gun. A good gun. It was my pay, from the captain.'

The harpooner looked the gun over. He sat down again, arms folded, dared the shaman to see how far he got. 'You may as well hand the gun over now, old man,' he laughed as the Inuit began to circle him, slowly beating out a rhythm with his feet. The shaman began flicking his hands from side to side, an amused snarl on the harpooner's face. The room was stuffy with smoke from oil lamps and tobacco pipes, a reek of spirits in the air. Oliver felt his eyes grow heavy in the monotonous chanting. The shaman moved closer, flicking his wrists up in front of the harpooner. To Oliver's amazement the harpooner's eyes closed, his head nodding. He suddenly rose like a giant puppet, lumbering and swaying side to side. The natives and the rest of the crew crowded in to watch and laugh. The shaman slowly began to walk towards the harpooner's bunk, the harpooner following with a shuffling gait. When they got there, as if in a dream the harpooner reached into the bed space and pulled out a sack. He followed the shaman out of the door, eyes glazed as if sleepwalking. Up on deck, he began taking out skulls from a bag as if they were turnips, hurling them into the sea one at a time.

When the harpooner was done, his bag empty, the shaman banged his drum twice and the harpooner sank down on the boards in a deep sleep. The bones of their people had been sent down to Sedna in her sea caves, from where she kept watch on all souls living and dead. Satisfied with this result, the shaman and the other natives crept away silently. The crew who had gathered to watch also melted away. No one wanted to be near when the harpooner woke up. The steward had two men drag him back below lest he get frostbite overnight.

The next morning he went roaring around the ship, wanting to know who had stolen his skulls, worth a fortune he cried. The captain and every man on deck swore there were many witnesses to the fact that he had thrown them all overboard himself, no doubt worse for drink again.

It took a few days before the harpooner had all the story from the cabin boy, and understood why it was that the children danced behind him in lumbering steps, ran away as soon as he turned round. He said nothing more, too proud to call for the shaman to be punished. But it was written in his glaring gaze that his revenge would come.

Oliver decided to keep a watch on the shaman's daughter.

When a rum cask was found breached and half-missing, the harpooner dead drunk in the captain's cabin with a knife in his hand, the captain ordered him to be locked in the hold and put off at the Hudson Bay trading post in Rankin Inlet. The harpooner spent his waking hours hammering on the walls, cursing the ship and everyone who sailed in her.

CHAPTER 25

Another week passed without sight of a whale, the captain's mood increasingly low, pushing the ship along the floe edge in search of the telltale fountain from a breathing hole. One morning a yell went up from the crow's nest. A blow.

Oliver heard banging on his door, the cook's boy shouting. 'Surgeon Gillan, if you want to go with the hunters they are lowering the boats now.'

He pulled on his clothes and hurried up to the deck. Most of the boats were already on the water, but one manned by the shaman and his tribesmen was yet to lower away and he ran over to beg a place. The Inuit's face showed no change of expression and he nodded but Oliver could see he was not pleased by this incursion. Oliver held on to the side as the small boat was lowered and hit the water.

The Inuit were pulling hard. The shaman stood at the back of the boat, facing the rowers, directing their course. Their harpooner stood in the bow, waiting to shoot. A figure sitting next to him, ready to manage the harpoon line once it began to spool out. When the sealskin-covered figure turned and looked back, Oliver realized it was the shaman's daughter.

They followed behind the other boats, the Scotsmen yelling and calling as they made chase. The atmosphere in the native boat, in marked contrast, was silent. When the shaman called out in a low singing sound, they veered away from the boats in front of them.

The natives exchanged oars for paddles, the boat cutting almost silently across a sea calm as a looking glass, the sounds from the other boats fading. A couple of hundred yards in front of them Oliver saw the fountain of a whale's spout misting against the sky, and moments later the great black tail of a whale appeared, signalling that it was going to dive.

Without warning, the beast came up again, leapt in the air so close to the boat that he could have sunk them with ease. Oliver felt his heart all but stop, sharply mindful that they were out in the deepest of icy water. For a moment its eye was level with the boat, a fellow soul looking into theirs, then the harpooner steadied himself in the bow and fired into the whale's side.

The line began to spool out at a speed of knots as the whale dived again, enough friction to set the boat on fire, the shaman's daughter pouring buckets of seawater over the rope as fast as she was handed them. When the whale surfaced again, the natives replied with two more lances that penetrated some four feet into its flesh.

By now, Oliver was heartily on the whale's side, distraught to see such a noble creature harried and slaughtered. The boat was almost upon the beast, a writhing black hill washed by the waves. Oliver waited for it to rise and flip the boat over like a piece of driftwood. But the shaman delivered one last fatal lance, piercing its blowhole. A fountain of blood shot up twenty feet, covering the boat and everything in it with oily, red gore. Yarat too was coated in it, her fur skins slick and shiny. The skin of her face painted in blood, the two eyes looking out at Oliver the only recognizably civilized part of her left.

But looking down at his hands he saw they too were covered in viscous red and realized that he had also been baptized in the whale's gore.

In the next moment the dying whale turned on one side. Its lower body dipped beneath the boat and with a last, mighty spasm, it flicked the craft high in the water. Oliver felt himself falling with the boat, washed from his seat as a surge of icy sea rushed in, the shock of the cold taking the breath from his body. He fought to the surface, gasping in air, before the weight of his fur suit dragged him under again. He could feel his consciousness fading, when with a sudden tug at his jacket he was forcibly dragged to the surface by a metal hook. Arms reached down to drag him back on board, crushing his ribs against the side. Only minutes from death, he coughed up a quantity of sea, someone banging on his back. He saw two concerned brown eyes and recognized the face of the shaman's daughter again, her bloody clothes now washed clean by the sea, slick as a seal. Her hands felt his frozen cheeks, and shouting out, she began to peel off his jacket, made one of the larger natives give up his parka. She held him tight as he drifted in and out of sleep, listening to the rattle, which, he assessed in a detached way, was the sound of someone with so much water in their lungs that they would likely succumb to pneumonia and die.

When he next came to, lying in a cabin, someone had removed his wet clothes and he lay in his blankets. The lamp was lit, a woman humming. Glossy dark hair shaded a face, and as she hummed her strange two-note tune, Yarat pushed her hair away and smiled.

Twenty years of gazing at lithographs of Madonnas painted by Italian masters or at Greek marbles in museums had led Oliver to appreciate one kind of beauty. But now he saw that humanity had other forms of loveliness. He thought how much he liked the planes of her face, the deep tan of her perfect skin and the high colour of her cheeks, the fall of her straight black hair, and the silky caribou skins that she wore. She sang as he fell asleep and in the morning he woke and found her folding blankets, realized she had slept on the floor by his bed, keeping watch.

He could feel his breathing much eased. A memory of her holding something warm and bitter to his lips to drink. But before he could ask her more, there was a hammering on the door. The steward came in, the white nankeen jacket that the whalers wore now bloody as a butcher's apron.

'We've a man on deck's crushed his foot with a block. We'll need you to take a look.'

Feeling unsteady, Oliver pulled on some clothes and made his way up on deck.

A scene of carnage and uproar met him. The boat crews had managed to catch a second whale. Crowded into every space on deck, lines of men, both native and Scots, were dissecting, chopping and throwing chunks of bright orange whale fat and red flesh. The boards swam with blood and oil, a hot stench of death and iron. A whale was roped fast to the side of the ship like a boat, men standing on it to slice off great strips of flesh, hauling them up on board for processing. On the upper deck MacKay was laid out, moaning in pain, white as the sails and the sky above him.

Oliver's two years at medical school had ill prepared him for such serious surgery but now he saw that he must amputate the foot, or lose the leg and then the man to rot. He undid his roll of instruments, laid them out on a chest, took out the bottle of chloroform and a cloth from his chest. He bound MacKay's upper leg with a leather strap as tightly as he could to lessen the bleeding. Then asking three others to hold him down should the administered drug wear off, he took out the strongest hacksaw blade and began to break through the skin. It seemed that he sawed for hours, cold sweat on his brow. When MacKay woke halfway through, his screaming echoed around the boat until he could be subdued again. A freezing rain came in, stinging like needles of ice, soaking through his jacket. Finally the foot was cleanly cut away, doused in spirits to purify the wound, and bound up in clean bandages.

Oliver returned to his cabin and sank down onto the bottom bunk, unable to stop a violent trembling from the cold and the shock, even though he wrapped himself in blankets. When Yarat opened the door and slipped in, he was shaking so hard that the tremors were exhausting, his stomach cramping in spasms. The frigid air seemed to have sucked away every last vestige of warmth from his flesh. Concern in her eyes, Yarat locked the cabin door, peeled off her clothes, lying skin to skin with the blankets and furs on top of them. Eventually, his shivering stopped as she whispered and sang him to sleep, her breath in his ear.

And later that night, he woke to the deep quiet of a creaking ship in the small hours when no one is awake but the watch up on deck. Realized that Yarat was still there next to him, in his arms, her eyes open and watching him in the dark. And as they explored each other's contours, it seemed to him that he had always known that she would come to him one day, that this was the time for which he had been waiting for so long. Content, awestruck by her beauty, Oliver asked Yarat if she would become his wife. She nodded, said she would be his woman, and with her serious brown eyes focused on his in the lamplight, they made love for the first time.

When they reached the far side of Hudson Bay night and day were of equal length. But from now on, the darkness would grow longer each night.

The first snow fell like stinging rain.

At Rankin Inlet they dropped anchor. This was where they would leave the harpooner. A trading station stood on the brow of the hill, a wooden hut hung with the drying furs of white foxes, rippling in the wind.

'I'll pay you back for this, one day,' the harpooner growled at his brother. 'No half-Yak gets the better of me.'

'Take the chance to make a new start. Keep off the drink,' Captain Grant said gruffly.

'Follow your own advice, man.' The harpooner climbed over the side to the rope ladder where a small boat was lowered and waiting.

After they had taken on fresh water and meat, the *Narwhal* continued north into Repulse Bay, the captain relying more than ever on skill and instinct to nose along the uncharted waters of the northern coasts. Within the fortress of a ring of small islands that the natives called Keewatin, the ship dropped anchor and waited for the delicate skim of ice that had begun to form on the sea each night to thicken and harden. And each night, the temperature dropped further below freezing, the frost sparkling on the rigging like a ship enchanted. The masts were taken down and stowed. The men were set to piling snow up around the ship for insulation. Even so, at night, the breath-filled air inside the ship condensed against the cold outer walls so that anything that touched them became wet.

Soon, the nights had grown so long that the stars were clearly visible from late afternoon, layer on layer of bright points appearing in the blackness. At the end of each short day, the red of the setting sun lingered on for far longer than it did in England, followed by a long blue twilight. One night Oliver and Yarat stood and watched curtains of light pulsing sometimes red, sometimes green, as a flame in a chemist's laboratory, swirling past with a swishing sound like wings.

The natives hunted for seals at ice holes near the floe's edge. The crewmen played cards and fought or they held dances with the natives, where Oliver found the advances of the men towards the younger girls aggressive and worrying. Yarat had told him about whalers who fathered children and then disappeared. It was left to the kindness of a tribe to care for these half-and-halfs. In what way was he different?

He asked the captain if he would conduct a marriage ceremony between him and Yarat. He took some convincing that Oliver was not simply assuaging his guilt with a more sophisticated seduction. Finally, after assuring the captain that he was indeed serious and getting him to agree to allow Yarat a passage home with him to Dundee, Oliver and Yarat were married on deck with the moon and the faint sun both in the sky, the captain officiating and the steward playing a hymn on the button accordion.

The Inuit had built a village of domed snow houses by the side of the ship. Now they built one for Oliver and Yarat at the side of the shaman's snow house.

That night they slept on a platform of snow covered in Arctic heather and caribou furs, Yarat tending the whale-oil lamp, its wick of moss laid on its side, the flame along it a luminous row of tiny mountains.

In the morning the joins of the snow blocks showed lines of blue light. Above them, the fog of their breath caught under the ice hut's dome like a small cloud. Yarat had taken Oliver's hand and placed it on her stomach for she knew, she told him, that she was expecting a child, and it was already a moon and a half old inside her.

CHAPTER 26

'Wait,' said Alasdair. Caro stopped reading aloud. 'So Oliver's diary is saying that it was Yarat he married. An Inuit girl called Yarat was my great-grandmother. Eugenia's mother.'

'It's certainly quite a lot to take in,' said Martha. 'I had absolutely no idea that Eugenia could be half Inuit, but now I think about it, she had very pretty regular features, such smooth skin and dark hair, it all makes sense. And so incredibly romantic.'

'And at last we have a name,' said Caro.

'Well, I think it's high time that we added her to the family tree, where it belongs,' said Alasdair. 'Right now.' He went and fetched the roll of paper from the library, spread it out on the table. Martha opened her fountain pen and carefully wrote in the name 'Yarat Gillan' next to 'Oliver Gillan'.

'Welcome back to the family,' she said. 'At last, we know who you are.'

Caro nodded. 'But don't you think it's sad that Eugenia hid the little Eskimo doll away, as if she was embarrassed about her own heritage?'

'She certainly never breathed a word about Yarat, whom she must have remembered very well,' sighed Martha. 'How awful for a child to be made to feel ashamed of her own mother.'

'Tomorrow we'll have to let Detective Cameron know what we've found,' added Alasdair. 'Especially now that a date's been set for the inquest.'

'But knowing Yarat's name still doesn't prove anything,' said Caro. 'We still have two women missing, Yarat and Charlotte, either of whom could be our body, I'm afraid. Though I hope not.'

'Darlings, I shall let you two carry on thinking about it all but I'm going to have to stop there,' said Martha, blinking. 'Almost two in the morning. Do you mind if we read the rest tomorrow? There's already so much to take in. I feel I will need to sleep on it before we read any further.'

'I think my eyes would welcome some sleep, too,' said Caro. 'It is quite slow-going deciphering Oliver's cursive – the words are so tiny. And Felicity will be awake bright and early. We'll follow you up soon.'

Hugging Alasdair and then Caro, Martha headed for bed.

The snow had continued to fall outside. Caro and Alasdair went out into the front porch, watched the soft flakes rising and falling in the currents of frozen air like the ghosts of a swarm of bees. The lawns glowed with a white covering, the air sharp with cold.

'I still can't take it in,' said Alasdair. 'My great-grandmother an Inuit in fur skins, born in the Arctic. I'm one eighth Inuit.'

'I like the sound of that,' said Caro. 'Very much. And I love to think that Felicity is a little bit Inuit too. It feels rather special.'

'They would have walked through this very door, Oliver and Yarat, with their child. Can you picture it?'

Caro nodded. 'But I still don't understand it. She and Oliver sounded so much in love, and with a child they clearly both adored. Whatever came between them to make her leave her own child?'

As they were walking up the stairs, hand in hand, Caro stopped.

'You know, whatever's going on, you and Diana, nothing is so important that I would ever give up on you. Nothing I couldn't forgive.'

Alasdair looked blank.

'I know you took Diana to lunch with your mother that day. When you put me off coming. I don't know what's going on, but I'm not someone who gives up. Even if Martha is encouraging whatever it is'

Alasdair let out a gasp. 'You mean you think me and Diana—? That's what you've been thinking? All this time? Oh darling, I didn't tell you because I didn't want to upset you any more than I needed to. Not before we were sure. I know how worked up you've been about Diana lately. But you're right. Diana can't be trusted. It seems she's been undervaluing some of the antiques from Kelly and selling them on at a large profit. Mother and I wanted to give her a chance to explain, and she did come up with some excuses, some problems with her maths, forgetting things, but I don't really buy it. Mother wants to give her the benefit of the doubt, for the sake of Diana's mother who's such an old pal of Ma's, but it certainly looks as though Diana is not a good egg. Quite a stinker, in fact. She's got the next couple of weeks to prove it was all a mistake, show us the books from her firm, but I'm not holding out any great hopes. I just didn't want to tell you until we were sure.'

'Darling, how does it solve anything if you don't talk to me about what's happening? I've been going mad. I don't know what I've been thinking. Oh, I wish you'd told me.'

'Just think this.' Alasdair wrapped her tight in his arms, kissed her. 'You must know you are my whole world. I'd be hopeless without you. A mess. And I'm so sorry.'

And if Caro had worried about Diana, then Diana was gone, a shadow on the periphery. Nothing real about her.

They went up to bed, hand in hand. And later, Caro lay thinking about Oliver's anguished letter as he tried to find Yarat again. She heard Alasdair turning in his sleep, felt the pressure of the mattress alter as his weight shifted, as if she were a boat floating on water. She stretched out her hand to lightly lie against his side, relaxed into a feeling of being harboured, at home. And cross as she had been about the lunch thing, her body told her that all she wanted and needed, more than anything in the world, was here, in Alasdair's soft breathing, in the baby sleeping nearby.

How could she have sat in the garden and contemplated leaving? She and Alasdair were a team. She'd go and see Daddy – it was time – but they'd visit him together, as a family. And she was going to do all she could to make her marriage happy and secure. Whatever it took. Even with Martha.

The weather turned nose-pinchingly cold, Felicity dressed in layers of Martha's exquisitely knitted baby clothes with their Fair Isle patterns and woollen pixie hats. Barbara had helped Caro to air out and wash them until they smelled fresh again. By teatime, the dusk had taken on a cold, bluish tinge, clumps of snow falling like feathers. Felicity's first snow. She toddled in the gardens, holding on to Caro's hand, reaching after the falling flakes, bright red cheeks, holding out her tongue to taste them.

That evening, Caro, Alasdair and Martha decided to resume the reading aloud down in the kitchen after a supper of lamb stew cooked by Caro.

'Darling, this was delicious,' said Martha. 'Nothing like proper peasant food, potatoes and carrots straight from one's own garden.'

Caro waited for the hint as to how Martha would have done it better in some way.

'I've been thinking,' went on Martha. 'I don't say often enough how much I appreciate my daughter-in-law. All the things you do so well, for Alasdair and Flissy. For me. This lovely meal. One of the cleverest things Alasdair did was to marry you, my dear.'

Caro was too surprised to answer for a moment.

Martha gave a rueful chuckle. 'I know how it is, Caro dear. Never thought I would, and I don't know how it happened, but lately I've found myself turning into Duguld's mother, anxious, keen to give away my well-worn advice. My way of giving a helping hand, I think. But I do remember how it was as a new mother, how easy to feel undone by well-meant advice. One needs to feel one's own with a first baby, time to get to know each other without too much well-meaning help. So I hope I do make it clear what a splendid job I think you're doing. How lucky Alasdair is.'

'Of course,' said Caro, feeling acutely embarrassed and grateful at the same time. She coughed. 'And you do know how important you are to all of us. Will always be. Felicity's only granny. I'm so lucky to get to know Alasdair's family, a different world, here in this place. One gets used to seeing things a certain way, according to one's habits as one grows up, but I love how you Gillans go about life, so interesting.'

'Interesting! Well then, that's good,' said Martha. 'Now, let's get on with that diary. Oh, isn't this nice?' She swept her hand vaguely around the kitchen with its vaulted roof of old stones, the pans above the range gleaming a well-burnished copper, but they both knew what she meant.

And it would have all been perfect, Caro thought, as Alasdair began to read from the pages, the kitchen warm, the snow falling outside, the baby sleeping in her carrycot by the Aga, but it still felt disturbing not to know who had been hidden away under the earth of the cottage grounds.

And the more Caro learned about Yarat and Charlotte, the more she hoped that it would not turn out to be either of them.

But if not, then who?

CHAPTER 27

The islands enclosed and protected them, the ice solid and stable within the archipelago's arms, but one night Oliver followed in Yarat's footsteps to the ridge of the small island, following her silhouette against the moon as she found a path for them. On the other side of the spit of land, the plates of ice ground against each other like millstones, rushing forward with the tides, heaved up into banks and hills tall as a ship's mast by the tonnage of ice pushing behind them. Easy to see how such a moving mass of ice might crush a ship like a matchbox – had done so many times. Leaving the creaking and roaring of the monumental tide, they walked back under the moonlight to the safety of their harbour, though the sight of the Arctic's force troubled Oliver's dreams and made him start awake at night.

They returned to the ship, sharing Oliver's tiny cabin, the moon spectacularly bright each night as daylight became just an hour of blue twilight around midday before it grew dark again. Oliver found himself drawn to go out and gaze at the moon as it circled the sky, the white landscape under its brilliant light so beautiful that Yarat had to come and take him back to the cabin, the temperatures dropping below forty. MacCree told him he should be careful if he'd fallen in love with the moon. Frostbite and being moonstruck went together.

Oliver's skin was indeed tingling when he went back to his bed.

He was reminded of the seriousness of frostbite when he had to deal with two bad cases, men who had fallen asleep on deck after drinking too much. Oliver commanded the cook to set water to boil, swaddled them in blankets and fed them with hot soup and coffee until the chill began to thaw from their bones. The captain was furious with them, but their punishment would be their pain as the nerves in frostbitten flesh began to feel the damage.

December brought blizzards. Famine weather, Yarat called it. Too bad to hunt. Each morning, the natives came on board to have mugs of soup and hard biscuits, their stores of meat running low.

Then late one evening, the snow falling fast through the darkness, blurring the eyes and stinging the cheeks, while waiting for their cocoa the children began crying that they had seen a tupilak, a hungry ghost, out on the ice.

The natives and crewmen crowded along the side of the ship, blinking into the blizzard, a host of snow clumps swarming in the dark. Intermittently, it was just possible to make out a shaggy, snow-covered shape, lumbering towards them across the ice.

'A bear,' the first mate said.

But like no bear anyone had seen, walking upright, head low. A musk ox? The women started calling to their children, taking them below to the hold. The natives shouting to the shaman who stood silent, squinting out into the snow.

A lull in the wind showed the dark shape closer, an absence in the moving snow, approaching as if through veils, staggering, lunging and coming ever nearer. Then it vanished in the mounting blizzard and winds. There was a long debate among the crew as to whether they should send out a search party to see if it was someone in need of help, but the captain said that to do so was to give the men a death sentence. And to chase what? A shadow.

Oliver peered into the snow as long as he could before the darkness and the blizzard obliterated the ice lands entirely.

If it was human, then they would not be alive by morning.

No one slept well that night. The figure on the ice lumbering through their dreams.

The morning showed itself calm and benign, the moon's steady eye looking down on the fresh snow.

Shouting from the Inuit men down on the ice. On the snow, next to an igloo, a long form was lying perfectly still, the fur glittering with frost in the moonlight. A man, six foot at least, broad as an old bull. Oliver wondered what sort of constitution he must have to endure the harshness of the blizzard at forty below.

The crew swarmed down onto the ice.

Shouting at the Inuit to bring a sled, Oliver helped heave the massive bulk up onto it, but turning the body over, they all jumped back at the sight of the familiar red-veined face, letting the body roll back onto the ice.

It was the harpooner, the captain's brother. A heavy arm thrashed out. He growled at them as if surrounded by a pack of wolves, then lost consciousness again and lay still.

This time they secured him with a rope, another under his arms so they could haul him up onto the ship like a great bull seal, tying another rope round him to keep his arms lashed down.

'He's like a bloody whale,' complained Nicolson as they finally hauled him up and dragged him inside the deckhouse where the stove was hot. The harpooner wore native caribou skins, two layers, beneath his musk-ox greatcoat, which explained how he had survived on the ice as long as he had. With a hot drink inside him, he came fully back to his senses – and amazed everyone by humbly apologizing for all the trouble he was causing.

'And thanks to you all who have saved my life from a certain death out there.'

'But how did you come to be wandering around in the middle of nowhere, heading surely for the wastes of the frozen sea?' Oliver asked.

'Thrown out of the trading station by a man made dangerous by drink. The steward there broke open the stores and drank every last drop of liquor he could find, then threatened to shoot me.'

Smiling and grateful, oily with pleasantness, he slept in the forecastle with the crew. No, he didn't need a cabin bed like the captain, though they were brothers. He wanted to make amends for all that had gone before, he said. His dearest wish was to set things right.

That night, Yarat woke, sniffing the air. Shook Oliver awake. Sounds of running above deck. A snapping sound like distant explosions.

'Oliver. Is the ice breaking up already?'

Pulling on her clothes, she opened the cabin door. A wall of thick black smoke bellowed into the cabin. Choking, they made their way up on deck, the crew readying to abandon ship. Flames leapt up into the night sky, showers of sparks mixing with the thick dusting of stars. The captain was roaring up and down the deck, ordering his men to save everything they could, the boats being lowered down. An enormous crash from below as the tank of whale oil was breached and the flames leapt even higher, a thick column of black smoke obliterating the stars. With a terrible creaking and snapping, the ice began to break and the ship, taking on water, to list to one side.

High on the main deck, a figure in a shaggy musk-ox coat stood waving his arms, shouting and bellowing as if with joy, a bottle of brandy in each hand.

'There's even for you!' he yelled. 'You'll be captain of a ship on the bottom of the sea, brother.'

Within minutes, all but the harpooner were off the ship. Everything that could be saved was now on the ice. Yarat and Oliver stood side by side, as with a deafening roar of flames and breaking ice, the ship began to slide down underneath the ice.

The harpooner fell against the bulwark rail, terror on his face in a moment of lucidity. He scrambled to hold on, to climb over as the ship rolled, but with a final and terrible creaking as if the doors of the underworld were opening wide, the ship tipped and slid from sight, leaving nothing but a jagged black lake in the ice.

The captain and steward began giving orders to pull the salvaged rations and tents away from the hole, but before all could be stored in good order, a blizzard came in from the north, peals of thunder ricocheting across the ice. Struggling to stay upright, the men made their way to the native igloos and crowded inside.

The cold and freezing snow brought back the fever on Oliver's lungs that had plagued him after his near-drowning, his breath crackling deep inside. A symptom he well understood. While the crewmen ranged their poor supplies and made plans to walk the ten miles down to the trading station, Oliver lay in a delirium of burning bones, swimming in aching cold seas.

Oliver cared not if he lived or died over the following days. He barely understood when the captain told him that the men were leaving with a sled of provisions to walk to the trading post. In a dream he felt someone peel away his garments, cool hands soothing him with dampened bird skins. He dreamed in words he could not understand, sung to him in a deep, reverberating voice, until it became his most urgent task to find the voice that sang and know all its messages.

He woke one morning to the feeling that his body had come back to him. No nausea, no pains, only a terrible weakness so that he could not rise to find water for his thirst. No sounds in the air other than his own breathing. He was alone, on a long ice platform covered in a double layer of animal skins. A white dome above him.

Oliver could not understand where he was, why he had not woken in his bedroom in Kelly Castle.

A square slab of ice had been set into the snow dome like a glass window, a pure light entering through it. Steps of hard-packed snow led down from a doorway above.

He felt a flickering in the white light and looked up, saw a figure in silhouette, one hand resting against the ice lintel. Dressed in a tawny caribou-skin parka, sealskin leggings and boots, dark hair parted and braided into two round coils, she looked down at him. She descended the steps, calm, gentle, her eyes fastened on him. She dipped a tin cup in a bowl of ice melt and sat on the ledge next to him, one of her hands under his head, the other placing the icy water to his lips. The light reflected back from the white walls, showing a delicate and sweet face. A pinched upper lip curved sweet as a bird, a small fine nose with the slightest up-sweep, slanted bright eyes, wise and innocent.

His wife. His Yarat. And he fell in love all over again.

CHAPTER 28

Yarat explained to Oliver that the whaler men had feared their journey on foot and sledge to the station would kill him, so sick was he. So she and Oliver must stay in her native village until he was well enough to travel. The captain had told her that if she was to get Oliver home to his people where one of their very powerful healers might cure him, then she must try to get to Nantucket. But they must first reach Chesterfield Inlet where the American whalers spent the winter at Marble Island. One of them would surely take them to Nantucket. And once there, there would be Scots boats travelling back to Dundee after the sailing season.

And she had another reason for not risking the journey with them, Yarat told Oliver. She gave him the journal she had taken from the boat as they fled, his story of how she and he had met on a ship and fallen in love.

'Remember, you must write a new page now,' she told him. 'By the summer, you will be a father.'

Yarat's belly grew rounder, reflecting the shine of the seal-oil lamp that she tended with a stick to keep the flame burning along the wick. Her breasts grew heavier. At night her long straight hair made a curtain around them, cocooned together under the warm caribou furs that she had sewn together into a blanket.

She showed Oliver how to wait patiently at the breathing hole of a seal to bring home meat for them, always sharing what they had caught with the others. Often they joined her father and other families in the largest snow house, the people in caribou skin ranged along the family sleeping platforms or around the edge of the igloo, talking and eating. Yarat would translate the stories they shared into English.

When the ice began to break up, the tribe moved onto the land. The bay was suddenly a mass of moving slabs, piling up, thundering past the shore. Then overnight, the great rivers of broken ice were swept away in a storm. A mist appeared across the sea, the snow disappeared from the land to reveal rocky tundra, which soon began to produce tiny flowers. The villagers built round houses made of turf blocks and covered them with roofs of brown and tawny animal skins.

Yarat began to sew a nursing amauti, with patterns of contrasting colours, and a curved flap at front and back. The hood was wide and capacious, its back roomy, tied tight at the waist so a small child could stand there.

She gave birth to a baby girl alone in her tent, Oliver not allowed to enter. They named her Little Star. A sweet round face now peered out from Yarat's wolfskin-lined hood, the child's cheek next to her own. Oliver marvelled at how Yarat swung the baby from the hood to feed her, gently slid her back again. There was not a moment in the day when Little Star was out of contact with her mother's skin, and at night the child lay close enough for Yarat to draw her near to feed.

They talked of travelling down to the depot at Rankin or Chesterfield, but Oliver was ill again for several weeks and could not travel. Another winter went by, Little Star now walking and talking. It seemed to Oliver that this was how his life had always been, helping the men hunt seal, sitting motionless on the ice by the breathing hole swathed in layers of thick caribou fur. Slow sunrises and sunsets that lasted for hours, apricot skies over luminous snows, each bump and outcrop with long turquoise shadows. When he was too weak to help, he stayed with the women in the large snow house as they worked the caribou skins, learning their tongue, each evening reading with Yarat from his precious box of books from the *Narwhal*. Yarat sewed a tiny doll that Little Star carried in her own hood.

In the spring the tribe moved north to hunt caribou before returning to the shore to hunt the sea mammals.

When the snow was firm enough, Yarat said it was time to go and look for the Qallunaat ship. Oliver found he could barely remember the time before his life with Yarat in the village. Did he want to return? Was it fair to ask such great changes of Yarat and the child? But she said they must go. A wife must follow her hunter and she knew that sooner or later, Oliver would wish to return to his lands. And Little Star should see the place that was one half of her, though the other half would for ever be made of snow and ice and the summer Arctic winds. They waited until the sea had frozen over again, when the runners of the sled were iced over enough for it to run smoothly. They took a team of six dogs and Yarat's brother, who would bring the dogs back to the villagers. Yarat carefully packed their best furs, their metal cups, their hunting knives and the stone lamp. They took two seal carcasses for the journey. Any other food, they would hunt for on the way.

The captain of the *Orry Taft* gave them a berth to Nantucket, in return for a promissory note from Oliver to pay an extortionate amount on his return to Scotland. They had a poor berth in the hold, where Oliver stayed awake as much as he could, a knife to hand. The crew of the *Orry Taft* was made up of a ramshackle class of men one step away from prison or destitution, it seemed, and a world away from the steady family men of the Dundee whaling ships who sailed with the same captain year after year and in spite of their rough ways took their pay home to their families. By the time they reached Nantucket, they'd had so little sleep the fever on his lungs had started again and Oliver was coughing up blood, as quietly as he could.

In Nantucket they learned that none of the crew who had set out to walk to the trading station at Rankin had come home alive. They arrived to find that a madman who stole all the drink had set the store on fire and burned down the trading station. They continued, poorly supplied, and had died of cold and hunger while trying to reach Chesterfield Inlet. The letter that Oliver had given the captain to send home, to tell his mother that he was alive and living with his wife north of Repulse Bay, never reached his parents. All this time, Oliver realized, they would have thought him perished with the crew. But there was no time left to send a letter ahead from Nantucket to warn them. He would be his own letter of good news.

He recovered greatly on the Scottish sealer bound for Dundee where they were given a cabin and ate at the mess table each night with the captain and officers.

But he could feel Yarat growing tenser as the coast of Scotland came into sight, and he felt filled with love and gratitude that she had been so brave in agreeing to travel far from all she knew for his sake. He tried to describe Kelly to her, but failed.

And he tried to imagine his mother's joy when she found that he was alive, that he had brought her a grandchild.

He wished that he had had more time to gradually introduce the idea of Yarat as his wife, but he was sure that, once the initial shock was past, his parents would see how very fine she was and cherish her as he did.

CHAPTER 29

The journey from Dundee docks to the castle was exhausting for Yarat and Little Star. Oliver had arranged for a carriage to take them from the ferry directly to the castle, but the jolting motion on the uneven roads made them both nauseous, even after months at sea on a ship. They had never seen horses before. Little Star asked if they were some kind of caribou. Yarat explained that here they had different animals. Little Star knew about elephants from the sailors' play at Christmas. She wanted to know if she would see one in Scotland. Oliver promised to take her to see one – though thinking it would probably be the poor captive creature in Edinburgh Zoo that he had seen as a child.

Oliver tried to prepare them for the castle. Imagine, he began, an igloo, or a sod house, made from stones and high as the hill at Arviat. Where rooms sit on top of other rooms, four layers high.

'It would fall down,' said Little Star. 'I do not want to live there, Papa.'

'You don't need to be afraid. The stones are held together so they do not fall, not in summer, not in winter.'

'So it is a magic house,' said Little Star. Who was clever enough to know that the summer sun melts all igloos, and the rain melts all sod houses.

It was dark by the time they arrived at Kelly, and he was glad they were not able to see the extent of the building and be alarmed by it.

Though he knew that their unease would be nothing compared to the shock that his parents were about to experience when he introduced his bride and child, about whom they had never heard even a rumour.

They would have had little enough time to get used to the news that their son was alive. Oliver had managed to send a letter ahead from Orkney while the ship waited at port, but had said nothing about his companions. He hoped that the meeting of them in person, their beauty, their intelligence, would forestall any prejudice his parents might hold on hearing the word 'Eskimo' – with all the savagery and misconceptions about them that Oliver had been raised to believe. This seemed the best cause of action.

But as the carriage came to a halt and lamps appeared at the front door, he began to have doubts. Yarat and Little Star were wearing their furs and beads; they had nothing else to wear save the thin cotton dresses that Yarat had sewn on the boat. And these were made from a length of gaudy material given to her by the captain from his store of trinkets for bartering with the natives – in return for a wealth of valuable furs.

Oliver picked up Little Star and stepped out of the carriage into the chill November night. Yarat followed, looking around and sniffing the air. He felt her press into his side as the oak door opened and old Tom Griddle came out with a lamp, even more bent and hobbled than Oliver remembered him. He held up the lamp and looked in disbelief as they came near, stepping back as though Oliver might be a ghost. Which he might as well be. From poor Tom's reaction, it was clear the letter announcing his return had not yet arrived.

'It's me, Tom. Came in on a whaler that docked in Dundee today. Alive and well. Are the master and mistress at home?'

'Lord save us. Is it really you, Master Oliver? I don't know what your mother will do when she sees you. Near break in half with joy. She's been that down since we were told you were lost and dead. As has your poor father.'

A boy was woken and sent to fetch his parents. Carrying Little Star, Oliver led Yarat into the kitchens, the warmest place in the castle at this hour. By now Tom's wife, Mary, had appeared, wrapped in her shawl and bonnet, to start heating water for tea, keeping her distance from the fur-clad creatures, but quickly won over by the red cheeks and sleepy face of his daughter. Little Star drank a cup of warm milk greedily but would not be put down from his arms.

'Well, isn't she the sweetest thing, Master Oliver. Where did you find her? Who is she?'

'She's my daughter, Little Star.'

Mary Anne tried to hide her surprise and shot a look at her husband, just as Oliver's mother came running in, her long grey hair in a loose plait, a chintz robe rippling out.

Sylvia ran to him, held Oliver's face in her hands, tears and smiles as she babbled, 'So it's true. It's true. You are here, alive. I thought they'd lost their minds when they came to fetch me. Oh, I will never complain or be sad ever again. You have been given back to me. Are you well? Are you surely well?'

Behind her stood his father, wordless, eyes moist. Sylvia pulled Oliver to sit down next to her.

'Mary Anne? Hot tea, rum – no, hot broth. But what is this? Have you brought back some little creature?' Little Star had hidden her face in Oliver's shoulder at his mother's outburst. Sylvia now pulled at the fur-clad bundle, her eyes opening wide to see a face within the fur hood. A child's face. Then she noticed a second fur-clad figure standing a way back in the shadows. Fear and revulsion crossed Sylvia's face.

'But why have you brought these creatures back with you, Oliver? Because I won't have them in the house, you know. They can go to the stables. Tom!'

Oliver held up his hand as Tom stepped forward. 'Wait. Mother,

Father, I would like you to meet my wife, Yarat, and my daughter, Little Star.'

A small half-laugh escaped from Sylvia's mouth. She stared at Yarat with horror and disbelief.

'Married to a savage. Don't be ridiculous. Not possible. Gregor, tell them it's not possible. If you have had some dalliance with a native, I can forgive you, though I do not wish to know about it. But I certainly would never have expected you to drag the creature back to the house with her pup. No, whatever this was, this can be no marriage in the eyes of God. Not with a heathen savage. Does she even speak English? Gregor, tell them to go.'

Oliver's father remained as if stunned, mouth agape. Yarat moved close to Oliver, anger in her eyes. It was clear to Sylvia that she understood very well everything that was being said.

'Mother, without Yarat and her people I would be dead. Her kinsmen are good, kind people, who have taught me so much. And you have a granddaughter now, your own flesh and blood.'

He set Little Star down on the ground where she stared up at the tall thin lady and her angry eyes. Yarat drew Little Star to her side, and the child buried her face in her mother's furs, moving them both slowly away from Sylvia. Yarat thought of the hungry ghosts that roam the high Arctic wastes, eating every living thing and becoming more and more ravenous as they grow in size, gathering the storm clouds around them and never satisfied or sated.

Sylvia drew herself up to full height, hands clasped in front of her breast. 'We are very grateful,' she said slowly and loudly to Yarat, 'for having our son brought back to us. But you will understand that we are a civilized people. It is not possible for you to stay. We will give you money and find a passage for you back to your people. You will return well provided for, along with the child. I doubt this marriage, as such, would be considered a legal marriage here, so by whatever rites you entrapped my son, we do not consider you a wife.'

'I can assure you,' said Oliver, looking as pale as death, holding on to the table as he swayed with a sudden dizziness, 'that we are man and wife in the eyes of the law and the eyes of God. The captain of the ship married us. I have the certificate.'

Sylvia turned to her husband. 'Then we will have to do something about the captain. And pay off the crew. Whatever it costs.'

'Mother!' Oliver cried again, more emphatically, but he fell backwards onto a chair. Yarat and Sylvia rushed to him. Pushing Yarat away, Sylvia held up his head and helped him sip water. Then he was escorted upstairs by his father and Tom, barely able to protest. He turned back and called out, 'Give Little Star the room next to ours, Mother, the Blue Room.'

As soon as Oliver had left the room Sylvia turned to the maid, ignoring Yarat and Little Star who were huddled together by the door, looking at her anxiously. She gave instructions for them to be put in the stable, in the groom's small room above the horses.

CHAPTER 30

'It must be that Oliver was too ill to write anything else,' said Caro when she had finished reading the journal aloud as they sat around the kitchen table after supper.

'Imagine the sort of reception that Yarat and their little girl must have endured, with Oliver's mother so horrified by his Arctic wife,' sighed Martha.

'Something clearly went very wrong after that,' said Caro. 'But what exactly?'

'According to the anguished letters that Oliver sent out, Yarat must have left the castle without telling him where she'd gone,' said Alasdair.

'If she did leave the castle,' murmured Caro.

With a feeling of dread, the next morning Caro telephoned Detective Cameron to tell him what they had found out through Oliver's diary.

'Is there any way you can tell if the body of the woman was that of an Inuit, from the bones?' she blurted out.

A few days later he called by with the answer to Caro's question.

'The coroner tells me that there's no definite way of telling if the skeleton is Caucasian or Inuit. She is, however, sending off some samples to Oxford University to try a new technique for dating the bones. That may give us some certainty around the time of burial.

And I also wanted to come in person to let you know that a date has been set for the inquest, where the most probable identity of the deceased and the cause of death will be ascertained as far as possible.'

'A public inquest?' asked Martha. 'With reporters?'

'Yes. But I'm sure you have nothing to worry about.'

'Perhaps,' said Martha. 'Though they always seem to want to put the most horrid spin on things.'

'There may not be much to tell. It is quite possible that we will never know who was buried in the garden,' said Detective Cameron. 'With so much time having passed.'

'And we may find out something we don't particularly like,' said Martha. 'But come what may, I really would prefer to know the truth. Have the matter settled.'

'Detective Cameron,' said Caro as they walked out with him to the drive where his car was parked. 'We know that Oliver didn't marry Charlotte Strachan. She's not our missing bride. But Charlotte does seem to have vanished. I was thinking we should still keep her in mind, regarding the body, as well as poor Yarat. Though I'd hate to find out it was either. I know you said that there's no marriage or death certificate for Charlotte, but could she be traced through other records connected to her education or her training as an artist?'

'I believe she went to an art school that has since been incorporated into the Edinburgh College of Art.'

'I might do some more research around that.'

'By all means, Mrs Gillan. And we are also waiting to hear from the solicitors dealing with Louisa Glenconner's family estate, although they assure us that they have no idea what became of Charlotte. They have been trying to trace any possible remaining relatives. No results so far, I'm afraid, but they will let us know if they do discover any.'

★

Caro telephoned the Edinburgh College of Art but was told that they did not have any records of a Charlotte Strachan. The secretary who took the call did, however, have a very interesting suggestion. She had previously worked at Dundee University and wondered if Caro was aware that there was a late-Victorian painting in the art gallery there by a woman whose name was Charlotte Strachan.

Caro could hardly believe it. As soon as she was able, she drove with Felicity to Dundee, taking the car on the ferry across the Tay. An hour later she was standing in the art gallery of the Prince Albert Institute, staring with amazement at a small oil painting. It was a scene of Dundee's Earl Grey docks, whaling ships silhouetted against a bronze sunset, behind them the smoke of the factory chimneys blowing away to the sea, everything filled with life and movement. But the most startling thing was beside Charlotte's signature. It was dated 1883. That meant that Charlotte must still have been living in Scotland while Oliver was away in the Arctic. If Charlotte had gone missing, then it would not have been until after that date. So had she still been in Scotland when Oliver returned with Yarat? Did Charlotte visit Kelly at that time? With a sinking heart, Caro realized that it looked possible that Charlotte might be the body in the garden.

Holding Felicity in her arms, Caro looked around to see if there were any attendants, and then stepped over the rope barrier hung between two brass posts, standing as close to the painting as Charlotte must have been as she worked on it. With a sudden impulse, Caro lightly touched over Charlotte's signature, would not have been surprised to take her hand away and find fresh paint on her fingertips. She stepped back over the rope. Felicity wriggled down and stamped across the expanse of wooden flooring in her new little shoes, enjoying the large echo around her, showing a creative appreciation for art galleries of which Martha would surely have approved. A uniformed attendant appeared and Caro thought they had better leave before they were asked to.

'We've still got two missing girls, then,' said Martha as they shared a supper of lentils and ham hock that Caro had cooked on the range, with slices of fresh wholemeal bread – both Caro and Alasdair turned out excellent wholemeal loaves from Martha's recipe – and with butter and a slab of cheese from the dairy at Pittenweem. Living in the countryside made it far easier to cope with the restrictions of rationing than in town where it was not possible to barter fresh eggs for butter, or buy bacon and mutton readily from the farmer. Tinned goods were still hopeless and clothes continued to need curating and patching, but things were getting gradually easier.

'The painting was a find, placing Charlotte in the area at the right time, and I'm certainly going to keep researching and enquiring,' said Caro. 'But unless we find some new information, we may never know who was buried here. Never be able to give that poor woman a name.'

'I couldn't bear to think it was Yarat,' said Alasdair. 'My guess is she must have been a rather special person from how much Oliver loved her. And I'd love to see what aspects of her might have been passed down to me and to Felicity, things that have been there all along without us realizing it. What I wouldn't give to know what she was like or to see a photograph of her.'

CHAPTER 31

'What do you think of this?' said Alasdair a few days later as he came in with the post. He showed Caro a letter. 'Do you think it's genuine?'

Caro took it, read it through a couple of times as she sipped her coffee. 'So this is a firm that traces lost heirs? Really? Do such things exist?'

'Seems they do. They say they've been looking for descendants who might inherit the Glenconner fortune after Louisa's granddaughter died, but they've come up against a problem. The solicitors dealing with the will are also acting as the executors for the estate – a bad idea, if you ask me, as it creates a conflict of interests. Seems they've been holding things up and obfuscating for five years while paying themselves vast fees for managing the estate. No incentive at all to find any actual inheritor.'

'For five years.'

'Indeed. Can you imagine the money they must be paying themselves to do nothing but stall? Anyway, a Mr Garvie wants to meet up with us. Things to tell us that he'd rather not put down in writing. Gosh, doesn't it all sound cloak and dagger. Ma's asked me to go. What do you think?'

'I think you should go, and I should come with you. I'd love to hear what he has to say.'

★

Caro and Alasdair met Mr Garvie in the public bar of the Peat Inn, an anonymous place by St Andrews standards. Alex Garvie looked like an earnest student, thin, with corduroy jacket and tortoiseshell spectacles. He was clearly keen as a whippet, however, when it came to tracing down likely leads.

'Can't thank you enough. We've been anxious to get our hands on the documents at Corcoran and Gillespie for years, but we can't just crash in there and demand to see them. We need someone with a reasonable legal claim, or even just a possible claim, to request access.'

'I still don't understand why you think we could help you.'

'I believe Charlotte and Louisa's father was close friends with your great-great-grandfather, Mr Gregor Gillan. And after his death, his daughters were more or less part of your family as children. '

'That's right. Though they grew apart as adults.'

'Even so, there's a family connection. A close one. You could say that Mr Gillan was an informal guardian. That might be enough for you to request to see the documents surrounding the will.'

'Really?' asked Alasdair, looking unconvinced.

'Well, it's not technically enough,' Mr Garvie admitted, 'but if you have a family lawyer, preferably someone who can sound fierce and go in and make a bit of a fuss, then I think they might let you take a peep at the documents. You see, the solicitors know that what they have been doing isn't strictly legitimate, milking an executive charge, so I don't think they will push back too hard. So long as we can make a vaguely credible case to see the estate's papers.'

'I don't suppose it could hurt,' said Alasdair.

'And we might even learn something interesting,' said Caro. 'We'd love to know if there might be any letters or diaries or photographs in Louisa's estate mentioning her sister Charlotte who seems to have vanished.'

'Yes. It's information on Charlotte that we're particularly hoping for. So may I have your permission to go ahead and set up an appointment with you and the solicitors?'

Alasdair nodded. 'Let us know when.'

'No doubt they'll be up to their old tricks and very slow to answer, but I'll contact you as soon as I have a date.'

After they had said goodbye to Mr Garvie in the square, they walked arm in arm over the cobbles towards the cathedral ruins, seagulls crying overhead, a brisk wind coming in from the coast. On the other side of the cathedral grounds, they came out through a door in the sandstone wall, the stones the same ochres and pinks and greys as the stones at Kelly. In front of them the cliffs and skerries of St Andrews, the ruins of the old castle, and in the distance Dundee.

'So it was over there,' said Alasdair, tucking Caro's hand into his coat pocket, the winds bitter. 'That's where Yarat and Little Star would have docked with Oliver, all those years ago.'

CHAPTER 32

There had been times, in the year and a half since Felicity was born, that Caro had felt completely broken and scattered by having a child. But of late she had begun to realize that she had not been annihilated so much as expanded. So much knowledge and experience and insight rapidly added to her old self: the precise feel of a tiny child's sleeping weight, the gift of your child's delight in your attention, the pain of birth. A singular focus on the unique being given into your care, the profound love it called up. And the way Felicity revealed something new about herself each day, one's expectations of what a child might be like gone like a vanishing tide to reveal a wide, unexpected land called Felicity who loved dogs and hated cabbage, had hair like her father, a dogged persistence like her mother, and a sweetness all of her own. At times, Caro could almost feel the creaking of her brain growing to accommodate each day's new experiences.

And sitting in the garden wrapped in a coat and woollen scarf while Felicity played on the front lawns with her push-along cart of bricks, her boots leaving tracks in the frosty grass, Caro tried to imagine a life where she had never known Kelly, never met Alasdair's family. Would it have been easier? Happier? She'd felt so ground down by the assumptions and yes, the prejudices of the Gillans' class at times, but it had also been an education, in people, in habits, in cultures. And now, because of it, she wasn't the same Caro. Not a worse Caro, or a better Caro, she simply knew more. Understood more. Saw more. And perhaps, as a result, she had more choices as to who she might become, and who she did not want to become.

She thought of the old photograph of Martha, in a silver frame. Martha at twenty, standing in front of her easel in the gardens of Kelly. She wore a simple slip of a cotton dress, her hair down. She was looking back and laughing at the camera. A picture taken by Duguld, clearly. You could see the love between them. That Martha looked like someone you might be good friends with, fun and young and interesting. Was she still there inside the needy, prickly Martha who subtly seemed to be in competition for Alasdair's attention? What if she made more effort to get to know the real Martha, the sunny girl in the garden? Martha a chum, not an adversary?

At least Alasdair had stopped panicking at the idea of competing claims from a mother and a wife.

'How can your mother understand that you are married if you can't show her that we're a team?' Caro had said to Alasdair. 'It's not disloyal to act as if we are. We're not drawing lines to exclude her, we're just sketching out a new way where she's included and valued. We love her. She's family and always will be.'

He'd nodded. He'd taken to reassuring his mother more that she was valued, and as a result she had relaxed a little, becoming less anxious and demanding of his individual time, happier for them all to spend time together.

As Christmas approached, Caro found that something had shifted in her relationship with her mother-in-law. She'd noticed how Martha made more supportive comments of late, not in a false overpraising way, but comments that showed she realized that Caro had her own way of doing things with Felicity, or occasionally making encouraging noises that brightened up a discouraging day.

And when Martha did go too far, then Caro tried not to notice.

Caro found she enjoyed finding out more about the real Martha, her interest in Arts and Crafts, how she'd managed to raise the children in such a rambling place while doing so much to restore it.

And it was Martha who began to talk about their long-term plans, for where Caro and Alasdair were going to live come the spring.

'Yes, we should make plans,' said Caro. 'In fact, I've applied for a research post in St Andrews history department. I mean, I don't expect to get it, but if we could afford it, I've seen a little house for rent overlooking Castle Beach. I mean, I don't know that you'd feel happy about me working, so few wives do. . .'

'Caro dear, I was lucky to have had so much help when the children were small. It never occurred to me that I shouldn't work – on the castle, on my painting. So when you get your post, then just let me know and I'll come over and help with Flissy any time. Though by then, who knows if we will still have Kelly.'

The dossier on the Gillan family history was now almost complete. Martha came up to Duguld's study to see it, trailing her hand over the desk as she passed, as though the wood contained memories.

'This is wonderful,' she told Caro. 'I can't see the National Trust turning us down with such a complete history.'

'I added a section on Yarat and Eugenia that explains their Inuit heritage, and the connection to the Dundee whaling fleet,' said Caro. 'If you feel that's appropriate.'

'Absolutely. That must be included,' said Martha. 'A vital part of this family's story. We'll send all this off to the committee with a rather hopeful outline of the finances. But I worry that the shortfall in funds to keep the place in repair might still be too much for them to take us on.'

★

Just before Christmas, Caro and Alasdair visited her father in London, a wonderful week, treats to the theatre and a concert at the Royal Albert Hall while Phoebe came and babysat. Her father had a way of finding sugar and chocolate even in rationing. Mrs Dawson, the help, making sure the house ran like clockwork. The cabinet with her mother's collection of china dogs still lovingly dusted every day by Mrs Dawson as if Mother might come back.

And her father, of course, missed nothing.

'So it's not hard then, keeping your end up in a house a bit set in its ways?' he'd said, tapping out his pipe and relighting it as she sat on the stool. 'Not easy, living cheek by jowl. I recall your mother's mother. . .'

He took the pipe out and pointed at her. 'What you need, our Caroline, is a little motor of your own for you to get about in with the baby. Go into town and wherever you like.'

She'd said no. Always too proud to ask him for help. And Alasdair found it embarrassing when his father-in-law did give them money. But he'd insisted. He knew someone who could give him a good deal on a Morris – not new, but a good runner.

Back in Kelly, Caro cheerfully answered the phone when it rang in the hallway, looking out at the little red Morris parked outside on the drive. Their own car. Her car.

'Is that Caro? Alex Garvie here. From the bureau of lost heirs, as you like to call it. Thank you again for meeting me the other day. We have been following up what you told us about the girls and Oliver, as in the photograph you showed me. I thought you might like to know that we've managed to find out something very interesting about the maid, Mary MacGrievy. Mary married and had a daughter, quite late in life. Shona Morris. The daughter is a doctor who lives in Dundee.'

'Mary's daughter lives in Dundee! Do you have an address?'

'I do indeed. And if you do happen to pay her a visit, you wouldn't mind sharing any new information on Charlotte or Louisa that might come to light?'

Shona Morris lived in a large granite house, its tall bay windows looking out over Magdalen Green and the Tay Estuary. A neat, fair-haired doctor in her late forties, she served Caro and Martha tea and scones.

'My mother kept in touch with Charlotte, you know, for a long time,' Shona told them. 'Of course, I never met Charlotte but I had the photographs and the letters, and other things. So I always felt I knew her. What was it that you wanted to know about her and my mother?'

'It's quite complicated,' Martha began. 'We never really had much information about my husband's great-grandfather, Oliver Gillan, and we knew nothing until recently about his friendship with Charlotte and Louisa. Nothing at all, either, about his wife. Then we found out that Oliver married an Inuit girl.'

'Oh yes,' said Shona, nodding.

'You knew?'

'My mother returned to Kelly at the request of Mr Gillan to care for Oliver and Yarat's child, Little Star, or Eugenia rather, after her mother disappeared and Oliver passed away.'

'So it was Mary who was caring for Eugenia,' said Martha. 'Mary was the beloved Nurse that Eugenia used to speak about. More or less saved her life, I believe. She must have re-married then, changed her name from Brown to Morris.'

'Aye, she did. Mr Brown was her first husband – he passed away in an accident at the docks. My mother was in fact a young widow when she went back to Kelly to care for Eugenia. Angus Morris, her second husband, was a groom at Kelly. They married late in life, after

Eugenia was eighteen. I was the surprise that came along when my mother was almost forty, just after they moved back to Dundee.'

'I still can't believe it,' said Martha. 'Mary lived at Kelly as Eugenia's nurse.'

Shona nodded. 'For several years.'

'Shona, I suppose you read in the papers about our recent problem, the body they found at Kelly?' said Caro.

'I did.'

'Do you think it's possible that your mother had any idea who it was buried at Kelly back then?'

'Oh yes.'

'She knew! She knew who it was. So was it Eugenia's mother, Yarat? Was it Charlotte?' asked Caro. 'But why ever didn't you say something? Go to the police?'

'It wasn't my story to tell. I thought I should wait until you wanted to hear it.'

Shona got up and went to a polished wooden chest of drawers with gleaming brass handles, opened a drawer. 'I have been waiting for you to come for this. I found it after Mother passed away. I wasn't sure what to do with it, with Charlotte's family all being gone. It has been a burden really. So I'm glad to give it to you. Do with it as you see fit.'

She placed it on the low table in front of where Martha and Caro were sitting. On the cover, *The Diary of Mary Brown.*

Shona made a fresh pot of tea, stirred it, and then poured them all a strong cup. Handed round thick slices of cake.

'I think you'll need this to keep you going. It's quite a journey you're setting out on. Have a glance through now, if you like, but since there's too much there for you to read this afternoon, do take it back with you. Then think about it, and let me know what you decide to do.'

CHAPTER 33

Charlotte moved into a handsome stone house in Dundee with good light that overlooked Magdalen Green and the Tay river with its brilliant light flashing silver and amethyst and golden depending on the time of day. She continued to make trips to the harbour in Dundee or the Grassmarket in Edinburgh to sketch bustling scenes of life, but now she dressed in sensible skirts and a coat with a velvet collar since this was 1885 and a woman was allowed to paint undisturbed. She had also begun a series of portraits in her studio, of mill girls from Dundee, some of them as rough and wild as any of the whaler men, others a little more educated but with the same readiness to take up the privileges of men.

It was Mary who had kept Charlotte informed of any gossip from the mill about Kelly, though there had been no news of Oliver, which was not unexpected, but still.

Then came the worrying rumours that Oliver was missing, Sylvia suffering from nervous troubles, Oliver's father increasingly withdrawn from the world.

'But you shouldn't worry, Mary,' Charlotte had told her. 'I can feel that Oliver is alive and trying to get home to us. I would know it if he were not.'

Then one day, Mary had run to the house with the news that Oliver was home. Charlotte had been beside herself with joy.

After a few wild days of hope, Mary brought the rest of the news, kept a closely guarded secret for as long as possible. Oliver was married. To an Inuit girl. Over the next few days Charlotte could see no way forward. The view from her window emptied to a blank space.

And now Oliver was bringing the woman here, to her studio, her sanctuary.

Mary came in and took off her hat and jacket, busied herself with putting together a tea that a child and stranger might like. She'd prepared tinned sardines on toast, pink sugar buns – hard to say what they might eat. Charlotte had stood at the large bay window, lips pressed together, arms over her chest, until Mary told her that she must help make the tea.

But when Yarat and Little Star came with Oliver to the studio, both in sealskin amautis, Little Star's hood up after the buffeting of the wind outside, Yarat as calm and steady as the North Star, Charlotte's heart thawed. Standing in her studio, the two of them seemed as elemental and true and right as the sea or the sky or a wood at evening. They changed the stale air of the closed room to something fresh with distant snows. They opened the world and made spaces in the heart for days to come.

Little Star's small hand in hers, Charlotte showed her paints and brushes, the solid weight of her as she sat on Charlotte's lap and Charlotte told her a story about her papa as a little boy, trusting and relaxed.

Yarat took Charlotte longer to see, first her eyes, then her steady small form, the inky sheen of her hair and how close she stayed to Oliver. But over the course of the afternoon, Yarat became a whole, a person who listened to the conversation seriously, replied in her oddly accented English, until Charlotte could feel the weight and worth of the woman's presence, other and foreign yes, but hewed from a fine rock.

'We have a very great favour to ask you, Charlotte,' he had said as he turned from the window, Charlotte covering the shock of realizing how ill he was with a quick smile. 'Would you stand as godmother and legal guardian to Little Star? I worry about Mama, ever more erratic in her opinions and moods. She has not yet shown the welcome I hoped for to this little family of ours. And Papa has retreated from the world, not helped by Mother's outbursts, I am afraid, almost broken by the strain of thinking me missing for so long. So you see, it is not a small favour I ask of you. There may come a time, in the future. . .'

'With all my heart,' Charlotte had replied.

And later, as they walked on Magdalen Green in front of the row of sandstone houses, Yarat and Little Star running in front with Mary, Oliver had said to her, 'Was I wrong to bring them home? So far from their people? If I had realized how ill I truly was. . .' he said ruefully.

'And you will get better,' Charlotte had said. 'With good food and loving care. We shall make you better.'

He had smiled gratefully, looking over at Little Star, a tiny figure spinning in the wind.

Each week Charlotte worked on the painting Oliver had asked her to do of Yarat and Little Star side by side in their sealskin amautis and parkas. They had been to the studio several times to sit for her. She liked painting the silky seal fur with its patterning of silvers and greenish greys, or the tan and gold of the caribou fur with its peppering of ashy black, the intricate beading on the front of Yarat's amauti. And how strange it was to see Oliver's face staring from that mixture of Inuit and Scottish genes blended in Little Star's small face, a beautiful combination of creamy skin and wise eyes and thick dark auburn hair. She and Yarat talked as she worked, Little Star playing on the rug. Charlotte only asked her to stand still when was necessary and for as short a time as possible. Through Yarat's eyes, Charlotte travelled to the far Arctic, over glaciers and frozen seas, and gleaned an idea of how much Yarat loved Oliver, how much Oliver loved her.

Her own feelings for him, though as heartfelt as ever, became less of a burden, more akin to the deep appreciation of a sky at dawn, or a seascape in winter, essential to the soul though one may never possess it.

At the end of each session, Charlotte would get down on the rug and play and talk with her goddaughter. Little Star with her own pencils and paper that she could use whenever she visited Aunt Charlotte's.

Little Star was too small to ask questions about why Charlotte never came to Kelly to visit them.

Meanwhile Oliver's eyes burned bright and glittered with his future plans, a ceremony in a proper church to bless their union, where Sylvia, he hoped, would finally be won over to Yarat as her new daughter.

CHAPTER 34

'What on earth is this?' asked Sylvia as she unpacked a delivery of white silk satin and pure white lace as delicate as snow, a sheen of early light on water as the silk moved.

'I've no idea, ma'am,' insisted the housekeeper. 'Expensive fabric too. And all white. I'd say there was enough for a wedding gown.'

'It must be a mistake on the part of Jenson's. Clearly it was meant for someone else. Very inconvenient. Pack it up and send it back to them. And tell them to be more careful with their deliveries in future.'

Oliver came in from the gardens, holding Little Star by the hand. She wore a checked woollen gown and cloak. Sylvia had confiscated the furs, citing fleas, though Little Star had asked for them back.

'I was expecting a parcel, Mother. Was that it arriving?'

'It was you who ordered this?'

'I've been thinking. Since this irregular way that we were married – though perfectly legally, I assure you – has been worrying you, Mother, then I thought we might have a small ceremony at the church to bless the marriage. It's done when people marry abroad. A fellow at college married a Russian girl and they had ceremonies here and there in Russia too. Yarat is happy to do it. So I have spoken to the minister. And I've hired a very good seamstress to come and measure her for a gown, see what kind of dress she prefers.'

'You think this will help?' said Sylvia, snapping over the end of the white silk. 'Trying to turn a sow's ear into a silk purse. Making a spectacle of the family. And can a heathen even be blessed in a church? How long are you going to go on with this impossible charade? Because sooner or later, she'll want to go back to her own kind. You can't civilize a savage.'

'Mother, how can you say such things?' He sat down, his head in his hands, as Little Star climbed onto his lap, looking up at Sylvia. 'We are man and wife. I have to tell you, Mother, that if you cannot accept Yarat, if you make me choose between you, then I shall go with her.'

'And how would you survive without your father's allowance? Because we won't support such nonsense. Where would you go?'

'Mother, you forget I will be fully qualified as a doctor once I return to finish my studies. Then we may go wherever we wish. Perhaps back to Canada, which is what Yarat would like best, though she is willing to make a life here. I promise you, my best and most fervent hope is that we will be able to make a life here. But I have to warn you, Mother, if it cannot be, then we shall leave.'

'Such dramatics and threats, when it is just your poor mother trying to get used to so many changes thrust upon me of a sudden. Not having you all to myself any more. Of course, of course, Yarat must have her wedding dress. Though I might advise against white next to that skin colour. I shall even send for my own seamstress to attend to it. We will hold a private ceremony of blessing here, in the chapel, with Father Macleod. He will do that for us. A private affair. Very select. No need to put in an announcement.'

'I know I have asked a lot of you, and very suddenly. Thank you, Mother, for trying. You will love Yarat, given time, as much as you are growing to love dear Little Star.'

'Eugenia is indeed a sweet child. Especially now that she has a proper name, thank you. And how can I be unhappy, when you are come back to us? When we thought for so long that we had lost you.'

Sylvia kept up her smile for as long as Oliver was in the room. Once he had gone, her face took on a sourer expression.

So the little minx believed she could take Oliver away from her with a wave of her hand. For the first time Sylvia felt a grudging respect for Yarat, for the power she had, a power akin to witchcraft, the wiles of a savage dancing in firelight dressed in animal skins and with sharp teeth to rip her prey into shreds. A power beyond understanding, which for Oliver's sake, Sylvia saw, she must endure.

But already she had plans to end Yarat's hold over him, completely and for ever.

As Oliver took Little Star outside again, she asked, 'Papa, what is a sozeer?'

'You mean a sow's ear,' said Oliver. 'The ear of a pig.'

And Little Star looked thoughtful, because she understood enough to know that her grandmother had been talking about her mother.

Yarat stood on a stool in her bedroom while Agnes Mitcham helped her try on the half-finished dress. Sylvia stood behind them, watching Yarat in the looking glass as she held up her arms while Agnes took out the seams a fraction around the waist.

'Must be the good Scottish food, miss,' said Agnes, measuring Yarat's waist. 'You're going to be very bonny at this rate.'

Yarat did not reply. Seeing in the mirror the white of the material against her complexion, she saw the cheerful faces of her family and tribe dressed in their tawny furs, so lovely against the glinting snow and bright blue sky. A memory that squeezed her heart with longing. But she lived here with Oliver now, Little Star playing happily with the dolls and the rocking horse in Oliver's old nursery.

'Such a shame Oliver's not here to see how well the dress is coming along,' said Sylvia. 'And how well Eugenia looks in the new dresses that Miss Mitcham has brought with her. There. See, child.'

Little Star stood in front of her mother who was standing on the stool, the hems of the dress falling to the floor; she looked like a creature from an Inuit story, made of snow, floating across the ice. With her long raven-black hair, and calm eyes the colour of winter leaves.

Little Star saw that she looked like her father even more now that she wore the dresses Sylvia had had made, with clear grey eyes, red wavy hair and pale skin. You could still see her mother in her face, around the eyes, the length of her smooth, even cheeks, but she knew that it was Oliver's shadow that Sylvia liked in her.

'When will Oliver be home, Mother?' asked Yarat.

Mustering a smile, Sylvia sighed. 'Not for another fortnight. He has many people to see before he can be approved to complete his studies. And still they may refuse him. Not that I blame you, dear, keeping him away in the Arctic for so long. The heart wants what it wants.'

Over the following days, Sylvia moved about the house listlessly picking up a book or gazing out over the grounds. The arrival of Yarat had left her feeling diminished in some way, less secure in her home and in herself. Her chest tight with the constriction of this new threat that Yarat held over her. But there was nothing she could do to reverse her dethroning. And every day, her dislike for Yarat increased, this strange slip of a girl. She could see nothing special or lovely in Yarat. When she thought of Lucy Lochinver, and all that Sylvia had dreamed of in that future. One could say that she hated Yarat then.

Her only consolation, Eugenia.

She was brought out of her reverie by the butler bringing up the afternoon mail. Noticing an envelope with Oliver's writing on it, addressed to Yarat. Sylvia opened it carefully. She could make an excuse to the girl that it had been opened by mistake. She read it with mounting dismay and anger.

Darling,

I have found us a place of our own. It is quiet and remote, where we can make a new life for you and for Little Star. We will find friends to help us, a school for Little Star, and I believe there will be openings for work as a doctor. I will tell you more as soon as I arrive home.

Your own Oliver

A thunderclap in her breast. Sylvia closed the letter, breathless at such treachery. After all she had endured, Oliver was still planning to steal away and hide himself with this woman and the child. A child who was, after all, Sylvia's only grandchild. Did she not have rights to see her raised well?

Sylvia hardly knew what she did as she put on her cloak and paced the grounds, tall and wrapped in her own dark weather. And out of her anger, there came a plan, clean and cold as a knife. Tomorrow, with Gregor away in Edinburgh for a week, would be the day to begin.

CHAPTER 35

When Yarat and the child appeared at breakfast, dressed once again in fur jackets and trousers, Sylvia gave the letter to Yarat, apologizing for opening it. She hadn't paid attention, she said, since she was used to letters from Oliver being addressed to her. And how well Yarat was progressing in her reading.

'So you will be moving away with Alasdair?'

'You do not mind?'

'Young people must follow their own path,' Sylvia had said with a gracious smile.

Over the following few days, Sylvia left the next part of her plan to steep like oak leaves in salt water, a bitter, poisonous drink. Messages were sent to Dundee docks. Money exchanged hands.

Sylvia greeted Yarat with a smile one morning, a piece of notepaper in her hand.

'Oliver apologizes that he has written to me, and not written to you directly, but the arrangements being complicated, he did not want there to be any misunderstandings about the details. He says −' here Sylvia scanned the sheet of paper − 'that he has arranged a berth on a ship leaving Dundee for Hudson Bay. Ah yes, very far to the north indeed. I don't know how I shall bear it, but bear it I must.'

'He has got us a place on a ship?' asked Yarat.

'Yes, my dear, an Arctic whaler, but a cabin that will be comfortable enough, I believe, so you need not worry. And Oliver is sending supplies to the ship for your life in Canada, near – let me see – Repulse Point.'

'I know of it,' said Yarat. 'And he is ready to return with us there?'

'For your sakes.'

Oliver's mother read out the letter twice, carefully, explaining the details so that Yarat would understand. 'So you see Oliver is coming home from university and he wants to take you and Little Star with him to Canada, to start a new life together, the three of you together.'

Yarat thought, it will soon be four of us, and put her hand on her stomach with a secret joy, but said nothing. She knew Oliver's mother would only find a way to use it against her. But was it true? Could Oliver really be going to take them home to Canada?

'"I have realized,"' Sylvia continued to read out, '"that my family's ways are not your ways. You can never be happy while you live here in the castle. I can see how much you long to return home to the Arctic. And I can never truly take my place in this family and be part of society so long as I have an Eskimo wife."' Here Sylvia paused, a catch in her voice. She coughed and went on. '"And so it must be that you will leave. It will be for the best. I can see that our skimpy Scottish cotton dresses and our woollen shawls do nothing to keep out the cold and the damp in winter compared to the furs you are used to."' She looked up sharply and caught a faraway look in Yarat's eyes. Yarat thinking with longing of her grandmother and her mother, sitting by the firelight chewing the seal leather soft with worn teeth. Sharing words of wisdom as they paused and sized up the softness of the leather between their fingers, knowing just when it was ready to make the most comfortable and waterproof boots. Sharing their kind words that would teach her how to live so that no bitterness would seep into her soul but she might know how to get on well with all people, since in the frozen snows she must often depend upon others for her life.

'Yarat, are you following what I am saying? What Oliver is saying.'

Yarat nodded. Oliver's mother stared at her shrewdly but Yarat's eyes showed only trust in the false words that Sylvia read aloud. For a moment, Sylvia felt guilt for what she was about to do, but she steeled her heart. She wanted only what was best for her son, what would make him truly happy.

'He says – and I will summarize – that he has arranged a passage on a boat leaving Dundee for Hudson Bay, the last to leave this year. So you must hurry to get ready and make your way to the quayside in Dundee tomorrow. Oliver will be waiting there, and since time is short, he wishes me to make all the arrangements to convey you there, though he knows it will break my heart to see you go.'

'Tomorrow? We must be ready to leave tomorrow?'

'Yes, girl. There. You have what you want. You have taken my boy from me, and I shall not see him again. And why do I not cry? My pain is far beyond tears.

'Well, why are you standing there with your mouth open? Go and pack your belongings. The maid will help you.'

A maid Yarat had never seen before, tall, thin as sticks with a rough complexion and an oddly blue nose, followed her upstairs. She stood in front of the door with arms folded while Yarat rolled the things she would take into a bundle and tied it with leather straps. For Little Star she packed a leather bag of her daughter's favourite toys and warmest clothes. By the bed, she laid out their amautis and their sealskin trousers and boots ready for early the next morning.

All night Yarat could not sleep. She sat quietly in the window, watching the stars. Watched as a white owl glided silently from the dark and landed in the branches of the great Scots pine on the lawn.

It was time to go home, but she wanted to remember this place. From the moment she arrived, she had been as homesick as Sedna in the kingdom of the birds. Yet she had already come to love much about Oliver's world, because it was part of him: the house, the gardens, and the kind servants, so unlike the brusque woman who had come in that morning. She wanted to see and feel it for as long as she could before it became a distant dream. She worried for Little Star who had settled quickly and trustingly into her flower-walled room with its soft bed and dolls and a wooden horse to ride. Little Star would remember little of living in the far North.

Yarat had been prepared to make a home for them at Kelly, for Oliver's sake, but she felt a fierce joy that he was ready to leave it, to return with her to the great land of snow. Her prince of birds would take her home. She only wished that Oliver were here with her so that they could talk and whisper of their life to come. But in the morning she would see Oliver again, waiting for her by their ship.

Long before dawn, the maid came in to rouse Yarat and roughly shake Little Star awake. She brought them a tray of tea and toast and bacon, made sure they ate it.

'Heaven knows when you'll next have something to eat. Best let the child drink her milk. And tea for you. Plenty of sugar in it. Drink it all up now.'

The air was solid and dark, smelling of rain and the distant sea, the hour before the world wakes, when secret deeds are carried out. The maid and the surly manservant chivvied Yarat into the carriage – come on now, miss, no need to stand there sniffing the air – pulled the blinds down. Little Star sat on Yarat's lap, soon asleep again, her cheek against the thick silky fur of her mother's amauti. The new maid and a manservant opposite, more like gaolers than servants, stared at these strange fur-clad creatures; the man swivel-eyed and sweaty, the red-faced woman with the blue-veined nose betraying a sneer of disgust. Yarat closed her eyes against their stares. How strange that the rocking of the carriage should make her feel sick even though she had never been ill on the seas, even more sick than that first time when she had ridden to Kelly with Oliver. A headache had come on since breakfast. She felt so tired. She tried to think on the happiness that lay ahead, Oliver waiting at the quayside, the boat with its sails unfurled, Little Star in her arms as they set sail for the far North. And the news that she would give to Oliver about the child she was carrying inside. Twice she startled awake from a deep sleep, her head rolling back and forth against the glass of the carriage window as they bumped along. She was woken by the maid shaking her shoulder roughly. It took a while to remember where she was.

'Mr Oliver will be on the ship, miss. You'd better hurry on board to greet him.'

Yarat tried to get up but her legs had turned to water and she had to be helped out of the carriage by the servants, half-dragged, half-carried onto the boat, almost falling as she crossed the gangway strung over black water far below. Behind her, an impression of a door closing and the carriage speeding away. No memory of walking down the companion steps to the lower decks, or entering a cabin, her last thought as she sank onto the bed of trying to protest that something was wrong, though no words came. For hours she wandered through hazed and anxious dreams, desperately searching for Little Star in the rooms of Kelly Castle, calling her name. But she could find no way out of the empty maze of rooms. And there was no sign of Oliver or Little Star.

She slept for thirty-six hours, did not see it grow dark and then light again, woke as evening fell a second time. She could feel the boat free of its moorings, rolling fast and steady through the seas. She sat up slowly, her head fugged and aching, took in her surroundings. But where was Little Star? In a rising panic she realized that the child was nowhere in the cabin, needing only moments to search every corner. And Oliver? And why was the door locked? She pounded on it. After a time, a man opened it.

'My child!' she cried. 'Where have you taken my child?'

The man shook his head. Kindly enough, but gruff.

'We don't have your child, missus.'

'What stupid things you say. Tell Oliver I want to speak to him. Now. Where is Oliver? Take me to him. I know he's on the boat.'

'No one called Oliver on this ship, missus.' And he began to close the cabin door on her, pushing her back inside with his wiry white arm.

'Let me out. I don't believe you. He's here on the ship. He said he would be here.'

'Looks like he didn't make it. That's the long and short of it.' He pushed her inside and locked the door again.

She felt something crushing her lungs; she couldn't breathe.

She screamed day and night for them to fetch Little Star, fetch Oliver. The captain locked the cabin.

'Best teach her some civilized ways,' he said to the first mate, who, having no papers for hiring, did everything the captain said.

No one dared voice a question about what the captain had hidden in that cabin. Old Tommy, bent over and with a few strands of tallow-white hair, scuttled in and out each day with a bowl of something but would tell no one what he saw inside. The surgeon also went in and out with a bottle of laudanum in his pocket. If the crew asked him about the moans and cries that came through the wooden partition, the surgeon, as chief consumer of laudanum on the boat, had nothing to say on the matter. Rumours grew that something terrible had been hidden in the locked cabin and many vowed to leave the ship and find another as soon as they reached Disco Bay, regretting that they had ever taken passage on this unholy vessel. For surely, a captain who would allow such evil things would have no luck, and a captain with a curse is the worst of all men to work under up in the frozen waters of the Arctic. The men began to believe that they would never come home alive from that accursed ship.

CHAPTER 36

Where was her mother? When the carriage had stopped, the maid had taken Little Star from her mother's lap and passed her to the manservant who lifted her down to the ground.

'Stand there. And don't move.'

She could smell the sea and hear the creaking of rigging. The air was cold and the dawn still an hour away. Along the waterfront, globes of yellow light from the street lanterns showed gangs of men working dockside, the sky breaking open, red and dark purple over the horizon.

The maid and the man had to help her mother down the step. Was her mother sick? Her steps were unsteady and strange, her weight leaning against the maid. Little Star went and held tight to her mother's hand, her cheek against the silky deep fur of her caribou amauti. But her mother's grip was loose and slippery and Little Star had to keep taking her mother's hand each time it flopped away. And it was so hard to keep in step, her mother moving along in strange jolts, half-pulled by the servants towards the great ships that loomed above them at the quayside. So many people and carts, even at this hour, bales of jute stacked like a fort. Noises made her jump and startle, rattling wheels, shouts and curses. Two seagulls swooped down, screaming at each other as they fought over scraps on the stones. Little Star put her hands over her ears. Closed her eyes. When she opened them again, there were legs and shoes and people calling, but where was her mother? There was no sign of her. She pushed her way through a forest of legs, looked up and down. Began to run this way and that, dodging between people. So many boats. But which one was theirs? She called out, in English, in Inuit, calling for her mother. Why did her mother let go of her hand? Frightened, confused, she walked from one end of the docks to the other, running back again. The sun climbed to its height, more people swarmed the docks, carts rumbled by.

She found a place to hide behind a stack of barrels until her mother should come to fetch her. The sun set and it began to go dark again. Then tears started running down her cheeks, because she could not believe that her mother had not yet come. It grew so late, the ships asleep on the water, the whale lamps casting circles of light. Hungry, exhausted, she lay on a pile of scratchy sacks behind the tarry barrels and cried herself to sleep.

When she awoke, she found herself in a smoky room that smelled of alcohol, a ring of men and women looking down on her.

'Well, well, here's a catch,' says a man. 'What kind of animal do you think this is?'

'It's no beast. It's a little Eskimo girl,' said a woman with a shawl wrapped around her shoulders, a breakfast of beer in her hand. 'Can you do us a dance, Eskimo girl?' The woman poked her with her foot and Little Star kicked back in fright. The woman jumped away, spilling her beer.

'Mind she doesn't bite you,' said another woman. 'Here, give it some of this to drink to keep it tame.'

Someone put a glass to her lips. A burning taste in her throat that made her cough. The faces around her laughed. Curled up in a ball of fur, she lay still as a mouse under a table, the wooden floor giving off stale smells of beer and spirits and bad things, watching boots and clogs and faces as people came in to look at her, jostling to see. The landlady started to charge twopence to see the savage child.

By mid-morning, rumours of a child that was half-human half-beast had spread along the Dundee docks, travelling along Overgate and into the tenements and narrow streets passing between the mill workers as they left their shift in droves. And this was how Mary, coming home from work, came to hear of a small child clad in fur, found abandoned among the whaler boats. A child with red hair and grey eyes.

Mary had seen Little Star at Charlotte's studio, and she had been to lunch, in her best serge dress, with Charlotte, Oliver, Yarat and Little Star at a hotel in Dundee. Afterwards they had walked to the solicitor's office on the Perth Road where Mary was witness to a document making Charlotte the principal guardian of Little Star should anything happen to her parents. Which did not bear thinking about, but with all that Oliver had lived through, and knowing how Charlotte had been raised without parents, he had been anxious to put it in place. For though Little Star would also remain a ward of her grandparents while they lived, Oliver understood that they would do nothing to help her find pride in her Inuit heritage. Charlotte, however, he could trust to teach Little Star to value and understand her mother's people. And Charlotte was kind. She would bring warmth to a child who might need it.

Knowing Mrs Gillan and knowing Charlotte, Mary could see the wisdom in Oliver's provision.

'Though these documents will never be needed,' Charlotte had said as she signed them.

Frowning, Mary now hurried to the Arctic Inn down by the docks, where the sailors went to pour their pay down their throats and break each other's heads. How could the child, if it were she, have ended up there? Pushing through the crowds, she saw a bundle of wet fur on the dirty wooden boards. A smell of urine from the frightened child, too terrified no doubt to move. Kneeling down, Mary called her name.

At first, Little Star would not open her eyes. Mary crept under the table, began to tell stories about the times she had met the child, about Oliver and her mother. The eyes flickered open, fastened on Mary's, and she let herself be coaxed out. For the gawpers crowding round the table, Mary used the voice she served up to lazy mill girls or thieving trolley boys, the one that could be heard above the thunder of machinery, even by those made hard of hearing from years in the mill.

'I know this child, and her father is a respectable man of means who you would do well not to cross. And why has no one given her a cup of warm milk with sugar in it to stop her shivering? She will come with me and I will contact her father to take her home.'

Carrying Little Star, Mary cleared a path through the onlookers, the landlady mumbling that she'd no right to take the little circus girl and stop her earning an honest penny.

Out on the dock, Little Star hot and feverish, Mary looked for a cab, and using her own hard-earned pennies to pay the driver, took the child back to her lodgings in Shepherd's Loan. She paid a neighbour's boy a shilling to go and send a telegram to Oliver in Edinburgh, and one to Charlotte asking her to come. Charlotte would know what to do.

She did not send a message to the castle. Mary's instincts told her that Sylvia would somehow be behind this neglect.

Mary tried several times to ask the child what had become of her mother. Little Star turned fearful eyes on Mary, but said nothing. It seemed that Little Star had forgotten how to speak.

The child slept in the alcove bed in the kitchen that night, Mary sitting up to watch over her. Charlotte came the moment she got Mary's message. They whispered together about what could have happened for Little Star to be wandering alone without her mother as they waited for Oliver to arrive.

'But where is Yarat?' said Charlotte. 'She would never willingly part with Little Star.'

'I heard that someone had seen a woman in fur clothes on the docks, who looked dead drunk or ill. But where she is now, no one could say.'

'The whole story fills me with foreboding,' said Charlotte. 'Nothing sounds right. We will give the child only into Oliver's care. Because if what I suspect is true, then Sylvia cannot be trusted with Little Star. We'll send no message to Sylvia yet, not until we have spoken with Oliver.'

When the child woke, her eyes wide and terrified, Mary put a bowl of bread and milk before her, and though she ate a little she remained mute. In spite of Charlotte's gentle questions, Little Star still gave no clue as to where Yarat had gone. When her father arrived, distraught and shocked, she clung to him.

'Where is your anaana?' Oliver asked her. 'Little Star, dearest, where is she?' But Little Star just shook her head.

Sylvia had been in a panic all night. The two servants she had hired to escort Yarat onto the ship should have returned with the child long ago. She had waited for them expectantly until long into the morning. She wanted the child home. Without the mother's pernicious heathen influence, then dear little Eugenia – and enough with the ridiculous name Oliver still used, let her have a Christian name – would learn to behave like a civilized creature. She would become a true grandchild to Sylvia.

But dawn broke, the hours went by and still there was no sign of the carriage or a small child with auburn hair. Convinced Yarat had managed to take Eugenia with her, Sylvia sat at the library window, stony faced and distraught. The truth was, she had no idea where the child was. She had lost her only grandchild, and she now bitterly regretted her plan. If she could only go back forty-eight hours, before any of it had been set in motion, and see Eugenia again. She'd even bear Yarat for that.

When she heard a carriage arriving, she rushed outside. She was shocked to see Oliver. How had he heard so quickly? What was she going to tell him? Sylvia gasped with relief to see that Little Star was with him – and that Yarat was not.

Oliver descended from the black hansom cab, white as a winding sheet, with a cough as rough as an old man's death rattle as he carried the child inside.

'Mother,' he called out as he came near. 'Is she here? Has Yarat returned?'

Little Star, in his arms, stared at Sylvia with large, angry eyes.

Sylvia launched into a tale of betrayal as they walked into the castle, wild-eyed, pacing and sobbing, how Yarat had sneaked away in the dead of night, taking his child with her. She did not seem aware that Oliver sat crushed, pale as a ghost, as she ranted on.

Sylvia bent down. 'Child, what a terrible time you have had. You must not be sure what was waking and what was a nightmare. How your mother ran away and abandoned you? You recall her leaving you, yes?'

'Mother, she won't speak. She is so terrified that she can't make a sound.'

Sylvia almost collapsed with relief.

'Come with me child, and I will take care of you. Oliver, go and sit by the fire and tell them to send you hot wine, or you will be sick indeed. And we all know who to blame for that.'

'The thing I find hardest to believe,' Sylvia told him as they sat in the library later, the roaring fire causing Oliver to sweat as he coughed every so often into a handkerchief, 'is that she could have abandoned the child so heartlessly. When I think what might have happened with the child so close to the water, and the people there are of low morals who will sell anything. Kidnapped onto a boat going anywhere in the world. If she hadn't been brought back by a servant who recognized her. . . It's a mercy we saw the child again.'

'Enough,' said Oliver. 'Mother, please let us try and piece together what actually happened. You say Yarat must have left before dawn, that she arranged for someone to come here and take the carriage without your consent. Then the carriage was abandoned at the dock and neither Yarat nor her helpers found again, just Little Star.'

'I believe so,' murmured Sylvia.

'But Little Star left wandering on her own. Nothing in this sounds like the woman I know, my Yarat.'

Sylvia gave a sour look. 'And yet there you have it. Eugenia was left to wander at peril of her life. Yarat gone, most probably on one of the whaling boats back to the Arctic. The dissembling, the deceit, insisting how much she cared for you when all the while she was planning to run away.'

'But why? Why? When we were talking of how we would make a new life together,' Oliver said, half to himself.

Sylvia bristled. Was there still no remorse from Oliver, no hint of feeling for how alone he would have left her, his own mother? The savage's influence was still strong as a witch's spell. Sylvia rose and took his cold hand in hers like a doctor feeling for an illness.

'Dearest Oliver, how can you, or I, or anyone know what goes on in the mind of a creature from a savage race, who lived as though the Bible had never been written, eating raw flesh, dressed in animal skins? Darling boy, if we can only save the child, bring her into the fold of all that is holy and civilized and good, for her own sake, then perhaps that is the best we can hope for.'

'Don't you see? Little Star will never recover from this. All I can do now is tell her that her mother would never willingly choose to abandon her. Never choose to leave me.'

'Yes, yes. I know. It is so hard to contemplate. Such treachery.'

'In the morning, I will go to the docks again and question every man and woman until I can sew together the truth, scrap by scrap.' Oliver's cough was now so persistent that he could no longer speak, his face grey and clammy. Sylvia had to call for Tom Griddle to help him up to his room.

'Tell me all you saw on that last night Yarat was here,' Oliver asked him, in between attempts to catch his breath.

'But, sir, I can't tell you what happened. There were no servants in the house. Mrs Gillan gave us all the night off to go home to our families. And very kind of her it was too. Who knew that it would turn out so badly here? Though I'm heartily sorry for it now, sir. She had a lovely way with her, Miss Yarat. So kind to us. She didn't know all our customs here, but she was a born lady.'

Oliver rose early the next morning, and feeling a little better packed a small travelling bag. Little Star was still asleep in bed. He woke her gently to tell her that he would be gone for a while. And when he came home, he would bring her mother back to her.

CHAPTER 37

Little Star stood at the window in the upper hallway looking out across the drive. The second time she had been there all day, refusing to eat, falling into a limp mass that the maids could barely lift, so determined was she to slip back down to the floor and stay by the window. Besides, if they touched the child, her screams were terrible. Like a dog in pain, or lowing for hours like a calf taken from its mother. Worst of all, the long silence. Little Star stayed there until the sun went down, clutching some fur garment that smelled rank, eyes full of grim anger, staring at the window as the daylight disappeared.

They came by with plates of food that she kicked at. Or they talked to her in their language. Eugenia, they kept saying. Why didn't they call her by her name? She stared into their eyes and tried to convey the importance of her own words. Anaana. Mother. I want to see Mother. And sometimes she called out for Nuturalak. Nuturalak. Baby. Where is the baby?

'What's that she's saying?' said the stable boy who had been sent up to try and lift her into her room. He was good with difficult horses, though even he had never known a kicking and biting like it. He too had left the child sobbing on the floor, standing back, a little afraid of her.

'It's that savage gibberish they talk,' said the under maid. 'What's the mistress going to do with a little heathen like that in the house?'

'Hush,' said the second maid. Remember, she might be your mistress one day.'

'I doubt that,' said the groom, watching the child rigid and screaming.

'And remember, not a word of this to anyone, how savage the child's become, showing her true nature now. Not until the mistress has got her tamed into Christian ways.'

The maid bent down. 'Wouldn't you like a nice cup of milk, miss?'

The child screamed louder.

'Perhaps she has forgotten all her English.'

'She understands well enough. She chats happily with Master Oliver when he's here. Well, if you don't want anything to eat or to drink we'll take the tray away and leave you then, Miss Eugenia. Bring it back when you've nicer manners, and when you're finally hungry enough to eat something. Though goodness knows when that will be.'

Her name was Little Star, the one that stood by the brightest star in the sky; just as she and her mother were never parted, so those two stars were never parted, dancing in the sky among the mountains and streams of red and green lights when the winter was at its darkest.

Her mother was the warmth she lay against day and night, cradled against her mother's back inside her amauti, deep inside the silky caribou skins that were warm and never dampened by her small breaths, the skins part of her mother's skin, part of her, Little Star. If she was hungry, then her mother would read her movements and swiftly pull her forward to feed against her breast, holding the child inside the fur layers safe from the most bitter storm that the gods could throw at them. She slept soundly, her heartbeat calm, a smaller, faster clapping inside the steady drumbeat of her mother's heart.

When she woke, the two women in white aprons and caps were back with the tray, a cup of water, cold toast.

'Pity that mother of hers didn't take the child with her when she ran off,' said the under maid. 'Is there any news of when Master Oliver's back?'

'Nothing as yet. Though if I was him I wouldn't bother chasing after her.'

'I hear he's been down to the docks in Dundee for days now, asking everyone if they've seen her. Though I don't know what he intends to do if they have – get on a boat and sail after her into the Arctic seas?'

'I wouldn't put it past him. Seemed to think his savage woman was better than the finest lady in Fife.'

'Maggie Silver says she was an Eskimo witch. Says she put a spell on Mr Oliver.'

'We'd better be careful this one doesn't put a curse on us then.'

They moved back a little. Agreed to leave the child to scream, come back when she was quieter.

Sometimes that tall woman in dark Qallunaat clothes came, stood and watched her.

'Nuturalak. Nuturalak,' she said to Sylvia, urgent and pleading. She was old enough to know that a baby was coming. Her mother was gone, she wanted her mother back, but the baby was gone too. She had promised her mother to care for her little brother, this gift from Sedna, but how could she now? Her mother had told her that when it was time for the baby to take her place against her mother's skin, she would win new freedoms and should feel proud to be so grown, but at night Little Star had still snuggled close to her mother and her mother said she would have enough milk for both her children if Little Star asked. Though often she preferred the red meat that her mother chewed and put in her mouth when the family ate in the snow house so many moons ago.

Her father she loved too, taller and paler than all the other men in the tribe. When they came to the white men's place, he had cast off his furs and put on the Qallunaat clothes with ease, because he was of them, but her mother refused to remove her caribou and sealskins for many days. She had walked around the big house – it was bigger than any meeting igloo – wearing her amauti, holding Little Star by the hand.

Now, the tall woman in dark clothes looked down on Little Star, shook her head with an expression of disgust on her face. Little Star's hair was matted, her face streaked with dust and tears.

'Let me go home!' she shouted. 'Let me go to my mother.'

'There is no point punishing us with your screams, child. Don't you remember? She left you. Abandoned you on the quayside and left you to drown for all she knew or cared. Your mother, child, did not want you.' And in case Little Star had not understood, she repeated this message slowly, twice, until a hurt registered in the child's eyes.

Little Star went limp and quiet. She lay and thought about the words. They were not true. But they crept inside her heart like cold fingers. She left me. She left me alone, little Star whispered silently, while something cold and hungry wound itself around her heart, and she felt that she had died and turned into a hungry ghost that would never feel satisfied.

Sylvia looked down at the limp mass, shook her head. 'So you're remembering now. You see, we did not want you either, but we will do our duty and keep you. And at least you will have your papa when he returns from the dockside, running around in this weather trying to get news of that woman, your mother, when it's quite clear she does not want to be found.'

The maid appeared behind her. The child raised her head, understanding that there might be a message. News of her mother?

'Marion, is Master Oliver back yet?'

'No, ma'am. But he sent word. He's looking for a boat, ma'am, to go to the Arctic, on one of the whalers. Says we must send his luggage. Says he'll find her and bring her back. And he's sent this letter for the child.'

Sylvia screamed. 'On a whaler! His health won't take it. Send Thomas and Arnold at once. They must find him and bring him back. His life depends on it. Give me the letter. And go.'

Sylvia broke open the seal.

My darling little one,

I know your mother would never leave us and take your sweet brother or sister with her. I know that something has befallen her. My dear heart, I will find her and bring them back to you. Be very brave, be very good, and I will be home as soon as I can. I will kiss you every night.

Your fondest Papa

Little Star sat up, arms held out for the paper. 'What does he say?' she asked, her English clear of a sudden.

'He says he doesn't want you, child. It says you can stay here and rot for all he cares.' And taking the letter with her, Sylvia ran quickly up the stairs in a rustle of black silk.

Little Star lay down, quiet as a fallen leaf. She was not even a ghost now. She was nothing. She lay until the moonlight came through the tall window and she felt herself turning to ice and stone, her heart bitter and brackish as the winter sea.

That night, they brought Oliver home in a carriage, barely conscious. No boat had wanted to take such a sick man on board, even though he had offered to pay for his passage north several times over. The doctor was sent for, and explained to Sylvia that she must prepare herself for her son's final days.

Oliver spent the next few weeks writing letters from his bed, begging for news of his wife, sending them out across Canada and the whaling ports of Greenland and Nantucket. Sometimes he was able to get up and play with Little Star, each time shorter than the last.

CHAPTER 38

Desperate for news of Oliver, Charlotte had decided that she would present herself at Kelly and demand to see him. Mary brought some second-hand rumours from the mill. Some reports said he was getting better, others that he had but days to live. Everyone agreed, however, that his mother was becoming stranger by the day, talk of her sacking staff, putting the child on strange diets with no flesh, then days when Little Star was allowed nothing but milk and beef broth.

Charlotte worried for Oliver and she worried for Little Star. She remembered the night she had held Little Star on her lap while Mary made soup and tried to get the child to drink a little. Each time they tried to lay her down on the bed, she had clung on to Charlotte and refused to let go. When Oliver arrived, full of questions about Yarat that they could not answer, she and Mary had been horrified at how sick he had become in such a short while. With a twist to her heart she had realized that what had seemed academic, her position as a guardian to Little Star, might soon become reality.

She and Mary had seen Sylvia in one of her nervous crises before when they were children, how Aunt Sylvia had had to go away to rest in a sanatorium for half the summer. The rumours of what was happening at Kelly, Sylvia screaming blame at the child, Uncle Gregor unable to contain his wife, now made Charlotte determined in what she knew she must do.

She asked to see the lawyer who had drawn up her guardianship of Little Star. Her pretext for going to Kelly would be to deliver the painting of Yarat and Little Star, now finally finished. But before she could order a carriage to take her there, Mary came running to the house, her eyes puffy from tears.

Oliver had passed away in the night.

A few days later, Mary and Charlotte sat at the back of St Monan's church, holding tight to each other's hands, Oliver's coffin on trestles at the front. The church was full, but Sylvia still picked them out with her eyes as she followed the coffin out at the service's end, shooting them a look of hate. Behind her walked the small figure of Little Star, dressed in black, her head bowed under a wide black hat. Charlotte wept to see the pain and confusion in her face. Uncle Gregor walked behind, his eyes seeming to see nothing, an old and broken man.

Charlotte and Mary followed the crowd into the windswept churchyard, the sea hushing and sighing as the coffin was lowered into the ground. Little Star threw her handful of earth before the grave was closed, and Sylvia yanked the child back when she lingered a moment too long at the graveside.

Charlotte knew what she must do. She had the lawyer's letter, she had Oliver's request, and she had the means to care for Little Star. In the morning, she would go to Kelly, invited or not.

Sylvia swept down the staircase. She wore full mourning, jet jewellery glinting in the cold light from the window. She stopped when she saw Charlotte standing inside the door in her travelling suit, her gloves in her hand. Sylvia's face was gaunt, the colour of parchment. She looked to have aged ten years in a few weeks.

'You,' she spat out at Charlotte. 'You have no invitation. What are you doing here?'

'I've come for the child, Sylvia. You must know that Oliver made Little Star my ward. If I am not convinced that she will thrive here, then it is my duty to take her into my care. And after what I have heard and seen, the changes in the child, I feel that that is what I must do.'

'Are you completely mad? Eugenia belongs here. Oliver was sick when he wrote that very odd coda to his will. Not at all in his right mind. And after all the trouble I have taken, to civilize the child – my only grandchild, mark you – I can tell you that I am not about to allow you to take her away. Ruin her again with your ideas.'

'That's exactly why I will take her with me. To stop you poisoning the child against herself and who she is.'

Charlotte took a letter from her satchel, opened it out and held it in front of Sylvia.

'And there is more. Something you cannot fight, unless you wish to spend time in a jail. I have been sent information from a certain crewman. I know Yarat is still alive, how you tricked her into leaving without her daughter.'

Sylvia snatched the letter, her eyes moving over the lines. She looked stunned, trapped.

'And now my task is to find Yarat and bring Little Star home to her mother.'

Sylvia laughed. 'You think you will take my granddaughter to the Arctic, to live surrounded by savages? On the word of a common crewman from a whaling ship? What life would it be for her now that she's used to the comforts of this house? She does not even remember the savage life she was born into. And I'll not have it put about that the descendants of the Gillans have gone to live like heathens, in huts made of dirt and ice, wearing animal skins. Eating raw flesh. Living little better than the beasts. It would kill me to know she might live like that.'

'I'm sorry, Sylvia. I have a lawyer in Edinburgh ready to uphold my guardianship, and we are willing to get the police involved, if that is what you wish. Now, if you will please tell the maids to get Little Star's things ready, a case of warm clothes, any books or toys she would like, then I will wait here until she comes down.'

'I don't believe I will,' said Sylvia.

'The child has the right to see her mother again.'

'I can see my mother?'

Charlotte looked up to see Little Star standing on the stairs, her face pale, dark red hair pulled into two tight plaits. A pinafore over a grey dress. 'May I go with Aunt Charlotte, Grandmama?'

'Go back to the nursery, Eugenia. Go upstairs now.'

But Charlotte had crossed the hallway to the bottom of the stairs, hands together as if in prayer.

'Little Star, your mother is alive. I know she wants to see you. She must be so sad to have been without you for so long. Come with me now. We'll take a boat soon and find her again.'

The child frowned, shaking her head. 'But she left me. My mama didn't want me.'

'It's not true. They took her away. They stole her from you. And I can take you back to her one day.'

Little Star slipped past Sylvia and ran down the stairs. Charlotte opened her arms to welcome her.

With a shrill cry, Sylvia rushed at them. 'I'd rather die than let her go back there. Better that she die.'

Sylvia snatched a letter opener from the tray on the hall table. Charlotte saw the blade catch the light as it swung towards Little Star. Before she could form a thought or a plan, Charlotte had stepped forward and grabbed Sylvia's wrist. Sylvia bucked and bit as they fought. Little Star backed away against the wall. The knife flashed again, the two women pressed together in one mass, falling to the floor. Then they fell apart.

The silver handle of the knife stuck out from Sylvia's chest, her eyes open and unblinking.

Charlotte stumbled to a standing position. Oliver's father was at the top of the stairs. His face broken by sorrow. The day he had feared for so long had arrived, when Sylvia's madness would trigger a chain of events from which there was no coming back – when Sylvia in her madness would be lost to him entirely.

He walked down the stairs heavily, holding on to the banister as though the house were tipping on the seas. He told a maid to whisk Eugenia up to her room, administer brandy so that the child would sleep, all that she had seen put down to a nightmare while she had dozed that afternoon.

Then Oliver's father and Charlotte stood over the body, she rigid with the shock of what she had done. The old man with tears running down his cheeks because he remembered Sylvia as a lovely young bride, arriving at the castle with so much energy and joy. And weeping because he recalled Charlotte as a child playing in the grounds, and who would surely now hang for what she had done. He bent down, kissed his wife on the cheek, stroked her hair and then stood up.

'Listen to me, Charlotte. You must leave now. If anyone should say how Sylvia died, then you will forfeit your life. I saw with my own eyes that you only did what you did to save the child. The maids will be loyal to me, to you. But I tell you, you must go now, not a moment to lose.'

'I can't go,' said Charlotte. 'I promised Oliver that I would care for Little Star.'

'Which you cannot do if you are in a prison or worse.'

She shook her head. Looked around the walls for an answer. What choice was left to her?

'Then will you ask Mary to come? I trust Mary to care well for Little Star.'

'I promise, dear Charlotte. I may have been in a torpor not knowing how to manage Sylvia's outbursts of late, but I see now that I must care for the girl, my own grandchild.'

'Can I say goodbye to her?'

'Best not. No time.'

'Then tell her I embrace her, tell her that I will love her always.'

After Charlotte had gone, a groom covered Sylvia in canvas and laid her in the back of a cart. When it was dark he dug a hole in the lawns at the back of the Laundry Cottage. He and Mr Gillan laid Sylvia to rest and covered her over with the red earth of Fife.

Mr Gillan then sent a message to Charlotte's lawyer, saying that Miss Charlotte had decided to leave directly for Arctic lands and had left no message as to when she would return. The lawyer was to contact her through a post box in Canada.

There were few staff at Kelly that night. The two maids and the groom who knew what had occurred were too loyal to gossip, and were paid well to move far away soon afterwards. Mr Gillan let it be known that his wife, Sylvia, had become suddenly unwell and was away recovering in a sanatorium in the Swiss Alps. Two years after that Mr Gillan would send out a letter to say that his dear wife had passed away in the sanatorium, where the funeral had taken place attended by close family. And many evenings, Mr Gillan would walk along the woods at the back of the Laundry Cottage, stopping at a certain point to lay down the flower he carried from the gardens.

If Eugenia loved anyone as she grew up over the following years, then it was Mary. But Mary could see that Eugenia never quite gave all her heart to anybody, remaining for ever watchful, guarded and secretive, refusing to answer to the name Little Star or to admit that she had ever spoken in another tongue.

And if Eugenia had found the words to explain how she felt, then she might have said that in the end everyone abandoned her. There was something unseemly and ill-fitting about her, a half-breed that made them leave her.

As soon as she turned eighteen, Eugenia dismissed Mary, who was deeply upset, ready to stay on at Kelly as long as Eugenia needed her, and even more sad when Eugenia refused to keep in touch, perhaps because she knew too much of her shameful history. In the end, Mary accepted the proposal of the groom who had been sweet on her for so long and together they moved to Dundee.

Eugenia organized herself a year in a finishing school. She married very well at twenty-one. Over the years she became known in the best social circles of Fife as a very grand lady, who always insisted on things being done correctly.

No one knew of the little hand-sewn Inuit doll that she had hidden away in a secret drawer, or of her father's letters and diary, also hidden away like shameful secrets. And the beautiful picture of Yarat and Little Star in sealskins that Charlotte had painted, Eugenia asked Mary to burn it.

Far away, abandoned on the coast of Baffin Island, Yarat and her child were taken in by a tribe of her people. And though she never stopped seeking a passage back to Dundee on one of the passing whalers, none would ever take her.

CHAPTER 39

When Martha and Caro took the diary back to Shona, they had many questions – which Shona seemed to expect.

'I'm only so grateful your mother left the mill and went to look after Little Star,' said Martha.

'As soon as Oliver's father came to the mill, a broken man by all accounts, and called my mother into the office to ask her if she would come back and care for the child, my mother didn't hesitate. She dropped all her life in Dundee and went back to Kelly, even though Kelly had rejected her a few years before. She knew Charlotte wanted it, and my mother, you see, also loved the little girl already, as Oliver's child. Just as she had grown to love his wife, Yarat. And of course, my mother kept in touch with Charlotte after she had to leave, sent her letters and photographs to let her know how Little Star was getting on.'

'Mary knew where Charlotte was?'

'Yes. Charlotte wrote to her often as she travelled across the Americas. She went right up into Canada, painting, riding out with a wagon train at one time. And that was how she met Joe, a native American Indian. They never married officially, but they were together for the rest of her life. I have some of the sketches that Charlotte sent back to my mother, though she could never share them with anyone at the time. It was very hard that she couldn't tell Little Star that Charlotte was still alive, that she loved her and watched over her, but she did all she could to make Little Star feel that love was there for her.'

'It sounds as though Mary made her childhood happy in the end.'

'She did. Though it was always sad, my mother felt, that Little Star refused to breathe a word about her Inuit family, or even mention her mother's name. But the really hard thing for my mother was that when Eugenia ended my mother's role at Kelly she wanted to cut all ties to her own past and anyone who knew about it. She refused to keep in touch. She turned over a lot of the staff from that time, brought in new people. Didn't want anyone to remember her childhood. She even ordered the beautiful painting that Charlotte did of her and her mother in native costume to be burned.'

'What a pity. It would have been wonderful to see it.'

'You can if you like.'

'What did you say?'

'My mother couldn't bear to burn it. And I think it's time it went home to Kelly now. Come with me.'

They followed Shona through into the dining room. On the opposite wall, at the far end of a gleaming mahogany table, an oil painting hung on the wall. Two figures in brown and cream furs, a mother and a child against a sparkling background of white snow and blue sky. So beautiful that both Caro and Martha gasped out aloud.

Pulling up in front of the castle, with the painting wrapped in blankets in the back of the car, Martha paused to look up at the castle as though she had never seen it before.

'Somewhere, in one of those windows, a small child would have stood, waiting for a mother,' she said. 'If only we could go back in time, gather that child up and tell her she was loved. Nothing's more important in a family than the children. Those bonds between us make the net that keeps them safe. And poor Little Star, she fell right through a most terrible gap.'

They carried the painting in together, one at each end, as it finally came home to Kelly.

A few days before Christmas, the tree decorated in the hallway, all the candles lit – Alasdair on hand with a bucket of water just in case – they held the traditional carol singing at Kelly with family and neighbours. Caro looked around the smiling faces.

By next spring, would Kelly be in the hands of a hotel chain? The finances to keep the castle were still far from secure, even if the National Trust did get involved.

Especially now that Diana had siphoned off some of their funds. The week before, Alasdair had gone into Edinburgh to confront her in a meeting at the auctioneer's that she worked for.

When he got back, Alasdair had rubbed his head in his hands. How grey and tired his skin looked, the lines at the corners of his eyes and mouth that almost made Caro feel worried for him.

'How did it go?'

'The auction house had already had their suspicions but it took them a while to get the proof. Diana denied everything, of course, but the evidence was there.'

'So what will happen?'

Alasdair had shrugged. 'She says she'll pay it all back. At least, her parents will.'

'Her parents must be horrified,' said Martha.

'But won't the police need to be involved?' asked Caro.

'The auction house could report her, but it would do nothing for their reputation. She's leaving for Canada to stay with a distant cousin and that's probably for the best. Let's just hope she's learned her lesson,' said Alasdair.

Martha had sighed. 'Diana always did have strange ideas about what one could or couldn't do. I used to worry that she and Alasdair might end up together one day. Diana's never been someone to sow happiness around her, but this really was a shocker. Stealing from us. At least it's all over now.'

After the carol singing was finished, the guests gone, Barbara and Caro were washing up glasses and plates in the kitchen when there was a knock on the front door.

'Bit late,' said Caro. 'Probably one of the guests forgot something.' She hurried to open it.

A man in a trilby hat and mac was standing with his back to the door. He turned as she opened it and looked at her quizzically.

There was something about him that made Caro uneasy.

'Yes?' she asked. 'May I help you?'

'You said to come to the back door, but I wasn't sure where that was in a place like this. You haven't forgotten our appointment? I know it's been a while.'

He spoke with an American accent.

'I'm sorry. I don't recall.'

'You are Diana? Diana Stokes.'

'I see,' said Caro. 'Diana. And if you could remind me of your name?'

'Bob Brierly, from the Sunshine Golf Company. You said it would be a good time to show me around, with the family out this afternoon. And we've certainly been paying you enough to get them to sell this place, so a quick tour of what we'll be buying would be welcome. I take it they have agreed to sell at last.'

'Still one or two small things to iron out. In fact, plans were changed, the owner's son's here. This would be a very good moment for you to meet him. Why don't you come inside, admire the hall while you wait and I'll run and get him directly?'

'Thank you, Miss Stokes.'

A few minutes later, Alasdair and Caro came down the stairs together.

'I'm afraid there's been a mistake, Mr Brierly,' said Alasdair. 'Diana Stokes has no agreement with us regarding the sale of Kelly. And we have no intention of selling. So if you have been paying her for her help, then I can only say you've wasted your money. You do know that Diana is planning on leaving the country tomorrow?'

'That can't be right. We had an agreement. You were desperate to sell—'

'I think she must still be at her cottage, packing. Why don't you give her a call? Tell her you're at Kelly, waiting for her. Perhaps don't mention we are here, just say Barbara let you in to wait.'

When Diana unlocked the front door and came into the hallway she found Mr Brierly, Caro, Alasdair and Martha waiting for her in the hallway. She drew in her breath, paused, then smiled apologetically.

'I'm so glad you're all here. I wanted to explain. What a foolish girl I must seem, having tried so hard to help get a top price with Mr Brierly, only to realize that it was actually the last thing you wanted of late, selling Kelly. And poor Mr Brierly, I did try so hard but I have been quite useless to you.' She gave a little pout. 'And now I truly must dash.'

Mr Brierly moved to position himself in front of the door. 'I don't think you will be dashing anywhere at the moment, Diana,' said Mr Brierly. 'Not until you've explained how you plan to repay the cash you've taken under false pretences. Unless you'd rather explain to the police. Or perhaps, do you carry a cheque book?'

Diana stared at him with hatred, seeming to be calculating figures in her head. Almost stamping, she hissed, 'Very well. Come with me to the cottage. Though believe me, this lot will be crawling to you soon enough, begging you to take this crumbling pile off their hands.'

And not looking back, Diana left. Mr Brierly followed close behind.

Martha closed the door. 'Thank goodness they're gone,' she said. 'What a horrible evening.'

'Of all the blessed cheek,' said Alasdair, picking up Mr Brierly's business card from the side table.

'Let's just hope we don't have to use it to call him,' said Martha gloomily, shutting her eyes for a moment.

Christmas at Kelly was poignant with the realization that it might be their last one there, snow falling on Christmas Eve as they came out of midnight communion in the village church, Felicity thrilled with her doll from Grandfather, board games, a perfectly roasted brace of ducks, the Queen's speech on the wireless, everything conspiring to be the perfect Christmas.

Shortly after New Year's Day, the phone rang.

'That was Alex Garvie, ' Alasdair told Caro. 'Reminding us about our meeting with those rather tricky solicitors, the ones who've been dealing with Louisa Glenconner's estate. He's still hoping to get some information out of them. Mother, is it all right for your lawyer friend to come along with us, help us look a bit official? Not quite sure what Mr Garvie hopes to achieve but it could be interesting to hear what the solicitors have to say. We might even learn something new about Charlotte.'

A few days later, Caro and Alasdair sat in the offices of Corcoran and Gillespie, solicitors to the Glenconner estate. Martha's friend Duncan Ballintyre, KC, sat by their side. Across the desk sat Mr Corcoran, a plump man with a brown chalk-stripe suit, hair so oiled it filled the room with a sickly perfume.

He pretended to be delighted that they had come to enquire about the sad case of a bequest without heirs, though he regretted that he could see no grounds, unfortunately, to consider the Gillan family sufficiently associated with the bequest for him to bring out all the associated documents, which if he did would only serve to back up his case that the inheritance remained, at present, impossible to execute.

Alasdair lit his cigarette and became friend and man of the world. Caro wide-eyed as she asked difficult questions. The lawyer quoted articles and precedents.

Shortly afterwards, Mr Gillespie produced a key to a strong box and they gathered around the contents.

Sifting through the papers, they found a document signed by Oliver, naming Charlotte as Little Star's guardian in the event of his death. And a document stating that Charlotte had willed all her estate to Little Star as her ward and goddaughter.

'I think,' said the lawyer, holding up the two documents, 'that it may be time for you to hand over your executorship to another firm, Mr Corcoran, because either you have been rather negligent in failing to put two and two together, or simply fraudulent.'

'Mummy, did you have a couple of sherries this afternoon? You seem – how shall I say it – elated?' said Pippa who had dropped by for supper with her husband.

'I am elated,' Martha said. 'Though it is nothing to do with sherry. Shall we tell them, Caro?'

Caro nodded. 'A phone call came from the new solicitors to Louisa's granddaughter's estate. It seems that since Charlotte was named as Eugenia's guardian and she left a will bequeathing all she had to Eugenia, that makes Eugenia's descendants the only named beneficiaries to Louisa's estate. The solicitor believes that Eugenia should legally be considered an adopted child of Charlotte's, more or less.'

'And it is a considerable sum,' said Martha. 'Enough to keep Kelly going for many, many years. Although, since I've talked to the National Trust, I still like the idea of sharing the castle with people who would be interested to see it a couple of days a week.'

'Oh Mummy, we'll have to get you a little ticket machine,' said Pippa. 'But that is wonderful news indeed.'

'It is,' said Caro. 'But there is one other piece of news. Now that the inquest is over, the coroner is going to release Sylvia's remains for burial. We'll be able to have a small ceremony together to place her in the family plot in the churchyard, next to her husband. And at the same time I think we should add a dedication to Oliver's wife.'

Martha nodded. 'Yes, they may have died so very far apart, but they never stopped loving each other. It's time to write Yarat's name next to Oliver's.'

CHAPTER 40

They weren't expecting a reply. Goodness knows, Caro had written to enough places around Hudson Bay and Baffin Island, asking if anyone remembered a whaling ship called the *Narwhal*, on which an Inuit woman married a ship's doctor and travelled to his home in Scotland. She received various stories remembered by the Inuit elders, but nothing that matched Oliver's story.

Then a letter came from a woman called Astrid Lesage, Professor of People's Culture at the University of Toronto. She had a Norwegian father and an Inuit mother. She had spent the last few years travelling across the Inuit territories collecting stories and histories before the present generation of elders passed away, taking their culture with them.

She wrote to say that she had heard a story, from several different sources, of an Inuit woman who married a white shaman with red hair who could heal bodies, who came to the Inuit lands on a great ship named *Narwhal*. The Inuit woman had travelled far away to his land, to a great stone house, but she was tricked into boarding a ship that brought her back across the sea to the land of her birth and she was not able to find a way to get home to her red-haired shaman and the girl child taken from her. She had passed away not long afterwards giving birth to their child, a boy, who had been raised by her village in the care of a foster mother.

Yarat's grandson was a man called Anaturuk, who lived in a village near Cape Dorset on Baffin Island. He had in his possession a photograph of his father, Jonobo, Yarat and Oliver's son, along with his wife. He said that he could not part with such a precious article, but he had allowed Astrid to take a black-and-white snapshot of it with her camera, and she had enclosed it in the letter.

The photo was poor and grainy, but good enough to see that it was indubitably Oliver and Yarat's son, smiling broadly, standing next to his wife with her large serious eyes and a beaded headband, her long black hair brushed out over her shoulders like a cape. They wore sealskin trousers and parkas, hers with elaborate beading on the front and a wide hood to accommodate an infant. A little boy of perhaps two years stood between them, holding tight to his mother's hand. Anaturuk as a child.

'So, you have family in Canada, Alasdair,' exclaimed Caro. She showed Felicity the picture. 'Look, we have Inuit family, though I'm afraid they are far away.' Felicity smiled and waved her arms, sensing that this was happy news.

Shaking his head, trying to take it all in, Alasdair read through the letter a couple more times. Then he looked up. 'But you know what this means?'

'What?'

'We're going to Canada.'

A few months later they found themselves on a plane flying over the north Atlantic and looking down on the grey-blue expanses of sea. Caro held Felicity up to the window to point out the white birds seemingly flying above the waters, realized they were the tips of great icebergs floating in the sea. She'd misjudged the scale. The bare rock landscapes of the Arctic coastline came into sight, pink and grey mountains, with icy, fern-like encrustations of glaciers creeping down to the sea.

At Ottawa they changed for a smaller, eight-seater plane. Astrid was waiting to meet them at the tiny airfield at Nunavut. Being the summer, the ice had retreated to reveal wide landscapes of pale rock, miles of seas mirrored with sky.

They found Yarat's grandson at work in his studio. A man in his late forties, Anaturuk had high, strong cheekbones, sunburned skin creased with lines from smiling, straight dark hair down to his shoulders, and grey eyes.

He took them out in his boat, gliding over deep jade green water, past melting icebergs in translucent blue. A pod of narwhals went past, the sun-dappled water flowing over their mottled green-grey coats as if they were formed from the same element, their tusks emerging like chopsticks. They saw white belugas, ring seals and walruses on the rocky coast, hosts of seabirds flying overhead.

Back in the studio, a wooden cabin painted red that had once been a trading post for the Hudson Bay fur company, Anaturuk showed them his paintings of Arctic animals: elegant, stylized line drawings of owls and bears and seals, filled with complicated patterns and each with their own character, their spirits spreading out from their bodies like long shadows or wings. And later, while Anaturuk's wife cooked caribou stew, he took out a wooden box, unfolded a sealskin amauti. It had been sewn and worn by Yarat. He presented it to Alasdair and Caro. For Felicity, when she was older, he said, so she might know the people she came from.

They gave him a studio photograph of Charlotte's oil painting of Little Star and Yarat dressed in their fur suits, which he gazed at, shaking his head. The only sadness was that his father, Yarat's son, had passed away the winter before. But later, singing under his breath as he worked, he drew a picture of Little Star and his father, both children again, playing together on the ice as Yarat sat patiently at an ice hole, her spear ready to catch the seal that would give them food

The autumn cold brought a flush of colour to Martha's cheeks as she made a small tour of the castle gardens, pushing her walking frame in front of her. Every so often she stopped to pull at a flower head that should have been tidied up, or pointed out something to Felicity, the tall young woman with waist-length blonde hair at her side.

'We'd better get back inside,' Felicity said. 'Mummy will have lunch ready. Pippa's already here and Andrew should have arrived by now. It's months since I saw my brother.'

'But I hear he's enjoying his first year at university?'

'Too much, Mummy says. Not that he tells us a lot about it. He's been rather secretive of late.'

Inside the castle kitchen, Caro had laid the table for six, a large goose resting at the back of the Aga ready for Alasdair to start carving.

Martha came in and Caro helped her take off her mohair wrap, installed her at the head of the table, near the warmth of the Aga, with a restorative glass of Amontillado. Poured herself one, and a small one for Fliss with a large lump of ice. She smiled to see Fliss and Martha sharing stories about Edinburgh College of Art, Fliss's more recent but Martha's just as colourful.

And as for Caro, she had, she realized, developed a deep affection for Martha, from years rubbing along together, gradually learning who the real Martha was, the real Caro, not the shadows and expectations that they had had of each other, the bogeymen and the judges that they had built for themselves from the chilly snows of fear of disapproval. Of course, there would be a time, and sooner than they liked to think, when Martha would not be here any longer, but it was hard to contemplate. Martha had come to rely on Caro and Pippa to help her with the things that age and infirmity had made more complicated and even impossible, and Caro was glad that Martha trusted her enough to ask for help. Her mother-in-law had become a friend, a confidante, a comforting presence. Each week Caro and Alasdair would go over to Kelly, or Alasdair would fetch Martha in the car to have supper at their house overlooking the sea in St Andrews, a short walk between the departments in the university where they both worked. Alasdair had made professorship. Caro had been one of the first female lecturers to be employed by the university, though not a professor – yet, she liked to add.

Alasdair carried the goose over to the table and after a short grace, he began to fill up the warmed plates with rich slices of meat. Dishes of roast potatoes, cabbage in garlic, carrots and parsnips, redcurrant jelly, a large jug of gravy, were passed round the table amid the chatter, above them the painting of Yarat and Little Star. It was a moment poised on perfection, that Caro knew she must hold in her memory, leaning on the table with her strong arms as Andrew said, 'Mum, is it all right if I ask a friend to stay? I can't wait for you to meet her. She's called Celine. You see, she's really special.'

And hearing the joy in his voice, Caro felt a prickle of goosebumps along her arms, and knew this was the one. She saw a mysterious girl called Celine standing at Andrew's side – the pride in his eyes – a girl Caro was going to welcome with all her heart. Yes, there'd be hurt and misunderstandings over the years, but gradually, she was sure of it, as they listened and learned to see the world a little differently through each other's eyes, they would find the love that makes a family.

She felt Martha's arm around her shoulders, frail and emphatic, and looking up into the old lady's dear, beaming face, green trees outside dancing against a blue sky, Caro knew all would be well.

Very well indeed: For in the breaking and remaking that it takes for two families to come together, they would learn to welcome a new little earthquake, a small and unique person who'd need everyone to rethink the world all over again.

NOTES AND ACKNOWLEDGEMENTS

The new V&A Museum in Dundee is shaped like a ship facing out towards the Tay Estuary and the North Sea. The reason for this design is no quirk. The museum sits on what was once the Victoria and Earl Grey docks, Dundee's whaling port. Next to it is berthed Scott's ship, the *Discovery*, a whaler adapted for his polar expedition. Scott knew to go to the Dundee boat-builders for the technology to build an ice-resistant ship.

For over a century, while the Admiralty and gentlemen explorers were setting out with great fanfare to explore the Arctic, the working men of the whaling ships from Dundee and other UK ports had been there and back again many times with barely any comment from the newspapers. The whaler men lived alongside the Inuit, sometimes hiring them to work on their boats, and using their Arctic technology. For almost a century, there was a close link between the Scots and the Inuit, with many diaries and Inuit artefacts donated to the Dundee museums. Through them we can still glimpse a lost way of life from the peoples of the far Arctic.

I would like to thank Julie McCombie of the McManus Dundee Art Gallery and Museum for her help in viewing polar diaries and Inuit artefacts from the collection. Also many thanks to the staff of the Dundee *Discovery* Point where it is possible to view Scott's ship, which was constructed on the template of a Dundee whaling ship, and to the staff of Verdant Works jute mill museum in Dundee for their excellent exhibition and coffee and cakes!

I relied on Dorothy Harley Eber's collection of first-hand accounts from Inuit in *When the Whalers Were Up North*, to hear the voices of Inuit who met with the Dundee whalers at the end of the nineteenth century, along with Malcolm Archibald's *Ancestors in the Arctic*, a book of photographs and stories for The McManus: Dundee's Art Gallery and Museum. Gillies Ross also collected a wealth of first-hand accounts from whaler men and Inuit in *Arctic Whalers, Icy Seas*. The recent British Museum Arctic exhibition was a treasure chest of research opportunities, adding to the permanent Arctic exhibition which I have loved visiting over many years.

The beautiful Kellie Castle in Fife was the inspiration for Kelly Castle in the book. I recommend a visit. It is now cared for by the NTS.

I read and reread Terri Apter's book, *What Do You Want From Me?* to help understand the dynamics of in-law relationships, and hope this book gives a tiny insight into this complicated but rewarding relationship that seems to take everyone by surprise.

This book would never have happened without my wonderful agent Jenny Hewson at Lutyens & Rubinstein, and my fantastic editors at Corvus, Susannah Hamilton and Sarah Hodgson. Thanks also to editor Emma Heyworth-Dunn, to Hanna Kenne, to rights editor Alice Latham and to Kirsty Doole and all the team who do so much to get the books out into the world. Thanks, too, to the excellent copy-editor Mary Chamberlain.

My husband Josh and daughter Kirsty read through the text and offered support beyond the call of duty. Thanks to all my family, Hugh, Ali, Isaac, Luke, Kirsty, Hans Peter, Magnus, George and Anna for putting up with deadlines and plot twists. I owe especial thanks to the Dundee crew for their inspiration and to Hugh for sending me to listen to the 'voices of mill girls' at the Verdant Works jute museum exhibition. And lastly, every thanks to my dear parents, Joan and Frank.